THE
PLAYBOY

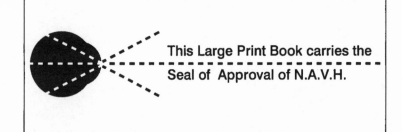

This Large Print Book carries the
Seal of Approval of N.A.V.H.

THE PLAYBOY

Carly Phillips

WHEELER
PUBLISHING

Published in 2003 by arrangement with
Warner Books, Inc.

Wheeler Large Print Hardcover Series.

The text of this Large Print edition is unabridged.
Other aspects of the book may vary from the original edition.

Set in 16 pt. Plantin by Myrna S. Raven.

Printed in the United States on permanent paper.

Library of Congress Cataloging-in-Publication Data

Phillips, Carly.
    The playboy / Carly Phillips.
      p. cm.
    ISBN 1-58724-444-6 (lg. print : hc : alk. paper)
    1. New York (State) — Fiction.   2. Brothers — Fiction.
  3. Large type books. I. Title.
  PS3616.H454P47 2003
   813′.6—dc21   2003045017

To Janelle Denison for being there day after day, page after page, line after line, word after word. And then starting all over again. This one couldn't have been done without you!

Special Thanks

Once again thanks to Lynda Sue Cooper for answering my questions no matter how small and for writing *True Blue*. You're a godsend! Any errors are solely mine.

CHAPTER ONE

Officer Rick Chandler brought his patrol car to a stop in front of a quiet house on Fulton Street and exited with caution. Yorkshire Falls was a small upstate New York town, population approximately 1,725. The crime rate was low in comparison to the big cities and folks possessed vivid imaginations. Case in point, the last major crime spree had centered around a panty thief with Rick's younger brother Roman as the town's most popular, if absurd, suspect.

Lisa Burton, the woman who'd placed the 911 call this afternoon, was a middle school teacher not prone to exaggeration or fright and though Rick didn't anticipate trouble now, he took nothing for granted. A preliminary check of the grounds told him everything was secure so he approached the front yard and strode up the bluestone steps. The door was shut tight and he knocked loudly. The shades on the side window ruffled as wary eyes peered out.

"Police." He announced his presence. The sound of unlatching locks followed until the door opened a crack. "It's Officer Chandler," he said, keeping his hand on his gun as an instinctive precautionary measure.

"Thank God." He recognized the home owner's voice. "I thought you'd never get here."

Lisa's breathless, husky tone didn't come as a shock. For all her schoolteacher conservativism, Lisa, he'd learned, had the hots for him. She'd made sexual overtures before and though Rick didn't want to think she'd call the police unnecessarily, her seductive voice had him clenching his jaw. "You reported a disturbance?" he asked.

The door swung open wide. He stepped inside — with caution at first — because she still hadn't come out from behind the protection of the solid oak door.

"I reported a need for police presence." She kicked the door closed behind him. "I reported a need for you."

His gut told him there was no cause for procedural safeguards and he released his hold on his holstered gun. But he remained wary and as he inhaled, his instincts were proven right. A heavy perfumed odor surrounded him and every male defense mechanism he possessed kicked in. He coughed, gagging on what he assumed was meant to be a potent aphrodisiac. It was potent all right but the woman who'd made the phone call was doomed to disappointment. The only thing that was going to be turned on were the lights.

He hit the switch on the wall at the same time Lisa stepped into view. He ought to be surprised by her appearance but figured he was too jaded by recent events. The plain-looking schoolteacher had transformed herself into a daring dominatrix. From her thigh-high black leather boots to her fitted leather bustier, up to her wild, dark, kinky hair, her getup shouted take me now, on the floor, against the wall, it didn't matter.

Rick shook his head. Though he already knew the answer, he asked anyway, "What the hell's going on?"

She propped her shoulder against the wall and assumed a sultry pose. "That should be obvious by now. You've turned down every ordinary woman's offer in town, including mine. I'm about to change that. Despite my day job and normal appearance, I can be *most* untraditional." She crooked a red painted fingernail his way. "Come let me show you my props."

A raised eyebrow was the most Rick could manage in response. Then he heaved a healthy sigh, certain of only one thing. His meddling mother, Raina, was behind Lisa's continued, less-than-subtle attacks.

Raina had vested every woman with the notion that her middle son would settle down if only he found someone special, someone who'd keep him entertained. Lisa, like many other females in town, had obviously taken his mother's words to heart. Though Raina was right in thinking Rick appreciated uniqueness, she was wrong believing he'd ever marry again, let alone have children. Given his past experience at the altar, his mother ought to know better.

Why put his heart on the line to be trampled when he could enjoy the vast array of women out there with no hurt involved? Though his playboy reputation was highly overrated, it was a fact he enjoyed women. Or he had until the Yorkshire Falls female population had launched their all-out attack on his bachelorhood.

"So are you ready to tie me up?" Lisa dangled a pair of fur-lined handcuffs his way.

Another time, another place, hell another woman and he might be interested in her charms. But with Lisa, the chemistry didn't exist and he preferred her friendship to her feminine wiles. He folded his arms across his chest and told her what he'd said the last two times she'd propositioned him, though not as overtly as this. "Sorry. I'm not biting."

She blinked, a sudden hint of vulnerability in her eyes. "That's fine. I can do all the nibbling necessary for us both." She smiled, baring her white teeth, her words dispelling any illusion of softness he thought he'd seen.

"Not now, Lisa." He rubbed his aching temples. "To be honest, not ever." The words didn't come easily. Rick worried about her feelings despite her predatory actions. After all, his mother had raised him to be a gentleman. But he'd bet even Raina, for all her pushing, hadn't anticipated how far the women of Yorkshire Falls would go to get his attention.

If Lisa favored leather over lace, she probably had a tough hide. Besides, she had to know

10

with a blatant gesture like this, she was risking rejection. Just as he knew that if he softened toward her at all, he risked a repeat episode. It had happened before, not just with Lisa. Other women, other outrageous stunts. This was the third attempted seduction this week.

She shrugged and glanced away, obviously more fazed than she wanted to admit. Yet once again she recovered, this time by licking her tongue over glossed lips. "One day I will strike the right chord."

He doubted it. Rick started for the door, but turned back. "You might want to take note of the fact that it's illegal to call 911 unless you're truly in distress." He ought to take out a reminder ad in the paper, but why waste trees and ink when the women wouldn't listen? Why should they when his determined mother wanted grandchildren and didn't care which son provided one first.

"I'll see you at the teacher DARE training program," Lisa said before he shut the door behind him.

"Swell," he muttered.

An hour later, his shift nearly over, Rick used the time to fill out a report, omitting select details of his last stop. He couldn't see causing Lisa any trouble by reporting the incident as anything other than a false alarm. But he hoped this latest rejection had taught the teacher a new lesson about calling the police unnecessarily.

He picked up a rubber band and aimed it across the squad room. At one time he'd found his mother and her myriad women amusing, but no longer. He had to find a way to get them all to back off but damned if he knew how. He narrowed his gaze and fired away. The rubber band hit his target, a torn magazine photo of a sappy-looking bride and groom hanging against the backdrop of the dingy beige wall. "Bull's-eye."

"Better not let Mom see that."

Rick turned as Chase, his oldest brother, walked up behind him, joining him at his desk.

Chase laughed but Rick wasn't amused. Raina's determination was legendary. Not even her heart condition had slowed her down. It wasn't enough that his mother had married off their youngest brother, Roman. No, now in her quest for grandchildren she'd set her sights on Rick.

Chase was the ultimate bachelor who'd already helped Raina raise his younger siblings after their father's death twenty years ago. Having done his familial duty, he'd been exempt from most of their mother's matchmaking schemes — so far.

Rick wasn't as fortunate. "You'd think Mom had her hands too full with her renewed social life to bother with mine."

After years of being a widow, his mother had begun dating. Weird term for a woman of her age, Rick thought. But that's what she was doing, dating Dr. Eric Fallon. Her loneliness had been a concern to all three sons and Rick couldn't be happier that she'd finally moved on. He'd just hoped she'd be too absorbed in her new life to bother digging into his.

Chase shrugged. "Mom's never too busy to meddle. Look at what she's juggling now: the good doctor, angling to get a baby from Roman and Charlotte," he said, speaking of their youngest brother and his new wife. "And being director of your social life." He picked up a pencil and twirled it between his palms.

Rick rolled his shoulders, trying to loosen the tightness from too much time spent on patrol. In their small town, hierarchy didn't mean squat, and the guys all pitched in for shift duty.

"At least Eric's keeping her busy," Chase said.

"Not busy enough. Maybe it's time to give her a job. You ought to offer her employment."

"As what?" Chase's tone didn't hide his shock.

"Gossip columnist seems appropriate to me," Rick cracked, getting a smile out of his brother too.

But Chase sobered quickly. "No way am I bringing her into the office. Next thing I know she'll be interfering with my social life too."

"What social life?" Rick asked with a grin. Chase was so damn private Rick couldn't help but give his more serious sibling a hard time.

Chase shook his head. "The things you don't

know about me." A wry smile twisted his lips as he folded his arms across his chest. "For a cop, you're awfully dense."

"Because you keep everything to yourself."

"Exactly right." Chase nodded, satisfaction glittering in his blue eyes. "I like my privacy so I vote we let Mom focus on your love life for a while longer."

"Gee thanks." Speaking of Raina reminded Rick of her meddling and took him back to his last stop of the day. "You seen Lisa Burton lately?" he asked his brother.

"In Norman's this morning, eating breakfast. Why?"

He shrugged. "Just wondering. I had a false alarm at her house this afternoon."

Chase perked up, his journalistic instincts obviously kicking in. "What kind of false alarm?"

"The usual kind." No point in telling Chase the school teacher was into S&M with her scrambled eggs now. She was probably embarrassed enough and Rick wasn't the type to kiss and tell. Chase had taught him to respect women whether they'd earned it or not. "Unfounded noises outside." He shrugged. "The place was secure."

"Probably just an animal of some kind."

Rick nodded. "Did she seem keyed up to you?"

Chase shook his head. "Not at all."

"Good."

"Speaking of dinner —" Chase rose from his seat.

"I didn't."

"Well I am. You ready to head over to Mom's?"

Rick's stomach grumbled, reminding him he was just as hungry as his brother.

"Sounds like a good plan to me. Let's go."

"Rick, wait." Felicia, the on-call dispatcher, walked into the room. "There's a woman in a vehicle stopped on Route 10 leading into town. Phillips came in late. Can you handle it while he's briefed for his shift?"

Rick nodded. "Why not?" It would delay dealing with his mother and her pointed questions about his social life. He turned to his brother. "Tell Mom I'm sorry and I'll be there as soon as possible."

"I won't mention that smirk on your face or the relief you're obviously feeling at being given a reprieve. But if she's got a woman there waiting, you're going to pay," Chase said.

Felicia strode up to Chase, confident and feminine even in her blue uniform. "I get off in five minutes. Take me with you to your mother's and I'll save you from her match-making clutches." She batted her lashes over her hazel eyes.

Rick watched, amused. Felicia had a good heart and an even better body, all rounded curves and femininity beneath her clothes. A

15

blind man couldn't miss the fact that she was a knockout.

"So what do you say?" she asked Chase.

He grinned and lay an arm around Felicia's shoulders, his fingers dangling precariously close to those curves Rick had noticed before.

"Now you know I can't take you home with me, sweetheart. Tongues would be wagging and by tomorrow we'd be front page of *The Gazette*," Chase said, speaking of his newspaper.

Felicia let out an exaggerated sigh. "You're right. One night with the oldest Chandler and my reputation would be ruined." She lay a hand on her forehead in an obviously dramatic gesture. "What was I thinking?" She laughed, then stood up straight, smoothing her blouse. "Besides, I have a date. We'd better let Rick get to that stranded car," Felicia said. "See you around, Chase."

"See you," he said, then turned to Rick. "And you'd better hightail it over to Mom's as soon as you can."

Rick shook his head. "Don't worry. I'm sure Mom considers home neutral territory. She wouldn't set you up while she's around to suffer the consequences." He grabbed for his car keys.

"Where Mom's concerned, I wouldn't get too complacent," Chase warned.

Rick acknowledged his brother had a damned good point when ten minutes later he realized he was on his way to another emergency call to rescue yet another damsel in distress. Based on prior experience, Rick had his doubts this was a routine stop, but rather a mother-initiated setup.

Despite the annoyance building inside him, he had to admit this time he was disappointed in the lack of creativity. Until now, the predicaments had been fresh innovative ways to get Officer Rick Chandler's attention. Running out of gas, if that's what had happened, ranked way down on the originality scale.

He drove to the outskirts of town and walked to where the driver of the fire-engine-red car awaited help. As he neared, he caught sight of frilly white lace that couldn't be anything other than a wedding veil dangling over the door. He rolled his eyes heavenward. First a dominatrix and now a bride. The dress backed up his suspicion that he was probably in for a setup. Brides didn't just happen through Yorkshire Falls and there was no wedding scheduled in town today. The nearest costume shop was located in Harrington, the next town over, and Rick wouldn't be surprised if this woman had stopped there first.

Apparently she had more creativity than he'd given her credit for, but she hadn't done her research. Rick Chandler loved rescuing women but a bride of any kind rated last on his list. Last time he'd responded to a similar S.O.S., he'd been home from college and on the force about two years. One of his best friends and a girl he'd had deep feelings for, Jillian Frank, had dropped out of college because she'd gotten pregnant and her parents had thrown her out of the house. Rick had stepped in without thinking twice. He had those damn Chandler genes. Loyalty ran strong, the need to protect even stronger.

He'd started by giving Jillian a place to live but ended up marrying her too. He'd planned to give the baby a name and he'd provided Jillian with a home. He thought they'd be a family. Considering he'd always been attracted to her before she went away to school, doing a good deed for a friend hadn't been too much of a hardship.

Falling in love had been a natural progression — for him. As they'd lived together during her pregnancy, he'd let down his guard and given his heart — only to have it trampled when the baby's father returned a few weeks prior to her due date. His once-grateful wife walked out, leaving Rick with divorce papers and wiser for the experience.

He'd decided then, he'd never again lose his heart, but he'd definitely have fun and enjoy his life. After all, he was a man who liked women. His brief marriage hadn't changed that. Short of taking out a billboard to announce his intent to never wed again, he'd always made his feelings to the women he got involved with perfectly clear. This so-called bride might as well

18

proposition a brick wall for all the response she'd get from Rick Chandler.

One hand on his gun, the other on the open window, he leaned down. "Can I help you, miss?"

The woman turned to face him. She had a unique shade of red hair and the hugest green eyes he'd ever seen. Maybe at one time her makeup had been bridal perfect but tears had smudged the mascara and streaked her blush.

Something about her rang familiar, but Rick couldn't say what. In a small town, he recognized most people, but every once in a while someone surprised him. "I take it you're having car problems?"

She nodded and sucked in a deep breath of air. "I don't suppose you can tow me?" Her husky voice sounded like she'd just taken a sip of warm brandy.

The desire to drink from her lips and see for himself took him off guard. Not only had he thought he'd steeled himself against this woman's charms, but he hadn't responded to any woman or seduction attempt since his mother's marriage push had begun. Yet faced with this so-called blushing bride, he started to sweat, the heat internal and not caused by the blazing summer sun.

He glanced at her warily. "I can't tow you myself but I can call Ralph's and he can send his truck over." He focused on her car problem and not her delicious-looking mouth.

"Do you think you can help me out of here first?" She extended her ringless hand. "I'd get out myself but I think I'm stuck." Material rustled as she tried to maneuver out of the car.

He still wasn't sure whether he had a real woman in distress and he weighed the odds. A bride minus an engagement or wedding ring didn't tip things in favor of a routine stop.

None of which mattered. She had to get out of the damn car. He opened the door, then extended his hand. As she placed her smaller fingers into his grip, a jolt shook him hard. He couldn't name the sensation, but when those shocked, vivid green eyes bore into his, he knew she felt it too.

Shaking off the unnerving feeling, he pulled her toward him. She clasped his hand tighter but when she pushed up, she teetered forward, falling into his waiting arms. Her full breasts smashed against his chest, her sweet fragrance enveloped him in sizzling awareness, and his heart picked up a fast and furious rhythm.

"Darn high heels," she muttered in his ear.

He couldn't help but grin. "I'm a leg man myself."

She grabbed hold of his shoulders and stood up straight. Though she now stood far enough away for him to think more clearly, her scent was emblazoned on his memory — a fragrance made more pure by the fluffy white dress and tiara perched on the side of her head.

"Thank you for your help, Officer." She

smiled and he realized she had dimples on either side of that mouth.

"You're welcome," he said, but he lied. He wished he'd never answered her S.O.S.

Rick had been exposed to many females in his lifetime and none had ever shaken him this badly. What he didn't understand was why *this* woman?

He let his gaze slide over her body in an attempt to figure out her allure. Okay, so her breasts pushed up enticingly beneath the fitted material of her dress. Big deal. He'd seen breasts before. Heck, all the women who'd tried to seduce him lately had made sure theirs were prominently on display, but none made him want to chuck all rational thought and drag the woman in question into the neighboring woods and make love until the sun went down — con-artist status be damned.

Rick's body shook in reaction to the mere thought and he forced himself to continue his perusal of her many assets. He took in her luscious mouth next. Her lips were coated with clear gloss and set in a naturally full pout that shouted kiss me. And he'd already confessed his weakness in wanting to.

Chemistry was obviously working overtime and he had to admit she was damned attractive bait for a woman his mother had sent. *If* his mother had sent her. Had Raina run out of women in town and decided to import one instead? Maybe that was his explanation. Perhaps

21

it was the fact that she was new to town, new to him, that intrigued him, setup or not.

"What's wrong?" She crinkled her nose. "You're looking at me like you've never seen a woman in a wedding dress before."

"It's something I've tried to avoid."

She grinned. "Confirmed bachelor, huh?"

Unwilling to touch that statement, he decided it was time to find out the truth. "Need me to get you to the church on time?" he asked, acting like the cop he was and not the man she'd aroused.

She swallowed. "No church, no wedding."

So if she had been a bride, she wasn't now. In fact she'd probably left some poor schmuck sitting at the church waiting for her to show. "No wedding, huh? Now there's a shock. Is the groom still at the altar?"

Kendall Sutton met the hazel-eyed gaze of the sexy officer staring her down. She'd never seen a man with such thick lashes or beautiful eyes. Or more skeptical ones.

The man standing beside her obviously thought she'd bolted minutes before saying "I do," and he wasn't impressed with her character. Not at all. She should be offended. Instead she was curious about this cynical streak he possessed. What would make such a good-looking man view women through jaded eyes? She didn't know but for some inexplicable reason, she didn't want him to view her the same negative way.

She blinked into the glare of the afternoon sun, remembering how she'd ended up stranded here, when just hours earlier she'd stood in the bridal room of the church where she'd planned to get married. She'd attempted to convince herself that the waist of the dress was too tight and the fitted material cut off her oxygen supply. When that lie didn't work, she tried to make herself believe she'd breathe just fine once nerves passed and she said "I do." She'd been lying.

Her impending marriage had been suffocating her. Clear, fresh air came easily once she and Brian had broken their engagement on their wedding day, but not either one of their hearts. She glanced at the policeman awaiting answers.

She didn't need to get long-winded with her reluctant savior, but she wanted to explain. "My fiancé and I amicably parted ways." She chose the most positive aspects of the morning, hoping he'd see she hadn't abandoned anyone or broken any vows.

"Of course you did." He ran a hand through his dark chocolate hair.

The long strands fell over his forehead in a manner way too sexy for her peace of mind.

"So why the tears?" he asked.

She swiped at the moisture dampening her gaze. "They're from the sun."

"Really?" He narrowed his gaze and studied her. "Then why the dried makeup stains?"

Observant, intelligent, and sexy. A potent combination, Kendall thought. He saw beneath the surface and she shivered despite the heat.

She sighed. "Okay, you caught me being a stereotypical female. I had a crying spell earlier." And she still didn't know if it was a delayed reaction to her aunt's recent death or pure relief she hadn't ended up trapped in marriage, or both. Either way, filled with relief, she'd jumped into her car and driven away. "I'm impulsive." She laughed.

He didn't.

Kendall knew she should have waited, then pulled herself together and headed west. Sedona, Arizona, was her dream, the place where she hoped to hone her craft and learn even more about creating jewelry designs. But while still in pain over her aunt's death, she'd been drawn to Yorkshire Falls, her aunt's old house and the memories there. The practical fact that she could settle her aunt's estate was a plus, not a well-thought-out plan. She still should have gone home to change before hitting the road.

When the officer remained silent, Kendall's mouth went into overdrive, nerves compelling her to talk while he scrutinized her. "My aunt always said impulse won't get you further than the next bus stop. Prophetic, huh?" She took in her situation — stranded in a wedding dress, no clothes other than honeymoon attire in the trunk, and little money in her pocket, headed

24

to her deceased aunt's house.

"Your aunt sounds like a smart woman," he said at last.

"She is. I mean she was." Kendall swallowed over the lump in her throat. Aunt Crystal had died a few weeks ago, in the nursing home Kendall had almost given up her freedom to pay for. Not that her aunt had asked Kendall for anything. She'd given willingly. There were only two people on this earth Kendall would do anything for — her aunt and her fourteen-year-old sister. Over the years Kendall had gone from resenting her sibling to loving her. Once Kendall finished with Crystal's house and things, she'd visit with Hannah at school before moving west.

The cop eyed her warily, squinting against the sun. Lines bracketed his hazel eyes, made more golden by the sun's glimmering rays.

"So." He stepped closer. His masculine scent surrounded her, more potent than the heat of the sun. "Come on. Admit the real reason you're out here and we can get on with things."

Get on with what things? "I don't know what you're talking about." But her adrenaline started to flow hard and fast.

"Come on, sweetheart. I've rescued you. What did you think would happen next?"

"Well, gee. I don't know. Sex in the back seat of your patrol car?"

When his eyes darkened to a stormy hue, she recognized the sexual attraction and could have

25

bitten her tongue in two for letting that sarcastic remark escape. Still honesty forced her to admit she felt the same way. Kendall was actually tempted to drag him into the woods and have her way with him herself. She still couldn't believe it but the policeman turned her on. More than any man ever had, including Brian.

"At least we're getting somewhere. So you admit to entrapment?"

"I admit to no such thing. As a matter of fact I have no idea what the hell you're talking about." She perched her hands on her hips. "So tell me, Officer. Is this how Yorkshire Falls's finest greets all newcomers? With rudeness, sarcasm, and veiled accusations?" She didn't wait for him to answer. "If so I can see why your population remains so small."

"We're picky who we let settle."

"Well, good thing for both of us I don't plan to remain long."

"Did I say I didn't want you here?" His lips twitched with an obviously reluctant smile.

Even when he was at his sarcastic, even accusatory best, he had a bedroom voice that dripped charisma. Sex. She trembled.

Then she licked her dry lips. She had to get out of here. "Much as I hate to ask you for anything, can you please drive me to 105 Edgemont Street?" She had no choice but to trust in his badge, his integrity, and her own gut instinct about the man, despite his disposition.

26

"105 Edgemont." His body stiffened in obvious surprise.

"That's what I said. Drop me off there so you can see the last of me."

"That's what you think," he muttered.

"Excuse me?"

He shook his head and muttered beneath his breath, then he met her gaze. "You're Crystal Sutton's niece."

"Yes. I'm Kendall Sutton, but how . . ."

"I'm Rick Chandler." He started to extend his hand, then obviously thought better of them touching again and shoved his fist into his pants pocket.

It took a minute for his words to penetrate, but when they did, Kendall's gaze flew to his. "Rick Chandler?" Her Aunt Crystal had kept just one friend after Kendall had moved her from her home in Yorkshire Falls to the facility near New York City. Kendall stared at his handsome face. "Raina Chandler's son?"

"That's me." And he still didn't look too pleased.

"It's been a long time. Forever, really." Since she was ten and she'd lived her one happy summer with Aunt Crystal before the older woman's arthritis had been diagnosed and Kendall forced to leave. She vaguely remembered meeting Rick Chandler or had it been one of his brothers? She shrugged. Having been there one summer and only ten years old, she hadn't gotten close to the people in town nor

27

had she kept in touch with any once she was gone.

Moving on was the story of Kendall's life. Her parents were archaeologists and traveled on expeditions to remote parts of the world. She'd rarely kept track of them as a child and took about as much interest in their specific whereabouts now as they took in hers.

Kendall had lived with them abroad until she turned five, when they'd sent her back to the States to be shuffled between family members. She'd often wondered why her parents had a child they never planned to raise, but she'd rarely been with them long enough to ask — until Hannah had been born and her parents had returned stateside for five years. At twelve, almost thirteen, Kendall had moved back in with them but she hadn't opened her heart to the people who'd essentially abandoned her, but came home for their newborn baby. The rift between Kendall and her parents had widened even though they no longer had oceans and continents between them, and remained until their departure. Kendall had then been eighteen and on her own.

"You've grown up." Rick's voice brought her back to the present. A wide smile pitched his lips into a charming grin.

No doubt about it, the man had a way about him. "So have you. Grown," she sputtered stupidly. Into a spectacular man. One with roots to this town deeper than any tree. Roots were something she knew nothing about and a sexy man who had those spelled trouble for a woman destined to wander.

"Did my mother know you were coming to town today?" Rick asked.

She shook her head. "It was another impulsive decision." Similar to her hair, she thought and lifted a hand to the pink-colored strands.

He exhaled and seemed to relax a bit. "Spurred on by the nixed wedding?"

She nodded. "By the mutual jilting." She bit down on her lower lip. "Nothing has gone as planned today."

"Including your rescue?"

She grinned. "It's been an experience, Officer Chandler."

"That it has been." He laughed.

The deep, husky sound curled her insides into warm, coiled knots of need.

"Look, I know this is going to sound bizarre but do you think we could keep the details of this first meeting between us?" An actual flush stained his cheeks, something she doubted Rick Chandler experienced too often.

"Just get me out of this heat and into an air-conditioned house and I promise I won't say a word."

He raised an eyebrow. "You haven't been back to Crystal's house in a while." It wasn't a question, rather a statement of fact they both knew to be true.

Only Kendall knew the reasons. She shook

her head. "Not for years. Why?"

He shrugged. "You'll see for yourself. Do you have luggage in the trunk?" he asked.

"A small carry-on and a suitcase." Filled with bathing suits and other vacation clothing. She sighed. Nothing she could do about it now, so she'd have to go shopping for more practical clothing later.

He retrieved her bags and stowed them in his car before returning to cup her elbow in a gentlemanly gesture — unlike the cynical behavior he'd exhibited so far today.

A few minutes later they were on their way. Sweat trickled down Kendall's back as the darn dress plastered to her wet skin. Despite the airconditioning in the car, the cool blasts of air had done little to relieve the intense heat. Being in such close quarters with Rick Chandler made her body temperature soar, while he apparently remained oblivious to her charms.

He'd become her tour guide, pointing out the sights, such as they were, in his small hometown. All the while, he maintained a respectable distance while he talked. Too respectable, she thought irritably.

"We're here." Rick called her attention to Edgemont Street.

She glanced up. From a distance, the old house was just as she remembered it, a huge Victorian with wraparound porch and large front lawn. A place where she'd shared tea parties and had her first taste of beading and jewelry design before her aunt's arthritis changed things. It was also the place where Kendall had nurtured childish dreams of staying forever with the aunt she adored.

But Crystal's home had been temporary, just like every place prior or since. And once her aunt had been forced to send Kendall packing because of her health, Kendall had learned not to invest too much in the way of hopes and dreams in any one place or person. But if she'd learned that lesson well, then why the painful lump in her throat now, as she looked at the dilapidated house up close, through adult eyes? She let out a frustrated sigh.

Rick shifted the car into park and turned, one strong arm wrapped over the seat. "It's gotten a little run-down over the years."

"That's an understatement." She pasted on a smile. No need to dump her troubles on the man. He'd done enough for her already. "Aunt Crystal said she'd rented out the house. And since she never asked me to take care of anything while she was in the nursing home, even when I questioned her, I assumed things were going well. Guess I was wrong."

"Appearances can be deceiving. All *is* well. It just depends on your perspective."

There was that wry humor again. She laughed aloud, liking him way too much.

"Are Pearl and Eldin expecting you?" he asked.

"The renters?" She nodded. "I called from

31

the road and said I'd be in town but I'd take a hotel. They insisted I stay in the guest house in the back." She wondered if it was in better shape than the main house in front of her. "I'd hoped to work out an agreement for *them* to buy." With her aunt's outstanding bills, Kendall needed to sell for a price at or above market value, not below.

She bit down on her lower lip. "If we reach an easy agreement, I could be out of here by the end of the week," she said with more optimism than she felt.

Rick remained silent.

"What?"

He shook his head. "Nothing at all. You ready to go inside?"

She nodded, realizing she'd been stalling. Before she could gather her thoughts further, Rick met her by her car door, ready to help her out. She grit her teeth before touching him, then placed her hand inside his. The electricity sizzled, even more charged than before. She couldn't shake it off, nor did she want to, but apparently he did because he released his grip fast, leaving her to gather her dress and head for the house.

Kendall made her way up the long drive. Her spiked heels kept catching in the broken sections of the driveway but she managed to stay on her feet — until the last step before the walkway, when her heel dug into the hot tar and wedged in good. While one leg stayed behind, her entire body pitched forward in what was destined to be a facedown sprawl onto the hard ground.

She yelped, then shut her eyes, not wanting to see what happened next.

CHAPTER TWO

What was it about women and high heels? Rick didn't know but this one looked damn cute, even in a wedding dress. He watched her wobble up the driveway and would have helped, but he had a suitcase in one hand and a hunch they were both safer at a discreet distance — until she lost her balance.

He couldn't prevent the fall, but he could cushion the blow and he dove forward, letting her crash on top of him instead of the solid ground. He took the hit with a hard grunt as his back made painful contact with the walkway step. He sucked in a ragged breath and was caught off guard by her fragrant, arousing scent.

Damn but she was something else. Even with the wind knocked out of him, he was aware of her, and not just because her soft flowing hair tickled his face. She was feminine and soft, everything a woman should be and yet this pink-haired enigma was uniquely herself.

"Are you okay?"

He wasn't sure who asked the question first.

"Nothing bruised but my pride," she admitted. "You?"

"I've taken harder spills sliding into second."

"Baseball?"

"Softball against neighboring police departments." The inane conversation did little to take his mind off the fact that he had her in his arms again. The desire licking at him grew stronger, something she couldn't possibly feel with all that plush lace between them. But despite the dress, *he* could feel plenty and it was time to untangle their bodies before he made an ass of himself by kissing her senseless. "Think you can get off before you crush me?"

"Is that a veiled reference to my weight?" she asked.

Only a confident female could joke like that, cementing the impression that she wasn't at all like other women. She rolled off to one side and he missed the light pressure against him.

He glanced over and stifled a laugh. Instead of an easy release, she'd tangled herself further in the dress. "You know what they say. If you want a job done right, you have to do it yourself." He let out an exaggerated groan and rose to his feet. Then he bent down and lifted the fluffy white bundle into his arms.

"What are you doing?" She grabbed for his neck and held on tight.

His back had taken the brunt of the fall and he wasn't about to risk a repeat episode. "Protecting my vital body parts from further injury."

"Funny, you felt pretty intact to me."

He sucked in a sharp breath. So much for the illusion of safety beneath the layered dress. He wanted her and she knew it.

A woman fresh from a broken engagement, one who affected him this strongly, was dangerous. She also was fun, something he just now realized he hadn't had in a long while. Life had become routine. It was a sad commentary if he could consider his mother and her small female army of recruits routine. But Kendall wasn't one of his mother's women and he liked her more for it.

He strode up the walk, leaving the luggage behind and even managed the steps leading to the house with her in his arms. Without warning, the door opened wide. Pearl Robinson, the female renter of her aunt's house and one half of an elderly couple living in sin, as Pearl was so fond of telling everyone in town, stood before them.

"Eldin, we have company," Pearl called over her shoulder. She'd been with Eldin Wingate forever. She smoothed her gray hair back in a bun. "I was expecting Crystal's niece, but not two of you." Her gaze traveled over both Rick and the woman in his arms. "You've been holding out on us, Rick. And you've been holding out on your mother too. Why just this morning, she was lamenting her grandchildless fate."

He rolled his eyes. "I'm not surprised."

Pearl glanced over her shoulder. "Eldin, get your lazy behind out here," she yelled, since Eldin hadn't arrived quick enough to suit her.

36

"And hurry up before he drops her."

"There's no chance of that," Rick whispered in Kendall's ear, not so much to reassure her as to allow himself another heavenly whiff of her fragrant hair.

"But you won't mind if I don't take any chances. Just in case." She gripped her small, soft hands tighter around his neck.

He liked the feeling.

"I'm coming, woman." Pearl's other half came up beside her, a tall man with white hair and all his own teeth. Or so he claimed. "What's so important you couldn't bring our guests inside —" He took one look at Rick and his words came to an abrupt halt.

"Hey, Eldin." Rick resigned himself to the inevitable questions.

"Hot damn, Officer."

"Didn't I tell you?" Pearl asked, looking at her significant other. "That's the reason I won't be marrying you anytime soon." She turned to Rick and Kendall. "We're living in sin," she said, lowering her voice, not that there was anyone else around to hear.

"Damn woman won't marry me for the most asinine reason."

"Eldin has a bad back and I refuse to marry a man who can't carry me over the threshold. Did I tell you we're living in sin?" She dropped her voice again.

As Kendall laughed, her breasts brushed against Rick's chest and his body completely overheated. "Can we come in before I drop her?" he asked.

"Excuse my manners." Pearl pushed Eldin back and they cleared a path. "You go on now, Rick, carry your bride over the threshold."

He'd never live this down. Rick paced the inside of the stifling hot guest house behind Crystal Sutton's main house. Eldin had brought them over so they could "get settled," while Pearl had insisted she needed to go to town for some groceries.

"Groceries, my ass," Rick muttered. She wanted to tell the world that she'd seen Rick Chandler carry his bride over the threshold. Never mind that there'd never been a ceremony or that the bride and supposed groom had just met. Pearl hadn't been listening.

The tightness in Rick's shoulders increased. All he could do was hope that when his mother heard the gossip, she'd put an end to the foolishness. Raina would know that Rick hadn't married or eloped again. She knew better than to buy into unfounded stories. But the news would spread, everyone in town speculating about Rick Chandler and the lady in the wedding dress he'd carried over the threshold.

He groaned and for the first time considered moving to a huge city where he could be anonymous in a large crowd. He shook his head, knowing it would never happen. Despite the memories here, he loved his family, friends, and the small-town feel of Yorkshire Falls too much to leave. But a man could dream, couldn't he?

He glanced at the closed bathroom door where Kendall had gone to change. His *bride*. He rolled his eyes at the absurdity and swiped a hand over his damp forehead. Damn but it was like a sauna in here. He'd have to make sure Kendall got over to the General Store and picked up an A.C. unit.

Where was she, anyway? She said she'd needed to change out of the gown but that had been over ten minutes ago. He strode to the bathroom door and rapped twice. "You okay in there?"

"Sort of," came the muffled reply.

He jiggled the handle and found the door locked. He knocked once more. "Open up for me or I'm kicking the door down." He hoped it wouldn't come to that. His back and shoulder muscles remained sore from the dive onto the driveway.

The door creaked open wide. He stepped inside in time to see her lower herself back onto the closed toilet seat and hang her head low between her knees. "I am sooo dizzy."

He glanced at her, concerned. "It's no wonder with that damn dress cutting off your circulation. I thought you were going to get out of it."

"I tried, but it's hot in here and I couldn't unbutton the dress on my own, so I sat down for a minute. Then I got to thinking about my aunt and all the years she spent here. I stood up, got dizzy again . . ." She managed a shrug.

She liked to ramble, something he'd learned from talking to her by the side of the road. Her thoughts jumped from topic to topic, but one thing stuck with him. Her pain. Rick had lost his father when he was fifteen. He'd been young, but not young enough so he didn't remember the man. He'd been a hands-on father, attended all his boys' baseball games and back-to-school nights.

"I lost my father a while back. I can understand what you're going through now," he said, compelled to open up to this woman for reasons he didn't understand. Reasons that made him wary. But he didn't censor himself. "It was twenty years ago. I was fifteen," he said, remembering. "But sometimes the pain is as fresh as if it were yesterday."

Rick met Kendall's moist gaze and his heart twisted with understanding. He hadn't expected to connect with her on any level, especially not on the emotional one he normally walled off. He was surprised he understood this stranger, this woman, so well. "I'm sorry about your aunt." He hadn't said so earlier and meant to.

"Thanks." Her voice held a rough timbre. "Same with your dad."

He nodded. She and Crystal had obviously shared a special relationship. Family bonding was something else Rick could relate to. The

Chandlers were closer than most, bonded by shared memories, both good and bad. With Kendall's pain both new and raw, he found himself wanting to be the one to ease her anguish — and not because to serve and protect was in his job description.

He swallowed a groan. He'd been down this road once before and received a punch in the gut for his efforts. "Once you got light-headed, didn't it dawn on you to call for help?" He directed them back to the problem at hand.

She tipped her head to the side. "Such a simple solution. Gee, why hadn't I thought of that?"

He chuckled. "Too weak, huh?"

"Something like that. Help me?"

Her wide eyes got to him and he couldn't resist her plea. "Where's the best place to start?"

"Back buttons." She hung her head forward, the pinkish red strands brushing against the stark white dress. When she felt better, he'd have to remember to ask her about the hair color, not that it mattered. He liked her anyway. And here he thought he preferred blondes, though he had to admit he hadn't a clue what her real hair color was beneath the pink sheen.

He reached for the first pearlized button when the intimacy of the act struck him. He stood in the small bathroom undoing a bride's dress. No memories rose to suffocate him since he and Jillian had eloped, Rick in uniform,

41

Jillian in a maternity dress. At this point he was long over the hurt and way past the love. Last Rick had heard, Jillian and her husband were happily married with three kids, living in California. Done, gone, and forgotten except for the lessons learned, Rick thought.

Which was why this bride and the feelings she inspired shocked him. Though Kendall wasn't *his* bride, that didn't change the proprietary way she made him feel. The notion didn't worry him as much as it would have if she was sticking around town.

Refocusing on his task, he released first one tiny button and then the next, revealing porcelainlike skin. She had a long graceful neck and an incredibly smooth back, one he wanted to kiss, as he trailed his tongue down her spine and tasted her, inch by delectable inch.

"Oh, that feels better already," she said on a long exhale that bordered on orgasmic in tone.

If he wasn't already damp from the heat, he'd have broken into a sweat. He leaned down, inches from acting out his fantasy, when she reached up and unwittingly swept some strands of hair off the back of her neck. Rick couldn't resist temptation further. As he inhaled her fragrant scent, his lips whispered across her silken skin that was warm from the heat, damp from the humidity.

She trembled and let out a soft sigh, but she didn't pull away nor did she deck him. All, Rick figured, a good sign that got even better when she turned her head and let her lips touch his.

His eyes closed as she answered his unspoken request, letting him taste her for the first time. Her mouth was warm, soft, and giving, feeding a hunger so strong it threatened to consume him. His heart hammered hard in his chest and his palms began to sweat, ridiculous for a nearly thirty-five-year-old man who'd kissed his share of women, but his reaction to this one had been intense from the start. He touched his tongue to her lips and fire leapt between them, the flames engulfing him from inside and out, but before he could seek entrance to her moist mouth, she broke the kiss.

She hung her head down and didn't meet his gaze. "Sorry but it's awkward."

And here he thought she'd been willing. "You didn't exactly say no," he said, feeling as though he'd been punched in the gut.

She sat up straight, looked at him, and blinked in surprise. "I didn't." Her eyes opened wide as understanding dawned. "You thought I meant the kiss was awkward? Oh, no. The kiss was amazing." An uneasy smile flirted across those lips. "But my position was awkward. Uncomfortable. Sort of like this conversation." She shook her head and a flush rose to her cheeks. Then she grabbed the back of her neck and began a steady massaging of muscles that had obviously been twisted during the kiss.

Ridiculously relieved, he laughed before realizing how much he'd cared if she rejected him.

"I'd offer to massage the kinks but I think we'd get in more trouble."

"And as an officer of the law you need to stay clear of that kind of *trouble?*" Her eyes twinkled with mischief, her subtle meaning clear.

"Not during my off hours." The words escaped before he could stop them.

She let out a laugh. "I do like you, Rick Chandler."

"Feeling's mutual, Ms. Sutton." He grinned. Damn but he could get in deep with this woman. And wouldn't *that* solve his current problem?

A relationship with Kendall would force his mother and the myriad women she sent after him to back off. Kendall's unusual arrival would definitely spark gossip. The more wary women in town would steer clear until they knew whether Rick was involved with the newcomer, while the more brazen ones, like Lisa, needed a blatant, can't-miss message. A message like Kendall, her pink hair, and wedding dress.

Not that he thought for one minute Kendall would go along with his insane idea to pretend they were involved in order to keep the women from Rick's door. He didn't even intend to suggest it, but he had to admit the plan had been a fun one while it lasted. "We still haven't gotten you out of that dress," he said at last.

"I'm right here waiting."

He grit his teeth and finished the buttons on

44

the dress with minimal fuss and conversation, focusing solely on his task and not the increasingly bared skin on her back.

He paused when his fingertips finally reached her waist. "How about I give you some privacy and you take things from here?" Because the next step would mean he'd be pulling down the top of the dress and revealing her bare breasts for view. It would mean he'd work the material lower, over her legs and then —

"That would probably be best." Her voice stopped his daydream just in time.

"I'll leave the door open." He stepped toward the exit. "Yell if you need anything."

"Will do." She shot him a grateful smile.

"Good. Good." Rick slipped out, escaping before he could indulge further in any need, be it his or hers.

The wedding gown hung from her waist as Kendall stared at her flushed reflection in the mirror. She wished she could blame the heat but knew her response to Rick's lips on her flesh, his strong hands on her bare skin, was responsible.

She hadn't expected him to kiss her, but the sexual tension humming between them couldn't be missed. Neither could the bond created over understood grief. Add to that he'd been stripping her out of her gown, for God's sake. How much more of an intimate act could there be? When his lips had touched her skin

. . . her body shook now with the memory, her nipples puckering at the remembered sensation.

Kendall didn't normally "do" brazen. But she'd needed to see his face and so she'd turned her head — and met his lips with hers. The kiss had rocked her world. He was so sexy he melted her insides with one look. So strong and sure he protected with a touch. He made her feel wanted. And in doing so, he answered a need she hadn't known still existed.

She'd always been the displaced child that no one wanted. And though Brian had desired her, he'd never given back emotionally. Their relationship had been a bargain. He'd gotten her the modeling jobs she needed to pay for her aunt's care and she'd pretended to be his girlfriend to help him through a transition period after a breakup. Though their fake relationship had turned into a real one, she'd never connected with Brian.

Not like she had with Rick. One kiss and she'd felt more than a physical pull. Enclosed in the small bathroom with Rick had been a confinement of a different kind. A sensual kind. The kind she'd like to explore further. *Why not?* The surprising thought flashed through her mind.

So did the answers. She'd ended her engagement to Brian and a huge phase of her life just a few short hours ago. Though she hadn't been in love with him, the whole ordeal had been traumatic. Though the dizziness had already passed, she splashed cold water on her face, then she shook her head and wrapped her icy, wet hands around the back of her neck for shock value.

She couldn't be thinking clearly, not if she was tempted to indulge in a romantic interlude with a virtual stranger. Yet he felt like anything but. After all, she'd seen the desire in his eyes, felt the tremor in his calloused fingertips. Kendall wasn't normally into affairs or quickies with men she barely knew, but Rick Chandler, his goodness and strength, his openness and giving, not to mention his sexiness, tested her resolve.

She changed out of the dress and reached for her casual clothes, leaving the bridal trappings on the floor in a discarded heap. The wedding was in her past. The open road awaited her in the future. Though it'd be wonderful to indulge in some T.L.C. and though Officer Rick Chandler might seem like the perfect man for the job, it wouldn't be fair to him.

She couldn't use him that way, no matter how good he made her feel. A man who lived in one place, who valued stability, and who was a family friend, was hardly the man to pick for an affair, assuming she was ready for one. Which she wasn't, she assured herself.

Too bad her body made a mockery of that promise. She straightened and started for the other room, steeling herself against the chemistry she couldn't control or deny.

Rick paced outside the bathroom so he could hear the thud if the heat got to her again and Kendall passed out cold on the floor. He was thankful when minutes later the door opened and she walked out, but gratitude evaporated when he got a good look at her newest getup, taken from the small suitcase he'd brought in for her earlier.

A pink floral cutoff T-shirt showcased her flat, bare stomach, while a pair of frayed cutoff white shorts hugged her hips and revealed her rounded curves and long legs. She was perfectly proportioned, making him want her more than he had before. Something he hadn't believed possible.

But as spectacular as she appeared, it wasn't her body he couldn't take his eyes from, but the frilly garter still hugging her thigh.

"What's wrong?" She glanced down. "Oh. Oh!" She blushed an amazing shade of pink that matched her hair. "I was rushing and forgot."

She bent down to remove the accessory, sliding the elastic over those long legs. Legs he could envision wrapped around his waist as he made love to her over and over again.

"Got it." She lifted her head and met his gaze. "You seem fascinated by this thing. Want to see it up close?" She dangled the blue and white lace midair.

And according to tradition be the next to

marry? "Hell no." But he was too late. She'd already tossed the garter through the air, leaving him no choice but to catch it or let it drop onto the dusty, hardwood floor. Resigned, he grabbed for the offending object.

"Good catch!" She clapped her hands in approval. "I'm impressed."

"Just tell me tradition doesn't work if the bride never said *I do.*"

A wry smile touched her lips. "You're afraid." She let out a loud laugh.

"I'm a cop. I'm not afraid of anything," he said. But if that was true, then why was his heart hammering hard in his chest and his breath coming in short, uneven gasps?

"Okay, no fear. But you do look like you're about to be sick." She came up beside him and placed a hand on his shoulder.

Her touch shot straight through him and he enjoyed the feeling more than was prudent.

"Anything I can do?" she asked.

He eyed that damn garter. "You can answer the question."

"Since I never got married and technically I'm not a bride, I'm sure the garter is harmless. Feel better?"

Hardly, he thought. Her fingertips still touched his shoulder, searing his skin through his department-issued navy T-shirt. His gaze dropped to her incredible body again. "You look a lot more comfortable," he said, changing the subject.

She grinned. "Amazing what getting rid of that albatross of a dress will do for you."

He raised an eyebrow. "A woman who shares my views on marriage? Impossible." He couldn't imagine a female who'd shake at the sight of a wedding dress. But this was Kendall and she was unique. No wonder she appealed to him.

"Are you telling me you've never met an independent woman before?"

"Not in this town. They all seem to be on the marriage plan."

Her eyes grew wide, her curiosity evident. "There have to be some women who want to remain on their own. Free to do what they want, when they want."

"Is that your M.O.?" he asked.

Kendall nodded. Rick had pegged her well. "I'm a transient," she said with a grin.

"Why?"

The answer lay in her past. By moving from place to place, she didn't allow herself to become too attached to anyone or anything. But she didn't think Rick needed or wanted to know her personal hangups, so she shrugged lightly and said, "It's all I know."

"Your childhood." He obviously remembered hearing of her past. "But there's no need to move around now. Did you ever consider putting down roots?"

"Not in this lifetime." She'd been there, she'd done that, Kendall thought. "I just spent two years in New York City to be with Aunt Crystal and cover her nursing home bills. It's time to put me first."

He nodded in understanding.

"Why don't we sit?" she suggested.

"This is the best you've got." He gestured to the couch with drop cloths covering it as well as the other furniture in the guest house. It had been so long since anyone stayed here that she obviously had her work cut out for her — even for just a temporary visit.

She joined him on the beige-covered sofa. "Sorry I can't offer you a better, cleaner place to sit."

He shrugged. "No big deal."

"So tell me about the Stepford wives." She changed the subject back to him.

He chuckled. "It's really not that bad. It's just that my mother's been ill and she's got this notion that it's time for her sons to settle down and give her grandchildren." He sobered at the mention of his mother's health. "Now she's launched an all-out campaign and the single women in town are only too happy to participate."

She recalled Pearl's words earlier about his mother lamenting her grandchildless fate. Obviously there was more to it than that. "Poor man. All the women in town throwing themselves at you." She clucked her tongue, though a part of her was actually jealous she wasn't the only one who found this guy incredibly sexy.

51

Not that she had any desire to marry and settle down, but she could see why those women who did found him the perfect catch.

"Trust me it's a lot tougher than it sounds considering I'm not interested."

"I'm surprised you're telling me about it."

"Oh, you'd hear about it soon enough. Especially after Pearl gets through letting everyone know about you and your grand entrance." He ran a hand through that gorgeous, dark hair. "You'll be branded."

Kendall started to laugh, remembering how Rick had carried her over the threshold to the tune of Pearl's humming "Here Comes the Bride," in between chiding Eldin and using his back as an excuse to avoid marriage. Kendall would have mentioned that Eldin seemed anxious to put a ring on her finger, but she sensed Pearl had a mind of her own. Just like Rick's mother, apparently.

But Rick wouldn't find this situation amusing, so she clasped her hands and tried for sincerity. "No one could possibly believe you'd gotten married without letting anyone know."

"They just might considering it's happened before." His eyes clouded over, memories obviously pushing at him and making him uncomfortable.

He'd been married. Eloped, it seemed. No wonder he resisted his mother's marriage push now. She leaned forward, surprised beyond belief. "Do tell."

"Not in this lifetime," he said, quoting her. He rose from his seat. "So what are your plans?" He tossed the volley back to her.

Apparently they both had emotional walls they didn't want to let crumble. Much as she was dying to know more about him, he'd shut her down. Since she didn't want to share any kind of closeness that would bond them, not when she planned to leave soon, she had to respect his privacy.

He wanted to know her plans and she assumed he meant short term. She took in the dusty trappings around her, and recalled all the things that appeared to be old and decrepit in the main house. She rubbed a weary hand over her eyes. "For tonight I guess I'll clean the room where I'll sleep and maybe the kitchen." She crinkled her nose at the thought of all that dust swirling around her. "Tomorrow I'll get started on getting the house in shape. Oh, and I suppose I should contact a realtor and see what my possibilities are, even though I know now I need to finish fixing before I can show the place."

He nodded, hands shoved in his back pockets as he, too, surveyed the damage. "I'll help you clean."

His offer touched her but she couldn't accept. "You don't need to do that. Honestly, I can get one room in decent shape by myself."

"With what? You're going to need supplies and if the weather forecast is correct, an A.C.

unit. No way will you be able to sleep in this place without air."

She tried to inhale but choked instead. Rick was right. The air was stagnant and oppressive. Concern and a wave of depression settled over her. "Oh, geez. I really didn't anticipate all these extra costs." She mentally calculated the money in her account. Unfortunately she'd need more than she had in the bank just to live the next month or so here.

"I take it you thought you'd arrive, list the house, sell, and be on your way?"

Kendall nodded. "A little overly optimistic, huh?"

"A little." He grinned. "But I like your attitude. Why deal with problems until they crop up?"

"You're just being nice to me. You don't want to call the new girl in town a ditz or an impulsive idiot."

His sexy grin turned into a scowl as his lips took a downward turn. "Hey quit being so hard on yourself. You've been through a lot. Now do you have an immediate plan?"

For money, she did have her credit cards, and Brian would be more than happy to overnight her jewelry and supplies. If she could find a store to place them on consignment, maybe she could scrounge up some extra cash. Okay, so she had a plan. Of sorts. She glanced at Rick. "Just point the way to town and I'll . . ."

"Fly there on your magic carpet?"

54

She let out an exhale and added fixing the car to her list of expenses. "I don't suppose I could bum a ride?" She bit down on her lower lip, realizing that for a man who was tired of women who wanted something from him, Kendall was probably more trouble than she was worth.

"I'm heading toward town myself. And before you ask, yes I can give you a lift back home afterward."

Home. Had she ever really had one? Not wanting to delve into deep thoughts right now, she flashed him a grateful smile instead. "You're a regular knight in shining armor, Rick Chandler."

He grinned. "What can I say? I never could resist a damsel in distress." A mixture of humor and unexpected sadness touched his voice despite the sexy outward smile. Was the sadness related to his past marriage, she wondered.

Once again, when it came to this enigmatic man, Kendall wondered why. What made him tick, what happened in his past that drove him to avoid another marriage yet make it a habit of rescuing women in need? Knowing his pull and effect on her, she was glad she wouldn't be around long enough to find out.

CHAPTER THREE

An hour later Rick had shown Kendall through Herb Cooper's General Store, helping her pick out household necessities. More than once as they walked the aisles, Rick had the sensation he was being watched. But each time he glanced around, the aisles were empty.

He'd chalked it up to too many hours on call when from behind a jostling noise startled him and he turned in time to see Lisa Burton. She lingered at the end by the cheese and cracker section, staring when she thought he wasn't looking. He groaned and jerked away before she could catch his eye. He didn't need another confrontation with the oversexed schoolmarm.

"You're quiet all of a sudden." Kendall spoke into the silence. "I'm almost finished and I appreciate your taking the time to wait around while I shop."

"My pleasure," he said. And it was. He enjoyed Kendall, her quick wit and sense of humor. He preferred her to any other woman he'd spent time with, lurking Lisa included.

A quick glance over his shoulder told him Lisa had disappeared. No doubt she'd gone down the next aisle, planning to meet up with him at the far end. In that instant, Rick formulated his plan. If he anticipated running into her and acted before she came up to him, Lisa and her marriage aspirations could be a distant memory — leaving him with one woman down and a town full to go, but he'd make a start.

"Dinner." Kendall grinned and tossed a package of hot dogs into the cart, basketball style.

Dinner. "Dammit." His mother and Chase were expecting him — he glanced at his watch — over an hour ago. He wasn't surprised neither had tried to reach him. When out on a call, his family had learned to wait out his often long delays.

"I admit they're not gourmet, but they boil quick and they're not too expensive. Perfect bachelor's food, so why the expletive?" Kendall studied him with large eyes.

"I forgot I was supposed to be at my mother's for dinner."

"And instead you're busy with me." She reached out and touched his arm.

The sparks crackled between them, making a mockery of her words and cementing the notion that his idea to get Lisa to back off would work.

"I'm sorry to have held you up," Kendall said.

"I'm not." He'd enjoyed hanging out with this woman who amused him, aroused him, and yet wanted nothing from him except what he was willing to give.

He pulled his cell phone from the array of

equipment hanging around his waist and punched in numbers from memory, waiting until Raina's voice sounded on the other end. "Hey, Mom. Sorry about the delay. I got sidetracked."

"Your new bride?" She chuckled, sounding lively and not at all like her out-of-breath, usual self.

Ever since his mother had been diagnosed with a weak heart a couple of months ago, he worried about her health. Both he and Chase alternated checking up on her, making sure she ate regularly and didn't overdo. Since their father had died, the three Chandler brothers looked out for Raina constantly. "I hope you've eaten?"

"Chase and I ate," she assured him. "He got called back to the paper but I'm keeping yours warm for you. And I saved my dessert to eat so I can keep you company. I'm looking forward to hearing all about your recent marriage."

He rolled his eyes. Rick knew his mother didn't believe the gossip, but the story had obviously already spread. A glimpse at the other end of the aisle told him Lisa was just where he figured she'd be, lying in wait and no doubt trying to figure out who he was with. Rick needed to give Lisa a firm and final reason to believe he didn't return her interest. At the same time, he needed to provide his mother with a female to focus on instead of the hoards who drove him crazy.

"I appreciate you holding dinner, Mom. I'll be there in . . ." He glanced at his watch, calculating how much time they needed to finish up. "About half an hour. Oh, and I'm bringing a guest."

Beside him, Kendall shook her head. "You don't need to do that," she whispered. "I'll be fine."

He waved away her objections and caught the end of his mother's question.

"Female company, Mom, and you'll be pleasantly surprised." Before his mother could begin the interrogation, he hit the STOP button, flipped his phone closed, and rebuckled it into the holder.

"Now that was stupid." Kendall glared at him.

He stepped closer, mindful Lisa was snooping around the corner. "A little ungrateful considering I saved you from boiled hot dogs and dust for dinner."

"You just got through telling me your mother is out to marry you off. Everyone in town probably thinks we've done the deed, and now you're bringing me home for dinner? Are you insane?"

"Probably." He met Kendall's shocked gaze and treated her to a grin. "I have a plan. A quid pro quo of sorts and you need to hear me out before you say no."

A hint of wariness flashed in her eyes, making him think she'd nix the idea before he got the chance to propose it.

She perched her hands on her hips and faced him. "What makes you think I'd say no?" she asked, surprising him with a challenge instead.

He figured she was out to prove she could handle anything he dished out and after that kiss, he wouldn't mind proving the same thing.

"So what kind of exchange did you have in mind?" The wariness in her voice hadn't changed.

If he wanted a chance of convincing her to go along with his plan, he needed to alter her attitude. He propped an arm on the glass door behind her head, bracketing her between his body and the frozen food case in an intimate position. One any observer couldn't mistake, and one meant to lower her defenses and make her his. "I'm proposing a housecleaning of sorts." His voice dropped a deeper octave, spurred by her nearness and the sizzling awareness raging through his veins. "I'll clean your house if you'll clean mine."

She shook her head and light laughter bubbled from deep inside her. "You aren't talking literally."

"About your house I am. My house I'm not." On impulse, he reached out and grabbed a strand of her hair and rubbed it between his thumb and forefinger, liking the sensual feel of the strands against his skin. "I'll help you get your aunt's place in shape to sell, and you'll help me get my house in order. My personal house."

What more could he say by way of explanation? *Be my lover, Kendall?* His skin prickled with awareness and his body trembled. In words and fact, all felt right. *She* felt right. So how could he offer a proposal that sounded so hard and callous?

"Quit beating around the bush and tell me what you have in mind."

Drawing a deep breath, he opted for the unvarnished truth. "I want you to pretend to be my lover. Keep the tongues in town wagging and the women off my doorstep." His eyes bore into hers. "What do you say?"

A nervous tick pulled at her mouth. "What I said before. You're crazy," she said as her huge eyes stared into his.

Was it his imagination or did hurt flash in the green depths before she masked the emotion. "Not crazy," he corrected. "I'm just a man who's had it with unwanted female attention. I also happen to enjoy your company and this arrangement would benefit us both." Didn't her body tell her what his already knew? That they were a perfect fit waiting to be soldered together?

He shook his head, reminding himself he'd suggested a fake relationship. But his body wasn't listening as she bit down on those generous lips.

"I don't know."

"You said you're short on cash. Can you afford a carpenter?" He grasped for the facts necessary to convince her he had what she needed. *He* was what she needed. "A painter?" he continued. "Anything else that house needs?"

Kendall exhaled a whoosh of air. "Probably not." Definitely not, she thought. Even if she worked on her jewelry in between fixing up the house, she still couldn't guarantee enough income to pay for the repairs. Rick was offering to do them — for a price. A price she'd paid before with Brian and had ended up in a wedding dress.

A shiver having nothing to do with the frozen case behind her rippled along her spine. She no longer wanted to rely on anyone to meet her needs or achieve her dreams. Most importantly she didn't want anyone to stand in the way of her goals. And Rick, with his golden eyes, sexy grin, and charming personality, was much more hazardous to all of those things than Brian had ever been.

But she couldn't deny his bargain made sense. His forehead still touched hers, the intimate contact making it difficult for her to sort out and weigh her options. Intentional, she had no doubt.

"As an added incentive I happen to be good with my hands."

How good, she wanted to ask but refrained. Her body had already reacted to his deliberate double entendre and a delicious warmth curled her stomach while a pulsing throb of desire settled lower between her legs. His voice oozed sex and Kendall let herself be seduced.

She licked her lips for moisture and tried without success to focus on the mundane. "Don't leave me hanging. Tell me what those hands can do." Unfortunately every sentence came out sounding needy, much the way she felt at the moment.

He grinned. "I've done odds and ends around my mother's house on my days off," he said, more focused than she. "I can handle most anything you need and what I can't, I can call in a favor, and lucky for you I have liberal shifts. Four tens."

"In English, please?"

He rolled his eyes in a playful gesture she found incredibly endearing. "You lay people are so pathetic. I work four ten-hour shifts a week with three days off. Plenty of time to help you out around the house and give people the right impression at the same time."

She clenched and unclenched her damp hands. "And what impression would that be?"

He stroked a gentle hand down her cheek. "That I can't stay away from you. That I've finally met the woman for me. And that no one else interests me in the least."

He spoke so deeply, it could have come from the heart — but it didn't, Kendall reminded herself. This was but another bargain. He was a man bent on avoiding relationships and marriage. All he was doing now was proving to her he could act the part of her lover.

She'd have to do the same if she agreed. Coming off a similar agreement with Brian, she knew how intimate she and Rick could potentially become. But Rick wasn't asking for her future, he just wanted a temporary fix to his problem. Just like she needed a quick fix to hers. Quid pro quo. She barely had money in the bank and this man was offering the solution she desperately needed.

"Kendall?" He broke the long silence, interrupting her thoughts.

She could do this. If she locked her heart up tight and reminded herself that she'd be moving on soon, there'd be no chance of becoming attached to this solitary man or this town.

She could handle his bargain. She met his intense gaze. "Yes," she told him.

"Yes you're paying attention now or yes —"

"I'll be your lover," she said before she could change her mind. "Pretend to be, I —"

Before she could finish, he brushed a kiss over her lips, taking her off guard. His mouth settled for a brief moment, long enough for the inferno to erupt, for the embers to light and sizzle anew. Then too soon, he broke the kiss, raising his head and meeting her gaze. "Thank you."

Her lips tingled. Unexpected warmth wrapped around her heart and it scared her. Still shaken, she deliberately kept things light. "Whether you're welcome or not remains to be seen."

Without warning a loud cry suddenly pierced the air around them. Kendall jerked around to see a woman at the far end of the aisle wheel around and run the other way so quickly, she never saw her face. Kendall didn't even know if the sound had come from the woman who'd turned and run. She turned back to Rick. "What was that?"

He rolled his shoulders and shrugged. "Couldn't tell you." Some kind of emotion flickered in his eyes but the moment quickly passed. "I think this arrangement will work well for us both."

She shrugged, unsure. "I still say you're insane."

"Nah. I'm just a man who enjoys stirring things up." Light danced in his gaze. "Now let's finish up here and get going."

"If you say so, but I'm not taking responsibility for whatever happens next."

"You rode into town in a wedding dress, honey. No way I'm taking any of the blame." Something Rick proved minutes later when the proprietor began ringing up Kendall's purchases.

"Newlyweds, huh?" The older, balding man hand-punched in the prices. Scanning obviously hadn't made its way to the General Store just yet. "Moving out of your apartment and into Crystal's guesthouse?" he asked Rick, but didn't wait for a reply. "Sorry about your aunt, Ms. Sutton. I mean Mrs. Chandler."

Kendall started to choke. "It's Kendall. Call me Kendall," she said. "Kendall Sutton."

Herb looked up and scowled at them both. "You married one of them feminists?" he asked Rick. "Don't let her take her own name. Next thing you know she'll be demanding more rights, like the TV remote. Then a man's got nothing left, not even his pride."

Rick breathed in deeply and, Kendall noticed, smothered a laugh. But he didn't correct the man.

"Aren't you going to say something?" Kendall whispered.

"It won't do any good and besides it can't hurt to keep them speculating, right?"

"About a relationship, not a marriage."

"You'll learn this town soon enough, but I'll humor you." Rick patted her hand. "We're not married, Herb. And I'd appreciate it if you'd correct the misunderstanding when you hear people talking. Not that it'll do any good," Rick said, lowering his voice for Kendall's ears only.

Herb swiped a hand over his bald spot. "Now I know I heard Pearl say she saw you carrying this pretty lady over the threshold in a wedding dress."

"Well that's true . . ."

"It's a long story, Mr. . . . ." She realized she didn't know his last name. "It's a long story, Herb."

"And we'd like to explain it to you but we're late for dinner at my mother's." Rick squeezed

Kendall's hand tighter.

Kendall tried to process the split-second conversation and realized Rick was playing the part already — spreading the news she was having dinner with his mother, holding her hand in public. Heated warmth emanated from his touch and she swallowed hard.

Herb laughed. "Raina's gonna like having a daughter-in-law who actually lives in Yorkshire Falls."

"I don't . . ."

Rick elbowed Kendall softly, reminding her to go along. She might not be his bride, but from now on, she was definitely his lover — in the eyes of the town, anyway.

Let the charade begin, she thought and handed Herb her credit card so he could ring the transaction. He glanced at her name on the card, looked back and forth between Rick and Kendall, then muttered something about women and their damn independent streaks, but minutes later finished the purchase and had bagged the items.

"You see Lisa Burton fly outta here?" Herb asked.

"Was that the woman who shrieked earlier?" Kendall wondered.

"Yep. Dropped her basket and took off, leaving me to clean up the broken eggs and everything."

"You never know what will set a woman off, Herb." Rick grabbed Kendall's elbow in a gen-

67

tlemanly gesture. "It was good seeing you." Rick shook the man's hand.

"Likewise."

"Nice meeting you," Kendall said as she helped Rick gather the packages.

"I'm sure I'll be seeing you around. There's lots of things an old house needs to make it livable for two and —"

"Sure is. That's why we gotta be going now." Rick cut Herb off and herded Kendall out the door before another round of post-wedding discussion could begin.

A good thing, since Kendall figured they were probably in for enough questioning from Rick's matchmaking mother.

Rick looked like he'd been hit by a meteor, Raina thought, immensely pleased. She hadn't seen that lovestruck, glazed look in one of her boys' eyes since . . . well since Roman had seen Charlotte at the Saint Patrick's Day dance. It must have something to do with all that skin these women bared today. Or maybe it was the navel. Raina noticed that Rick couldn't tear his gaze from Kendall's bare stomach and belly button.

Watching the two young people together enabled Raina to find a measure of peace and happiness. With the return of Crystal's bright-eyed niece, Raina sensed her friend's presence. She wondered if Crystal had sent Kendall here to impact everyone's life in some way. If so,

Raina intended to help.

"So what do you plan on doing with the house?" Raina asked Kendall. "Lord knows Pearl and Eldin would be happy to stay on."

The young girl laid down her fork. "Really? That's wonderful."

Raina nodded. "I'm glad you agree, seeing as how they live on a fixed income. The arrangement they had with your aunt was the only one they could afford."

"Speaking of their arrangement, I need to find out the details of their rental agreement," Kendall said.

"Oh, there is none." Raina waved a hand in the air.

"What do you mean?"

"In this town, people who've known each other for ages still do things with a handshake. Silly I know. But that's how it is. When your aunt got sick, Pearl and Eldin were able to give up their apartments that cost money and move in as caretakers. To keep up the place in her absence."

Kendall choked on a sip of water. "Excuse me. I didn't realize they don't pay rent." She coughed again, then blotted her lips with a paper napkin.

Rick, Raina noticed, watched the action in earnest.

"You call what they've been doing upkeep?" Kendall asked when she'd recovered.

"Eldin paints in his spare time, which he has

a lot of since he's on disability," Rick said. "If you looked carefully, you might have noticed the odd splotches on the walls of the main house."

"Touch-ups," Raina explained.

"I still don't believe they didn't pay Aunt Crystal rent."

"Oh, Crystal didn't see any reason. She owned that house free and clear for years. She knew things were tight for Eldin and Pearl and asked them to move in when she went to the home." Raina reached over and patted Kendall's hand. "Your aunt was a good woman."

"One of the best," Kendall said, her voice dropping as the reminder of grief set in.

She smiled right after, showing inner strength, something Raina admired.

"But I'll still need to fix the place up," Kendall said. "And then I can decide what to do with it —" She cut herself off. She met Rick's gaze and something unspoken passed between them.

Oh, Raina remembered those days well. Little looks, glances only a couple in the beginning stages of a relationship understood.

"I mean I'm —"

"She's not sure what to do with the house," Rick interrupted, finishing Kendall's sentence.

"Well, you can't mean to *sell* your aunt's house. It's your heritage!" Raina didn't understand all the undercurrents going on, but she couldn't believe Crystal's niece would

70

give up her inheritance.

"It's none of your business what Kendall does with her property, Mom," Rick said.

Kendall sighed. "It's hard to even think of having a heritage when I spent my life moving from place to place."

"Oh, yes. Are your parents still abroad? Crystal used to tell me about their travels." Raina tapped the table with her fingertips, thinking. Transience wasn't a helpful trait but perhaps Kendall wasn't like her wayward parents.

"They're archaeologists. Somewhere in Africa now."

"And your sister? How is she?"

"Hannah's in boarding school in Vermont. She's okay. I've gotten a call or two leading me to believe she's a bit of a troublemaker, but she's always been spirited. I plan to go on up there and have a talk with her myself once things settle here."

Raina shook her head. "Sad when a family doesn't live like a family."

"Mother." Rick reprimanded her with his tone. "Kendall just lost her aunt. She doesn't need you hassling her. Her life and what she chooses to do with it is none of your business."

Protective, Raina thought, and though Rick had that streak by nature, this time she sensed his defense of Kendall had a more personal side. A sense of satisfaction pulled at Raina as she watched her son.

"Rick, I don't mind explaining. Most people don't understand my lifestyle. Truthfully, if I didn't live it, I probably wouldn't understand." She smiled at Raina. "Considering what an obviously warm, loving family you have, I'm sure my family's life seems strange to you."

"Nonsense. Well maybe," Raina admitted, opting for honesty. People could change, she thought, given the right incentive. "I want you to consider yourself a part of our family. Crystal would want that and so do I." More than Kendall knew.

From what Raina had seen so far, Kendall Sutton wasn't only beautiful, she was warm, compassionate, and intelligent. She also had a mind of her own. And Raina assumed her independence held the most allure for her son who'd been bombarded with more domestic-minded women. Raina had only herself to blame for that, but things had changed now.

Rick obviously had fallen for Kendall even if he didn't know it yet. Maybe if shown love and tenderness, Kendall would learn to love the stability she'd missed out on as a child. And who better to teach her the value of family than the Chandlers? Rick especially.

"That's so sweet. I don't know what to say." Kendall's eyes held a bright sheen.

"I do. You've been conned. By the best in the business," Rick said wryly.

Raina scowled at her son.

"What business?" Kendall asked.

"The marriage business."

"Ah, yes." Kendall leaned forward in her seat and grinned. "I heard all about your match-making tendencies, Mrs. Chandler."

"And I heard all about your auspicious arrival. Now tell me how you ended up on the side of the road in a wedding gown of all things?"

"Mother —"

"It's a fair question, Rick." Kendall's cheeks turned a shiny pink, but she carried on like a trooper. "I was supposed to get married this morning," she said, embarrassed at admitting she'd been an hour away from saying "I do," when things had luckily fallen apart. "But we both realized marriage would have been a mistake and my fiancé and I parted ways."

Raina had been happily married for almost twenty years before John died. She couldn't imagine agreeing to marry someone she didn't love or ending things so abruptly. "To call off a wedding so suddenly. Did he cheat on you?" Raina asked, appalled and affronted on Kendall's behalf.

Rick kicked her lightly under the table.

Kendall shook her head. "No, but we were more good friends than anything else. He'd done me some favors, bailed me out by getting me some modeling jobs to help pay for Aunt Crystal's nursing home, and I felt I owed him. Things just got carried away from there, but we realized it in time, thank goodness. I was so relieved I didn't really think. I just walked out, got in the car, and drove."

The impulsive act shocked Raina, who'd spent her whole life in the same house doing the expected things in life. "Just like that?"

"Just like that."

Raina blinked, stunned. But since she'd gotten this much information, she might as well get it all. "And the pink hair was for a modeling job?"

Kendall raised a hand to the pink strands. "I wish. Actually it was an impulse."

"Another one?" Rick asked, devouring Kendall with his gaze.

Raina wanted to clap for joy.

"Last night I panicked. I stood in front of my bathroom mirror and I just . . ." Her eyes seemed to glaze. "Panicked. I couldn't imagine marrying Brian. I love him as a friend, but I've never been tied down to anyone or anything in my life. I saw my reflection and I was afraid I couldn't go through with the wedding." Her voice dropped. "But I'd given my word, I'd promised, and he'd been so good to me. I thought maybe if I didn't look like me, the new me could take on this new life."

"So you bought pink dye?"

She laughed. "No. I had red dye in the closet at home. Cherry Cola actually, but I've got pale blond hair and the color just didn't take the way I thought it would. Instead of cola-colored

red, I got pink." She shrugged. "There are worse things."

"I should have known you were really a blonde," Rick said, his voice deep and husky.

"Because of my impulsive, ditzy behavior today?" Kendall asked, laughing.

"Because he has a thing for blondes," Raina offered helpfully. "And if you ever want to change back, I could take you into town and introduce you to Luanne and her daughter Pam. They own Luanne's Locks. The only hair salon in town."

"You're supposed to stay off your feet," Rick said sharply.

Dammit, Raina thought. This fake heart condition would be the death of her yet. She hated putting her boys through the charade, hated the crimp it put in her social life, but it was necessary. She'd concocted the idea after she'd been rushed to Emergency a few months before with a diagnosis no more dire than indigestion. But her boys didn't know the truth and Raina had used the situation to help her show them the error in their bachelor ways.

She'd allowed them to think she was seriously ill and in return, they'd grouped together to give her her fondest wish. Roman had been the son designated as the one to give her a grandchild. Raina still held out hope he and Charlotte would do just that, though Roman insisted he and his new bride needed time alone before starting a family.

But grandchildren weren't all Raina desired. She wanted her sons settled, living happily ever after with the woman of their dreams and families of their own. She didn't want them living lonely lives. She was one-third of the way there. Chase and Rick were next.

"Are you sick?" Kendall asked, concern in her voice.

Raina drew a deep breath and covered her heart with one hand. "I had an episode a little while ago."

"A weak heart," Rick explained. "She's got to watch her routine and her diet and that's just a start."

"So Norman's been delivering meals and the boys hired a housekeeper." While Raina had been keeping a bank account to pay her sons back when this charade was over. She hated their stubborn refusal to let her pay for her own care. And she was growing to dislike their hovering more and more.

But she'd created this situation and she'd see it through. So far, Kendall seemed like her best prospect for daughter-in-law number two.

"You're lucky to have such devoted sons, Mrs. Chandler."

"Raina, please, and yes my boys are the best. They'll make wonderful husbands too. Just ask my first daughter-in-law. She nabbed Roman, the world traveler. Rick's a little easier since he doesn't have to be convinced to settle down. But you —"

"Ahem." Rick cleared his throat loudly. "Mom, I like to romance women on my own, without your help." Rick squeezed Kendall's hand and she blushed a shade darker than her hair.

"So you admit to a budding romance?" Raina asked, pleased.

"Just leave the dishes, Mom," Rick said, ignoring her.

But Raina wasn't deterred. Rick had never brought a woman to their family dinners before and Kendall's presence spoke louder than anything Rick could have said.

"Cynthia will be here first thing in the morning to clean. Meanwhile, Kendall and I need to get going. I promised I'd help her bomb out a room or two so she could sleep in a clean house tonight."

"Nonsense. She'll stay here," Raina said in the voice that shook her sons' composure when they were young boys. "That place is a pigsty, not fit for a human being and a couple hours' worth of cleaning won't change that. No insult intended, Kendall."

The young woman shook her head. "None taken. But I can't impose."

"You'd never be an imposition."

"You're sweet, but I'm used to being on my own."

"And you young people want your privacy?" Raina guessed, relieved Kendall had turned her down. With a house guest, she'd have killed her prime opportunity to walk the treadmill when her sons weren't around. When she'd concocted this scheme she should have labeled herself a heart patient, not a patient with a weak heart who had to curtail activity, but she hadn't been thinking ahead.

Rick rose and Kendall followed. Then he placed a lingering hand on the small of her back. "We're not going to answer anything private, Mom." He leaned over and kissed her good night.

Long after Kendall had thanked her and gone off with Rick, Raina's joy remained, making it difficult to wind down. She hadn't seen her middle son laugh so freely in ages, not with a woman as the reason, anyway. Not since that Jillian had broken his heart. But that was the past.

Kendall was the future. And though Rick didn't believe he'd marry again, Raina knew better. Thanks to Kendall and her impulsive nature, Rick would come to believe it too.

Rick held the car door open for Kendall, then strode around to his side and got in, buckling his seat belt before turning toward her. He held his hand high and she slapped it in return. "Mission accomplished."

"You think?"

"I know my mother and she definitely believes she saw sparks flying between us tonight." Because they had been, Rick thought.

But that was for another time. Shadows tinged the fragile skin beneath Kendall's eyes as exhaustion obviously set in. She needed rest.

"She'll call off the push for a daughter-in-law?"

He shook his head. "I didn't say that." He twisted his wrist and the ignition kicked in. "If anything she'll step up her campaign."

"So what was the point of tonight?" Kendall asked.

"She'll no longer be pushing other women on me. Instead she'll focus all her attention on the one with the most potential."

He glanced over in time to see her open and close those lips that tempted him so.

"You mean me?"

He grinned. "I most definitely mean you." But Rick sobered fast because he had something more pressing to discuss with her. "Kendall, what kind of relationship did you have with Brian?"

She stiffened in her seat, laughter replaced by intensity. "I don't think that's relevant."

"Sure it is. You said he did you favors and you felt you owed him." Shades of their bargain had risen when he'd heard Kendall's description, making him uneasy. "We're entering a similar arrangement. I just don't want you uncomfortable with me."

"If you're worried my past dealings with Brian will affect me pulling off the charade with you, don't be. At this point I'm a professional," she said wryly.

That's what had him worried. In Kendall's eyes, Rick didn't want to be another man using her for his own gain. "I know he got you modeling jobs to pay for your aunt's care. What did you give him in return?"

Kendall rubbed a weary hand over her eyes.

He grabbed her hand, squeezing it tight.

"Brian was coming off a broken relationship. He'd been hurt badly by a model whom he had to face often at industry events. He wanted what he called a pretty woman by his side to show his ex he was over her. He needed me to pretend to be his . . ."

"Lover." *Pretend to be my lover, Kendall.* Rick had asked her to do the same thing.

The same thing that had sent her running from New York City in a wedding dress. And because she was desperate, she'd agreed. Which made Rick feel like a shit for putting her in the same predicament again.

He exhaled hard. "I'm sorry."

"I'm not. I don't do things I don't want to do," she assured him. "And believe me I'm getting plenty out of this arrangement too."

"Besides my wonderful company?" He forced lightness into the conversation.

"Yeah, besides that."

She laughed, warming him inside and out. "What would that be?"

"By the time you're finished fixing up my aunt's house, I'll be on my way to a brand-new life." She leaned back in the seat and closed her eyes, satisfaction and a smile on those lips.

Well, he'd asked and she'd answered. Too bad for him if he didn't like her reply.

CHAPTER FOUR

For the duration of Rick's "off" days, Kendall and Rick cleaned, fixed, and focused on making the guest house livable. Dust and dirt flew fast and furious along with the sexual tension and incredible sparks. Sparks they did their best to ignore or avoid. Kendall had a hunch they were merely tiptoeing through a minefield that was destined to explode anyway, but once Rick returned to his shift, she was given a reprieve.

Left alone, she turned her sights to the work area for her jewelry designs. Apartment living in New York City had offered her unnatural light that hampered her color choices and hence her designing ability. When her jewelry and a suitcase full of clothes arrived courtesy of Brian, she scoured the house for the optimal working environment, and upstairs in the musty attic she found large windows that let in beautiful natural light.

Excited and working on adrenaline, Kendall spent an entire day bombing the attic, removing the dirt, and setting up the card tables stored there. Hours later, her plastic containers filled with materials had been strategically placed, beads organized by size and color, and her tools laid out for easy access. She stepped back and eyed her handiwork. The attic had been transformed into an artist's dream.

Ironic, really. She had the perfect studio set up in the same place she'd strung her first necklace, one made of varying sized pasta beads. It was here that Aunt Crystal taught her patterning, among other things. A wave of nostalgia along with the distinct feeling of loss enveloped Kendall. She missed her aunt as much as she missed what might have been, the life she'd have had if Aunt Crystal had been able to keep her on.

Kendall shook her head. No need to delve into the past. Live for the moment and move on, advice imparted by Aunt Crystal and wisdom Kendall had always followed. If the memories were choking her here in the attic, she'd just leave them behind and take on the town instead. Bracing her hands on her hips, she turned and walked out, grabbed her car keys and hit the road.

The sun shone overhead as Kendall drove her repaired, beloved red car into town. Her Volkswagen Jetta had had an electrical problem but the repair could have been worse and cost an awful lot more. So while the fates were still smiling on her, Kendall decided her first stop would be the beauty parlor to have her hair fixed.

She walked into Luanne's Locks, the place Raina had suggested the night before. The strong ammonia smell hit her immediately, clogging her lungs and bringing tears to her eyes. When she finally stopped tearing, she was able to look around. Pink wallpaper, burgundy chairs, and gleaming chrome and mirrors surrounded her. A glass case with hair products took up one wall at the front of the store, a perfect place for Kendall's jewelry to enhance the display — if the owner agreed to a consignment deal.

Kendall had approached many proprietors in various cities to take in her designs, and she hoped the owner would be receptive here. No one sat at the reception desk, so she headed deeper inside and paused at the top of one step that divided the entry area from the working one. For a small place, the salon was crowded with women and the chatter sounded loud and friendly, giving her hope.

Kendall drew a deep breath and paused by the first station. "Excuse me. Can you direct me to the owner or receptionist?"

"That'd be me." The stylist, a woman with a bouffant hairdo reminiscent of the fifties, turned to face her, teasing comb in hand. "How can I help you?"

Kendall smiled. "I'm Kendall Sutton and I'd like to make an appointment."

The stylist didn't have a chance to answer. A customer seated in her chair leaned over, speaking in a stage whisper to another woman with rollers in her hair at the neighboring station. "It's Rick Chandler's new girlfriend," she said, exercising her lungs.

The information traveled from the two manicurists sitting a few paces away and in seconds silence descended in the shop as all eyes looked at Kendall and none appeared friendly. The hope she'd held for winning over the store owner evaporated along with her positive mood.

Kendall had spent a lifetime as the new girl. She'd entered many a schoolroom or situation knowing no one, set apart from the crowd, and had learned early in life that she'd never be around long enough to let the opinions of others matter. As long as she felt happy and secure, as long as she lived an honest life and could look at herself in the mirror, that's what counted — more wisdom imparted by Aunt Crystal, and words Kendall took to heart and carried with her always. Wisdom that never failed to buoy her spirits.

Until now. A strange feeling of discomfort enveloped her. Odd for someone used to being the outsider.

"Her hair's pink." The statement sounded like a shout in the otherwise silent room.

As half a dozen wide-eyed, curious women continued to stare, Kendall clenched her hands into a fist to prevent herself from lifting a finger to the strands. Her stomach cramped and self-consciousness set in. Another unfamiliar sensation for someone who'd never before cared what others thought of her.

She forced a grin and ran what she hoped

was a carefree hand through her hair. "That's what I came here to have fixed." Though these people rattled her, she refused to let the insecurity show.

"Everyone go back to your gossiping and quit staring at the girl." From the back of the shop, an attractive redhead came into view and strode to where Kendall stood. "You ignore these people." She shook her head in disgust. "I'm Pam. I'm co-owner of this place, and the lady standing next to me with her mouth hanging open is my mother, Luanne." She jabbed her mother lightly with her elbow. "The other owner, and one who's usually a lot more polite to her customers."

"Forgive my poor manners." Luanne held out her hand and Kendall shook it. "Everyone was talking about Rick's new lady friend and then I looked up and there you were." Luanne lifted a hand to her mouth. "I'll shut up now."

Pam shook her head. "Good idea, Mom."

"It's no problem, really. Besides I'm sure this pink hair attracted the most attention."

Pam placed her hands on her hips and studied her. "You really don't know." She shrugged and leaned closer, whispering as she spoke. "Mom's serious. It's not your hair, it's your status that's got them talking. Do you have any idea how many of these women tried to land Rick Chandler for just one date and failed?"

"I'd heard rumors . . ."

"Not rumors. Fact. I'm probably the only single woman in this shop right now who hasn't made a play for the town's favorite cop. I prefer light-haired men, but most women in this town aren't so fussy. They just want the gold ring." Pam waved her hand Kendall's way. "Not that I think you're after such a thing. I just met you. I wouldn't know. But you get my point."

Kendall nodded, dizzy from Pam's speech. Used to big-city solitary living, Kendall wasn't comfortable sharing intimate information with a stranger. But obviously nothing was too personal to discuss when in a small town. "Can I make an appointment for my hair?" Kendall asked, changing the subject.

Pam smiled. "Lucky for you, I'd taken the morning off to run errands and I got back here early. I'll take care of it for you since —" She leaned closer again. "You don't want my mom changing you from pink to blue. Mom specializes in the blue-haired set."

Pam chuckled and Kendall found her light laughter infectious. "I'd appreciate your services."

"Then come with me."

Kendall followed Pam to the back room, doing her best to ignore the continuing stares, though she couldn't help but feel some of the women were actually glaring behind her back.

Pam seated her in a salon chair and wrapped a black cloak around her neck, covering her from head to toe. "Ignore them, honey. This morning's group of customers isn't representative of our town as a whole, I promise." Pam patted her on the shoulder. "Now, you want to go back to blond?"

Kendall nodded. "As close as possible."

"Okay, we're going to have to do some serious stripping before adding back some color." Pam headed for a small closetlike area, talking as she worked. "You may still have red tones even when we're through. Red's the hardest color to take and the most difficult to get rid of — unless you don't mind going green."

Kendall's eyes opened wide and Pam chuckled. "Just kidding. I only want you to understand what we're up against. It may take a few tries over a few weeks until the new color sets and takes."

Kendall doubted she'd be here that long but why get into that conversation with Pam. "Subtle red tones are fine. Anything more natural-looking than what I've got now," Kendall assured her.

"Cut?" Pam poked her head out of the working closet. "I've been dying to try that Meg Ryan shag on someone but no one in town's had the guts."

Kendall glanced at her shoulder-length hair in the mirror. "I take it you want me to be your guinea pig?"

Pam grinned. "I'll be your best friend," she said in a singsong voice.

The chant was reminiscent of the childhood

song Kendall had heard others use, but never about her. The happy lyric brought a lump to her throat and a longing for she wasn't sure what. Kendall inhaled deeply. "Sure. Why not. Make me look like Meg." She laughed, striving to shake off the unnerving feeling, the sense of loss that accompanied the knowledge that she'd never had a childhood best friend.

Once given permission, Pam squealed with delight. "You've got yourself a friend forever."

That thought not only cheered Kendall but gave her something special she'd never had. "Back at you, Pam."

For the next fifteen minutes, Pam chatted away while she worked and when she was through, Kendall had dye covering her entire head and a new friend in this town. But despite Pam's warm demeanor, no one else in the salon attempted a friendly wave or even a hello. Kendall tried to tell herself it didn't matter, but in her heart she knew it did.

In the four days she'd been in this town she'd come face-to-face with the things she'd never had in life — close friends and family. And for the first time, the loss hurt.

"Another twenty minutes and we'll rinse you." Pam set the timer and placed it on the counter. "Relax for a while, okay?"

Kendall did as she suggested and closed her eyes, ignoring the chatter around her, thinking instead of the best way to approach Pam about setting up her designs for display in the shop.

Finally, all noises drifted far away and peace descended on her.

"Hi, honey."

Without warning, a familiar male voice disturbed her rest. The seductive cologne excited her senses. She opened her eyes to find Rick, hands braced on either side of her chair, leaning over her.

"I love the hairdo." He grinned.

Ignoring the burning flush Kendall felt certain rose to her cheeks, she shrugged. "You know what they say, the things women do in the name of beauty."

"You are beautiful, even with that slop on your head. Not many women can say that."

"Please." She waved away his obvious exaggeration. "If any modeling agency saw me like this, I'd never have gotten my aunt's bills paid."

His sexy lips turned downward in a frown. "Some people don't know their own worth."

He stared into her eyes, almost willing her to believe until beneath his compelling gaze, she almost felt beautiful. The compliment warmed her, even as warning bells sounded in her head. "You flatter me, but I have a hunch you're awfully good at that," she said in an attempt to distance herself from her rampaging emotions and growing feelings for Rick Chandler.

"I'm good, period." He grinned, letting her know he was kidding. "Which of my attributes are you talking about, specifically?"

She rolled her eyes. "Your ability to flatter all

women, Officer Chandler."

"You never mentioned that you have a short-term memory problem. As of a couple of days ago, there are no other women. Only you." His hazel eyes danced with delight and he exuded charm even the most jaded female would be hard-pressed to resist.

"I remember." She licked her dry lips. "So, do you make it a habit of stopping by the hair salon?" She sought to change the subject.

"Only when a certain red car is parked outside."

"You came to see me?"

He winked, then brushed a kiss over her lips, taking her completely off guard. "Course I did. You're sitting in gossip central. What better way to get those tongues wagging?"

Her mouth tingled from his touch and the delicious hint of spearmint on his breath, but disappointment settled in her stomach. "Of course. That makes sense." Play out the charade, Kendall thought. How could she have been stupid enough to forget for even one second?

Now that her attention was properly refocused, she realized silence had once again descended in Luanne's as the gossips tried in vain to hear their whispered conversation.

"Smile." He reached out and touched one corner of her mouth, pulling her unwilling lips upward. "We have an audience."

She forced a grin, then reminded herself she

had no reason to be upset or disappointed. They had a bargain. She didn't want anything real with Rick Chandler any more than he wanted a relationship with her. But those sexual sparks wouldn't be denied and Kendall's gut told her they were both headed for trouble.

"Did you meet everyone here?" His hand swept around the shop in a grand gesture.

She shook her head. "As your . . . significant other, by reputation anyway, they didn't exactly roll out the welcome mat. Except for Pam. She's wonderful."

"Pam's a sweetheart. But you're telling me the rest of these women weren't friendly?" He frowned. "I never intended for you to suffer because of our agreement."

His serious expression did nothing to detract from his sex appeal, to Kendall's unending dismay.

"Hey, everyone," he called out, turning away from Kendall and toward the room at large.

"Rick . . ." She grabbed for his arm but missed.

"I want you all to meet Kendall Sutton. I know you all loved Crystal and you'll extend your friendship and sympathies to her niece."

Kendall noticed Rick didn't ask anyone to do him a favor, but his meaning was implied. Too bad Kendall didn't want friendships based on the fact that Rick asked people to be nice to her. Nor did she plan to stay here long enough for it to matter, she reminded herself.

He turned back to Kendall. "Mission accomplished." He treated her to a flirty wink. "I'll see *you* later." Another kiss, this one thorough and mind-blowing and then he was gone.

But his impact remained. Long after he'd walked out the door, her head still spun and her heart beat furiously inside her chest. She let out a long, slow exhale, trying to regain equilibrium.

"That's some guy you've got yourself." Pam's sigh echoed Kendall's previous one.

She bit the inside of her cheek. "You can say that alright."

"Ready to be washed?"

Kendall nodded. Once Pam had her settled in the sink, head tipped backward, lukewarm water rinsing down her scalp, Kendall realized she had her chance to talk potential business without anyone overhearing. "I have a proposition for you, Pam."

"Hmm. Sounds intriguing."

"Have you thought about setting up a jewelry or accessory area inside the store? Either where you walk in at the entrance or near the back wall?"

"No, but the concept sounds intriguing. What do you have in mind?"

"My designs. Wire jewelry and stones. I'm thinking if you let me leave some pieces here, we'll see if they generate interest. If things sell, I'll give you a percentage of the sale. It's a win-win situation." Kendall needed extra money badly right now. The cleaning supplies for the house alone put a dent in her wallet and her budget had been shot to hell and back.

"Hmm." Pam put the final conditioner in Kendall's hair. "I love jewelry and I hate turning down an offer like that, but you might be more successful talking to Charlotte about putting your pieces in her store." After rinsing her scalp with cool water, Pam wrapped a towel around Kendall's head, blotting her hair as she helped her rise.

Blood rushed to Kendall's head as she sat up, but the dizziness quickly subsided. Too bad the rush left by Rick's visit hadn't disappeared as easily. "Who's Charlotte?"

Pam walked in front of her so she could meet Kendall's gaze, then perched her hands on her hips. "Just how well do you know your boyfriend?"

"Well enough. Why?"

She narrowed her eyes. "Because Charlotte is Rick's sister-in-law. She's the first woman in this town to nab a Chandler man. And I'd think you would know that."

Kendall swallowed a groan. Rick's car had been parked outside her guest house through most of his days off. He'd arrived at six in the morning and stayed past ten most nights. They'd scrubbed, cleaned, and given everyone the impression they were new lovers, so head over heels for one another, they couldn't bring themselves to give up their private time just yet.

And lovers quickly learned intimate details about one another, including details about their families. Too bad she and Rick hadn't taken that into account before letting Kendall loose on her own.

"You were holed up in that house for days on end, but you obviously didn't spend much time talking." Pam grinned, giving Kendall the solution she needed.

Latching on to Pam's suggestiveness, Kendall nodded. "We spent enough time together to learn plenty." She wiggled her eyebrows provocatively. "But I just spaced for a second. Of course I knew which Charlotte you meant."

Pam eyed her as if she didn't believe a word and she was right. "Okay, well, if Charlotte isn't interested, just come ask me again and we'll work something out."

"I'll do that." Next time she saw Rick, she'd ask him about his sister-in-law, what she was like and if she'd be willing to consider taking in jewelry on consignment. "Thanks for the suggestion."

Pam led Kendall back to the chair and began combing out her now blond hair. "Like it?"

She gave Pam a truthful smile. "Very much."

"Good. Now let's cut!" Pam lifted the scissors and started snipping.

Rick kicked his chair back at his desk and fired off a rubber band at the bridal picture again. But this time, it wasn't the bride he was pissed at, it was himself. When he'd concocted his plan to make the town and his mother think he and Kendall were lovers, he'd blundered. Twice. He'd never meant to duplicate Kendall's painful recent past and he sure as hell had never meant to isolate her in the process. He'd never given the possibility a thought.

Then again he'd never taken women's personalities into account. He'd seen Lisa in the back of the salon and knew she had to be behind the cold reception Kendall had been given. Lisa had probably gotten everyone to treat her as the outsider who'd taken one bachelor off the list of available men in a small town.

"Messages." Felicia slapped a small stack of pink paper in front of him.

Rick glanced up at the petite brunette. She'd had her share of relationships with men and she had many women friends. Maybe she could offer insight into the thinking of the females in this town and why they'd be out to ostracize a perfect stranger. "What is it with women?"

"You're asking me?" Felicia settled into a metal chair beside his desk. "I thought you had written the book on the fairer sex."

He leaned back in his seat and folded his arms behind his head. "I never claimed to understand the female psyche."

"Lance says the same thing," she said, speaking of her current steady. "So is your new girlfriend giving you fits already?" she asked, a knowing twinkle in her eye.

Actually, Kendall wasn't the problem, he was. He wanted to ease her transition to town, make her happy and comfortable here — something he'd never given a thought to with other women who came and went from his life. Kendall, with her pink, now who-knew-what color hair and her sunny attitude, had gotten under his skin.

"That's okay, you don't have to answer," Felicia said. "But if she's making you work hard instead of falling at your feet, I can't wait to meet her."

Meet her. Maybe that was the solution. Let people meet and know Kendall, as he was coming to know her. Felicia had just given him his solution. He'd let Kendall meet his friends and family, people who'd like her and who she'd like in return. She'd be more comfortable in town once she had allies on her side. No one in town would challenge the Chandlers when they came out in force.

He jumped up and hugged his dispatcher. "You're a genius, Felicia."

"Genius, huh? I don't know what I said, but I ought to tease you more often. Did I mention I want a raise?" She let out a good-natured laugh.

"I'll put in a good word to the chief." He winked and grabbed for the phone.

The clean smell of disinfectant greeted

Kendall as she entered her house. The fresh odor offered a huge improvement over dust and mildew, but she wasn't nearly through. Still on her list to make the place more appealing was cleaning out the closets filled with old junk, painting inside and out, lawn maintenance and more.

She ran a hand through her freshly cut hair. The tasks were infinite. Her bank account wasn't. She opened her bag and searched for the card Rick had left her with his phone number, called and left a message that she needed to speak with him. She didn't want an "in" with Charlotte, just a little background and a push in the right direction. Kendall felt confident her designs would sell themselves.

With a little luck, Charlotte would be more friendly than some others she'd met today. While paying for her hair, she'd been snubbed by two women in a matter of seconds. Terrie Whitehall, a bank teller, and Lisa Burton, a teacher, both stuffed prigs according to Pam, had rebuffed Kendall's attempt at a friendly hello. Pam had retaliated with a verbal barb, giving Kendall a laugh, and she'd left the salon on a high, knowing she had at least one female friend in this small town.

Her cell phone rang and she answered it on the first ring. "Hello?"

"Ms. Kendall Sutton please," a nasal but otherwise toneless male voice requested.

"This is Kendall."

"This is Mr. Vancouver from the Vermont Acres Boarding School."

Kendall gripped the phone. "Is Hannah okay?"

"Physically she's fine. However she's been acting up lately." His monotone voice never wavered, making Kendall dislike him intensely. He could have been talking about a stranger for all he seemed to care.

"Hannah mentioned a few detentions, but promised she'd pull things together."

"Well she hasn't. I tried to reach your parents, but they're out of touch and you were the next emergency number. The only one actually and you're the only relative in the States. Ms. Sutton, your sister is on probation."

"Academic probation?"

Mr. Vancouver let out a haughty laugh, but he didn't sound the least bit amused. "Academics seems to be the least of her concerns, and right now it's less important than her behavior. To be frank, Ms. Sutton, your sister is a menace. She stuffed the toilets in the teacher's lounge and pulled off the conductor's toupee in front of an audience while he was taking a bow."

Kendall pressed hard against one temple to alleviate the headache she felt coming on. She stifled the urge to laugh at the absurdity of it all. It wasn't funny. Hannah's behavior was about as amusing as Mr. Vancouver's arrogant tone. "I'm sorry, Mr. Vancouver. I promise to talk to her today."

"You'd better or you'll be coming to get her before sundown. I can't allow such upheaval in my school."

"Where's Hannah now?"

"In detention. She should be back in her room within the hour. I have another call waiting." He dismissed her without a second thought. "Good day, Ms. Sutton."

The stuffy-head principal hung up the phone, leaving Kendall with cramps in her stomach and a growing urge to strangle her sister. Kendall needed answers as to why Hannah would suddenly act out in a way destined to get her expelled from school.

A frustrating ten minutes later, Kendall had left a phone message for Hannah, instructing her to call ASAP, and tried every available means to get in touch with her parents through the organization that granted her father money for his studies, to no avail. She sighed and glanced around the kitchen. The chipped paint and stains on the walls were the same in every room of the house, a symbol of the problems surrounding her. Troubles that seemed to grow over time.

"I wish I wasn't alone," she shouted to the walls. Her voice echoed in the empty house, startling her.

The sudden need to share her burden took Kendall off guard, as did the growing desire to call Rick again just to see if he'd answer so she could hear his voice. Even her hand, still on the telephone receiver, tingled, urging her to dial.

No. "No," she said aloud, to reinforce the notion. Though he knew she wanted to sell the house and knew she was short on cash, he didn't realize how tight things actually were. Nor would he, for the same reasons she wouldn't share her concerns about Hannah with him now.

She'd kept him distant from her personal problems out of necessity — she couldn't afford to rely on him. His presence had the ability to make her feel better and her entire life and history taught her she had to rely only on herself. Now wasn't the time to change what worked.

Even without calling a realtor, Kendall knew the key to selling high was to invigorate the interior with a fresh coat of paint. Rick had already scraped and sanded many areas in the guest house, so she felt comfortable beginning the painting of the main house on her own. She'd moved around enough to have sublet and rented many apartments and repainted many a wall.

She ran to the back bedroom, changed into old workout clothes, then surveyed the damage in the entry. She'd already bought gallons of fresh white paint and decided to begin there, where a potential buyer would get their first impression. Then she could work her way through to the rest of the house, so she'd see improvement each time she entered. In the meantime, she also hoped to pass time so she wouldn't keep looking at her watch, waiting for her sister or her wayward parents to call.

After turning on the radio and ruthlessly squelching another urge to contact Rick for his shoulder or any other body parts that tempted her, she got to work.

Rick thought his shift would never end. By the time he made his way to Kendall's house on Edgemont Street, dusk had fallen. She wasn't expecting him but he had an invitation to issue. One he hoped she wouldn't refuse, partly because he wanted to help ease her transition to Yorkshire Falls but mostly because he'd missed her and wanted to spend time with her again. Considering she wouldn't be staying in town long, Rick knew his first rationale was lame and pathetic but he didn't give a damn. He'd caused her hurt and he'd damn well fix things before she moved on.

He knocked on the door and when she didn't answer, he let himself inside. Apparently she wasn't that much of a newcomer if she'd left her door open. No one in Yorkshire Falls worried much about locks, much to Rick's and the rest of the force's chagrin.

Once inside, music reached his ears. He glanced around to see Kendall, singing while she painted a wall with broad strokes of a roller. Her effort reached only as far as her arm length, leaving a ragged horizontal difference between the new bottom finish and the old paint on top. Though what she'd done looked great, the initial impression was unprofessional at best.

Rick shook his head and laughed. "You could give poor Eldin a run for his money."

"Rick!" Her voice held a combination of warmth and pleasure as she scrambled to put down the equipment so she could greet him. "I probably should have gone out and bought a ladder, huh?" A sheepish grin spread across her face. "I was just so anxious to get started and keep busy, I didn't want to wait."

"Why didn't you call and ask me to pick up a ladder?"

"Didn't think of it."

He stepped forward, moving toward her, propelled by a force stronger than his mind or his will. "I suppose you expect me to fix what's left?"

She bit down on her lower lip and treated him to an adorable grin. "We do have a deal."

"Yeah we do." That damn deal. The one that named them lovers in public but gave Rick no rights over her body in private. Damned if he didn't want to change that.

The thought had been rushing through his mind the entire day. This woman he barely knew, one he for some reason wanted to protect emotionally and possess physically, had gotten to him. More than any woman had in a long while. He stepped forward and trapped her close to him. She couldn't step back or she'd hit the wet wall, so she inched closer to him instead.

He inhaled and was enveloped by her luscious scent. He took in her lithe body, covered only by a spandex exercise outfit. No doubt the oppressive heat explained her choice in clothing. The air-conditioning unit she'd bought only cooled off the bedroom in which she slept. The rest of the old house was on its own, Kendall refusing to spend another penny on a place she'd be leaving soon anyway.

Her departure was something he refused to contemplate. He wasn't ready to say good-bye. Not when he hadn't yet begun to say hello.

He intended to start now.

Her wide-eyed gaze met his and she waited for his next move. He braced his hands above her head and with the cold, wet sensation on his palms, he realized his mistake immediately.

"Wall's wet." She laughed.

"Gee, thanks for reminding me." He had paint on both hands.

"Just being neighborly."

"Surely you can think of a better term than neighborly — for your lover."

"In name only." She spoke the facts, but her eyes questioned.

Asked the same thing he'd been wondering. Could they allow themselves more?

She sucked in a shaky breath.

The deep inhale had the effect of squaring her shoulders and pushing out her chest, her round breasts tempting him through the tight spandex.

"We could change that," he offered.

She tipped her head to one side. Her freshly blond, newly cut hair brushed her shoulders, surrounding her face in a sexy shag. Damn, but he had a thing for blondes. For *this* blonde.

"We could." Her words came out an exhale.

He tilted his head and captured her lips with his. Earlier today he'd been performing for an audience. This kiss was theirs alone. Despite the blood rushing through his veins, he took his time, nibbling on her lower lip and savoring the sounds of delight she uttered in response. And when he cupped her breast in his palm, the gesture felt natural and right, causing an ache in his groin and a pulsing, pounding rhythm inside his head.

He wasn't content with the simple touch when his body demanded so much more but before he could take what he wanted, Rick was interrupted by the distinctive ring of a cell phone. Out of habit, he reached for the phone clipped on his belt buckle.

With obvious regret she stepped away. "It's mine," she said in a husky voice.

But she was his, Rick thought, as his handprint, stark white against the black fitted material of her top, pointed out. And he planned to pick up where they left off as soon as this unwanted interruption was over.

"Hello?" She grabbed the phone and spoke as if she were expecting an urgent call.

He didn't eavesdrop but he couldn't miss her raised voice either and by the time she'd hung up, Rick realized the moment between them had vanished. Sexual tension had been replaced by plain aggravation as an agitated Kendall paced back and forth on the other side of the room, muttering to herself.

"What's wrong?"

"Family problems." She crossed the floor and came up beside him. Her brows furrowed, puckering her forehead.

He wanted to smooth her skin and remove her worries. Her distress drew him toward her, even as his head warned him to mind his own business. "Anything I can do to help?" he asked anyway.

She shook her head. "Thanks but nothing you need to concern yourself with." She spoke as if they hadn't just been locked in a heated embrace, as if he couldn't possibly care about more than her body.

He expelled a frustrated sigh. She was shutting him out. Physically she stood close, but emotionally she'd withdrawn and was miles away. The handprint that once branded her as his now acted as a glaring STOP sign.

In the silence, his beeper went off and he glanced down, the number reminding him of why he'd come to Kendall's house in the first place. Chase was calling him from Norman's where his family and friends were waiting to surprise Kendall.

Rick didn't know what was bothering her, what kind of family business she had to take care of, but it was obviously serious, and he doubted she'd go anywhere now. Not without good reason.

She met his gaze, a mix of emotions in her eyes and expression. "My sister's half a step away from being expelled from boarding school," she said at last.

He stepped toward her, wrapping one arm around her in a show of support, the only gesture he sensed she'd accept. He was right. She sighed and rested her head on his shoulder.

Things couldn't go more wrong, so Rick steeled himself and said, "I don't suppose now's the time to tell you my family and friends are waiting at Norman's for a welcome to town party?"

Kendall sighed. His admission surprised her and despite her fury with her sister, she softened toward Rick once more. She was in no mood for people but since Rick cared enough to bring family and friends together for her benefit, the least she could do was put her personal problems on the back burner and accompany him to Norman's.

She turned toward him with a grateful smile. "Thank you."

He inclined his head. "My pleasure."

She inhaled his potent male scent and the desire to lose herself in him and forget her problems and the party grew stronger. She couldn't. "Give me a few minutes to shower and change."

"You got it."

Quicker than she'd thought possible, she doused herself in hot water, washed off the paint, moussed her hair, and quickly chose an outfit. It helped that Brian's package had also included most of her wardrobe. He'd turned her keys over to her landlady, who packed up items in her closet and drawers for him to send along. She thanked herself for having foresight to think ahead for once. A quick glance in the mirror and she squared her shoulders, set to go but not quite ready to face Rick. How could she be when the tingling in her veins from their mini-makeout session hadn't dissipated?

But forcing lightness into her step, she bounded down the stairs, skidding to a halt in front of him. "I'm all set."

He let out a long, slow whistle. "You sure are." He grabbed for her hand and twirled her around.

For a full view, she assumed. Her leather pants were courtesy of her modeling days, same with the lace top. Neither were overly expensive since she hadn't modeled for designer catalogue companies but she knew the clothing would make her stand out in a crowd. Despite the fact that this party was nothing more than a means to cement the idea of them as a couple, she wanted to make a good impression. Though she was loath to admit it, she wanted Rick's family and friends to like her. She wanted *him* to like her too.

He squeezed her hand tighter. "Kendall, about before —"

"Forget it." She didn't want to hear the kiss never should have happened, not when awareness still sizzled and made her feel alive.

"Not possible." His gaze lingered, as warm and hot as his lips had been earlier. On her mouth and almost on her breast. She sucked in a gulp of air.

"You're right," she admitted and exhaled hard. "So what did you want to say?" She refused to run from whatever he needed to tell her.

Once again a telephone's irritating ring interrupted them. This time the distraction came from Rick's cell and he answered it, regret in his gaze. "Hello?" He listened and then said, "We'll be right there." He flipped his phone closed. "We're late."

She nodded, accepting the reprieve. She shouldn't be engaging in intimate conversation with Rick. She couldn't deny the attraction but letting herself get close to him wasn't smart. Kendall intended to leave this town — and Rick — soon. No one and nothing could change her views. Not even the sexy cop with the drop-dead smile and warm heart.

CHAPTER FIVE

Kendall took in her surroundings, enjoying Norman's different ambience. The man had probably been a bird-watcher in another life because various species dominated the walls in photographs and decorative birdhouses hung from the ceiling.

"Rick's always known how to utilize his best assets," Raina Chandler said, bringing Kendall back to the conversation at hand. "He used his good looks to charm women even back when he was a kid."

Izzy, the wife and co-owner of Norman's, nodded in agreement. "At twelve years old he'd come in here and compliment me, hoping to get a free pack of gum. Imagine someone who looks like me" — she pointed to her gray hair and overweight body — "buying into the notion that I was as good-looking as Cindy Crawford. Rick always was a charmer."

Kendall laughed. "I can believe that." He still was. Dressed in faded blue jeans and a navy and white striped polo shirt, he was the epitome of sexy. But more importantly, he had a good heart.

He'd introduced her to his family and friends, people who were warm, caring, and treated her much differently than those in the salon. People who welcomed her and helped her to forget about her family problems for a little while.

"So, Kendall, how long do you plan to stay in town?" Raina asked, not for the first time.

Kendall was running out of ways to change the subject. "Well . . ."

"You've monopolized her enough." Rick's brother Chase stepped in.

With his pitch-black hair and blazing blue eyes, he didn't resemble Rick or Raina. From what Kendall had heard, both Chase and the youngest but absent brother Roman were the epitome of their deceased father. But according to rumor, all three Chandler brothers had always caused a stir among women. Chase was just the most reserved of the three.

"Now, Chase, let me enjoy my time with Crystal's niece."

"Grill her is more like it." Chase snorted and took Kendall's elbow in a gentlemanly grip. "I'd like to get to know her for a little while." Without waiting for his mother's reply, he led her away from the chattering women.

"Another Chandler brother who rescues women in need?" Kendall asked, once they were alone.

Chase raised his eyes toward the heavens. "Hell no. That's Rick's job. I just saw my mother gearing up for the inquisition and decided to spare you." He propped one shoulder against the wall, studying her through piercing blue eyes.

Sexy eyes if she weren't so attracted to his brother instead. "Well, I appreciate you running interference. So tell me a little about you. I understand you run the local paper?"

"*The Gazette.*"

He shoved his hands into his pockets, a gesture so like Rick she almost laughed. "Oh, yes. You're a weekly, aren't you?"

He nodded.

Unlike Rick though, this brother was a man of few words. Yet Kendall liked him, if for no other reason than he'd raised his siblings and obviously had a good heart. Something else the brothers had in common. Kendall glanced over to where Rick stood talking on his cell phone, gesturing with one hand. She grinned. Even when he wasn't working, he was working. She admired his dedication to his job. Oh, heck, she just plain admired the man.

"Don't get too attached to him," Chase said into the silence.

She blinked and turned back, embarrassed at having been caught staring. "I hadn't planned on it." But she did want to know why he'd felt compelled to issue the warning. She bit down on her lower lip. "Any chance you want to tell me why?"

"Not really." His eyes twinkled with mystery and knowledge. "But I will. Rick will walk before he lets you get close to him."

"Because of his previous marriage?" she asked, speaking the words before thinking them through. She doubted the oldest sibling would discuss his brother's past.

Sure enough, his eyes narrowed. "Rick told you about that?"

Kendall wouldn't lie, not even in the name of getting information she'd rather have come from Rick himself. She shook her head. "No, he intimated as much."

Chase nodded, understanding smoothing the lines in his forehead. "Well, let's just say once a man's been dumped by his wife he tends to be more cautious in the future."

So that was the story. Kendall had sensed as much and a vise clamped her heart at the thought of Rick being hurt by anyone. Especially by a woman.

Chase gave her a steely-eyed stare, as if assessing *her* character and gearing up for more to say.

"And?" she asked, not wanting him to hold back or censor himself. Though she had a hunch this newspaperman would always state the cold, hard truth. Whether she liked it or not.

"Don't count on him giving his heart to any woman. Especially one just passing through." His voice eased as if attempting to soften the blow.

She'd liked Chase from the start. Now she respected him too. But her heart sank anyway.

Sank unreasonably she knew, since she wasn't giving *her* heart any more than she was capable of settling down.

"Is that right?" she asked Chase in an attempt to play it cool.

He tipped his head to one side. "Yes, it is. You see, I deal in facts."

"Spoken like a true journalist," she said wryly.

"I am what I am." His mouth lifted in a half smile.

"I'm curious about something though. There's got to be a dozen women in this town banging on your brother's door. Do you give them the same speech?"

"No, ma'am. My mother cared for your aunt, so by extension that makes you like family."

There was that word again. Family. The Chandlers tossed it around so easily, but for Kendall things weren't so simple. Not when it came to family, the one thing she'd never had. Her throat swelled. Glancing at Chase, she managed a grateful nod.

He lifted her chin in his hands. "I'm just trying to help. So consider this conversation my welcome to town gift, okay? Maybe you'll even thank me one day."

Perhaps she would. In the meantime, she grappled to get her feet cemented on the floor and fix Chase's notion that she was the one about to be hurt. "Journalists don't work on assumptions, do they?" she asked him.

"Nope. Why do you ask?"

"Because you're assuming I'll be the one to fall hard for your brother." She leaned toward Chase and whispered in his ear. "News flash: I'm not sticking around long enough to worry about being hurt or dumped. But I've been known to make a pretty big impact on a guy." She hoped her words would be prophetic. No falling, no heartache, not for her. "So maybe it's your brother who needs this warning, his feelings you need to worry about. Not mine." She forced a grin.

Chase let out a loud laugh. His first full smile of the night tilted his lips, giving Kendall a glimpse at the sexier side a woman could fall for. Another woman, she thought wryly. She'd already fallen for Rick.

"You know I can see why Rick likes you. You need anything while you're in town, just give me a call."

"Thank you." On impulse, Kendall touched his arm.

"Ahem." The sound of Rick clearing his throat interrupted the moment.

Kendall's heart leapt at the sight of him. She hadn't realized she'd missed his presence, but now she was glad he'd been able to get away from police business, the phone, and the people demanding his attention. Glad he'd come to stand by her side.

Uh-oh. She recalled Chase's warning, and issued a strict reminder to tread carefully while she was here. But her pulse tripled and her mouth grew dry, the attraction stronger than rational thought.

"What's going on?" Rick's steady gaze settled on their physical connection.

She'd been so caught up in the joy of seeing him, she'd forgotten her hand lingered on Chase's arm and she jerked her hand back at the same time Chase let out his second laugh of the evening.

"Jealous?" he asked Rick.

"If you hadn't taught me to be a gentleman in front of a lady, I'd tell you to shut the hell up."

Kendall stifled a chuckle, though she liked the possibilities inherent in Chase's suggestion. Despite her better judgment.

Chase turned back to her. "The one fact I forgot to mention during our conversation earlier was that during the time he's with you, he's possessive." He gave her a meaningful glance, then slapped his brother on the back and walked away, shaking his head and chuckling as he left.

"What was that all about?" Rick asked, a scowl on his handsome face.

Kendall shrugged, not really certain whose interest Chase had been looking out for, hers, Rick's, or both. "Your brother was just issuing me a friendly warning."

"A little too friendly if you ask me." Rick's jaw ticked, tight with tension, tempting her to reach out and smooth the razor-stubbled skin and ease his muscles until he relaxed under her touch.

Her stomach curled with unexpected excitement. Could Chase be right? Could Rick be jealous? At the possibility, she took a mental step back to examine her own feelings. Impulse would be deadly now and she forced herself to think clearly. Jealousy would indicate interest. Interest she already knew existed after their encounter in the house earlier. But the surprise here was the realization that the emotion didn't have to pose a threat to Kendall or her heart. How could it when even Chase, who knew Rick better than anyone, admitted his brother would run before committing to anything serious? Just like Kendall would be gone before she could get hurt or attached?

With both those facts being true, clarity seemed to descend upon her. Why was she fighting the attraction? Why wasn't she letting herself indulge in what promised to be the most passionate sensual affair she'd ever had? There was no reason *not* to embrace the opportunity they both wanted.

She stepped closer. "Friendly isn't threatening, Rick." She didn't want him to feel competitive with his older brother. She inched nearer until she couldn't breathe without inhaling his masculine scent. She knew without a doubt she wanted their bargain to be a reality. She wanted to be his lover until she left town and she wasn't just falling into the convenience of their charade.

No man had ever affected her as deeply or kindled desire in her as quickly as he did. Her previous relationships were like her moves from town to town, quick and distant. Only Brian had gotten closer than most because they'd needed something from each other. They'd grown fond of one another in the process yet intimacy had always been missing. Nothing was missing in her feelings for Rick. The sexual attraction sizzled, the emotional connection was secure and reciprocal.

He'd been hurt once. She didn't know how long ago or by whom, but she could help him heal, the same way he'd been helping her. He'd provided a shoulder from the first time they'd met and he gave comfort as much as he aroused a physical need that had been dormant for too long. He obviously cared enough about her feelings to arrange this impromptu gathering. A gesture Kendall believed came from his heart, not from the need to further their façade as lovers. There were plenty of other ways of establishing them as a couple — his performance at the beauty salon being one of them. Not once had he attempted any overabundant display of affection or attention.

Until now.

She no longer worried about using him to get over a rough patch in her life, not when he obviously wanted the same kind of relationship she did. Short and sweet, but one that would build memories and good feelings to carry with her always. They seemed to be two kindred souls seeking the same thing. And he seemed to read her mind as he grabbed her hand and dragged her into the back hall.

Rick enjoyed women, and jealousy was a foreign emotion. Possessiveness was even more alien. But seeing Chase deep in conversation with Kendall and her hand on his arm set off an intense burning in his gut. Without stopping to think further he pulled Kendall down Norman's back hall.

"Rick?"

He ignored her for now. He had plenty to say, but not in front of an audience. He expelled an annoyed groan and pushed open the nearest door, which turned out to be an empty ladies' room. Thank God.

"Rick, talk to me —"

He cut her off, pulling her into an embrace and sealing his mouth over hers. Her warmth melted the hours of frustration he'd endured in favor of making sure she was accepted in his small town. She stirred carnal needs he'd ignored for too long. Or maybe he'd never felt this much before, but he was damn well feeling now. His heart beat fast and furious in his chest and his groin pulsed hard against his rough denim jeans, and all the while he made love to her with his mouth, his tongue mimicking the act his body desperately craved.

She kissed him back, matching him move for move, her mouth hard and demanding against his. Her eager submission dissolved his earlier annoyance and frustration, while the fire in his gut burned hotter. The flame she ignited didn't just smolder, it burst into a raging inferno he could barely control. But a small semblance of rational thought remained, enough for him to take advantage, flipping the lock on the bathroom door.

He needed to get her alone and cement where things stood. For the time she remained in Yorkshire Falls, he wanted to know she was his. He'd lost one woman in his life because he'd worn blinders. He wasn't about to screw up his short time with Kendall.

For the moment though, talk could wait. He slipped his tongue inside her moist mouth and placed his arm around her until he cupped her bottom in his hand. She groaned and wiggled closer, her body molding perfectly to his, making him want to ease those leather pants down her long legs and bury himself deep inside her willing body. And he had no doubt she was willing.

She lifted her head suddenly, her eyes bright, her lips moist and damp from his kiss. "We need to talk."

Though he'd thought the same thing minutes earlier, now he was hard and aching, wanting nothing more than to slip inside her moist heat and claim her as his own. Not that he'd act on their hunger here. When he made love to her, there would be no phones, no people, no distractions.

Right now, despite the glazed desire in her eyes, concern furrowed her eyebrows and Kendall looked distracted. And that wasn't the emotion he wanted her feeling. "What's wrong?"

"I think we should clear the air." She licked her already moist lips. "You know. Set parameters."

"Okay." He'd dragged her back here for the same reasons.

"I'm leaving when the house is ready to go on the market."

"I know that." It was the source of his churning gut. Rick had been in a relationship where he'd been caught off guard by a wife who'd left him for another man. Since then he'd kept his distance from women, telling himself that way he wouldn't get hurt again. But now, seeing his overwhelming reaction to Kendall, he realized he hadn't had to work hard at keeping other women at a distance. None had affected him this strongly before.

And damned if she didn't have one foot out the door before their relationship ever really began. Well at least this time he could say he was forewarned. He should be grateful Kendall chose to be honest with him now, before he fell hard for an impossible dream. But knowing how easily she drew him in, he'd realized he'd have to work harder at building those walls and keeping her out of his heart.

Starting now. He forced a casual shrug. "I'm not into long-term relationships anyway," he told her. And his stomach cramped harder. Not a good sign.

At his words, emotion flickered in her gaze. Good, Rick thought. Maybe she was more affected than she wanted him to believe. At least then they'd be on even footing.

"So we're in agreement. A short-term affair." She bit down on her lower lip.

Another sign of vulnerability, he thought. This conversation wasn't easy for her either and he sensed she was forcing the issue.

For both their sakes, he'd go along. "What else could we have? I'm the town playboy," he said lightly.

She flinched at the term and he took a perverse pleasure in the fact that his exaggerated status bothered her. Still he didn't want to drive her away, but bring her closer, taking what he could get while he could get it.

If she was going to leave as promised, he wanted all the time he could squeeze into her visit and intended to tell her so. He stroked a hand down her soft cheek. "But while you're here I'm all yours."

Her shoulders relaxed, her body easing closer to his. Awareness shimmered between them. Her lips beckoned and he lowered his head for another deep drugging kiss but before his mouth touched hers, a loud banging noise sounded from outside the door.

Kendall jumped back, knocking her head against the air dryer on the wall. "Ouch."

He reached out, running a hand over her newly cut, shaggy hair. "You okay?"

She nodded. "One second," she called out to the person on the other side of the door. Then she turned to Rick with wide, inquiring eyes. "What now?"

"Do you mean what do I want? Or is that a rhetorical question?" His heart pounded hard in his chest and his body told him not only what he desired but what he needed. Rick was the master of glib answers but right now, only the unvarnished truth would do. I want to take you home." Her home, his home, he didn't care as long as the place had a bed. He held out his hand.

Kendall placed her palm in his. "I'm hoping that's an invitation." A smile tilted her luscious lips.

"A very private, personal invitation," he said in a deliberate drawl.

Her cheeks heated to a flushed pink. He grabbed for the doorknob. Once outside, he planned to orchestrate a quick thank you and good-bye, then make their way to the street. They never passed the hall. The minute he stepped out of the bathroom, they were ambushed.

"Rick!" His sister-in-law Charlotte grabbed him in a huge embrace.

"Well, this is a surprise," he said into her hair, since he couldn't untangle himself from her bear hug. "I thought you were in D.C."

"We were." Roman's voice sounded from behind Charlotte.

Rick's brother and sister-in-law commuted between Yorkshire Falls where Charlotte owned her business and Washington, D.C., where Roman had a job as an Op-Ed columnist for *The Washington Post*.

Charlotte released her hold, mostly because Roman pried her arms free, then glared at her husband. Rick would have laughed at his brother's proprietary actions as he had in the past, but having dealt with his own reaction to Chase and Kendall, Rick understood his little brother better now.

"We heard there was a lot going on at home and we came as soon as we could." Charlotte grinned.

"Raina summoned you," Rick guessed.

"No, she just said she thought we'd like to come meet your new lady friend. Her words," Roman said. "I assume this is her?"

Rick glanced at Kendall in time to see her head ping-ponging, attempting to follow the three-way conversation.

Before he could begin the introductions, Kendall interrupted. "I'm her." She shook her head. "I mean I'm she. I'm Kendall Sutton."

Roman grinned. "Nice to meet you." He extended a hand and Kendall shook it.

"Likewise," Kendall said.

Charlotte took her turn next. "Did you know Roman kissed me for the first time in this hall? Remember?" Charlotte turned to her husband and devoured him with her eyes, making Rick, Kendall, and anyone within viewing distance feel disposable and irrelevant.

There was a time when Rick would have rolled his eyes and laughed. And there was also a time, pre-marriage and divorce, when he'd wondered if he'd ever feel that unique pull with another person. Like his mother had shared with his father. Like Roman now shared with Charlotte. Post divorce he'd spent more time running from relationships and commitment than pondering them. But now, watching the newlyweds, Rick felt a brand-new emotion — envy. Because he wanted Kendall to look at him that same covetous way.

He recalled the time he'd taken a look at his pregnant wife and seen more than a friend in need. And believing she was his by law and by word, he'd allowed himself to let down his guard, never once thinking Jillian would walk out on him, leaving him alone.

What he wanted from Kendall now transcended anything he'd desired from Jillian then. And this time Rick knew beforehand she had no intention of sticking around. Shit.

Rick glanced from Roman, who looked at

him as if he'd lost his mind, to Charlotte, who possessed an amused grin, to Kendall, who just looked confused.

"We were just leaving," Rick said. He wanted to get Kendall out of here and pick up where they left off. He wanted to get lost in the physical and forget the emotional pull she exerted — because around his close-knit family, emotions and the past were always too close to the surface.

"Now?" Charlotte asked. "You can't run out when we just got here."

"We made damn good time too," Roman added. "The least you could do is hang out awhile."

"He only got stopped by one cop." Charlotte sounded proud, then glanced at Rick. "I mean he only got stopped by one police officer doing his duty. And he had a very valid reason for pulling us over."

"Sitting in Roman's lap while he was driving?" Rick asked.

Charlotte blushed. "Something like that."

"We can stay awhile." Kendall tugged on his shirt. "Can't we, Rick? You wanted me to get to know your family and besides I've heard so much about Charlotte's shop. I'd like to talk to her."

"And she really wants to get to know you too. Besides, I'd like to catch up with my brother." Roman grinned.

Rick groaned. Catch up? Bullshit, he

126

thought. Roman knew damn well they'd spoken on the phone last night. But being the pain in the ass Rick had always loved, Roman was knowingly putting a wrench in Rick's plans to be alone with Kendall. And damned if he wasn't obviously enjoying it.

But Rick had no intention of letting his brother win. They'd have plenty of family time tomorrow while Rick had no idea how much longer he'd have with Kendall. And he both wanted and needed her tonight.

"I'm sure Charlotte's exhausted after flying into Albany and driving for over an hour." He met his sister-in-law's gaze, pinning her with his stare and hopefully reminding her she owed him a favor.

When the panty thief business had been going on and Roman was the prime suspect, Charlotte had discovered Samson, the town eccentric, was responsible for the thefts. His reasons had been benign — the older man had some misguided notion that he was somehow helping Charlotte by drawing attention to her store. Charlotte had informed Rick, but refused to speak on the record and swore she'd deny any knowledge if Rick arrested the man. Rick had let the old man's crimes go, marking the file unsolved. So Charlotte owed him and he now intended to call in the debt.

He held her gaze until she blinked first. Then she yawned, stretching her arms out beside her. "You're right, Rick. I'm beat. Can we have breakfast tomorrow instead?"

Roman exhaled an exaggerated groan. "Fine. I'll take my wife home for some R and R, and you two can get back to whatever you were doing before we arrived." He gave a meaningful glance back at the ladies' room from which they'd escaped.

Kendall sighed. "This doesn't look good, but I swear to you . . ."

"Please don't explain," Charlotte said. "Considering Raina's in the other room, I'm certain you were just looking for privacy."

Kendall laughed, but Rick wasn't amused because he wanted to be alone with her *now*. He nodded at his brother and Charlotte. "We're leaving."

"How's breakfast tomorrow?" Charlotte asked Kendall as Rick led her down the hall.

"Good for me."

"Nine A.M.," Charlotte called, her voice trailing off on a laugh, Roman chuckling along with her.

Rick didn't look back, not stopping until they'd reached the street.

"You were rude to Roman and Charlotte," Kendall scolded him as soon as the door to Norman's closed behind them.

"They're newlyweds. They'll understand." He squeezed her hand tighter.

His skin was as warm as her body was hot.

"I live upstairs." He pointed toward an alley on the side of what was Charlotte's Attic.

She glanced around the corner. "I knew you lived in town. Just not where."

He nodded. "When Roman and Charlotte got married, I moved into her apartment and they bought a small house in the new subdivision."

Though he made small talk, Kendall knew his intent was anything but trivial. He said no more, waiting for her to make the next move. He lived up those stairs and wanted to know if she'd go home with him. Sleep with him. Make love to him. A tremor started slow and worked through her body, a long, leisurely vibration that began as a low twisting in her belly and ended with a distinct throbbing between her legs.

His deep eyes met hers and she swallowed hard. She'd never been more aware of a man or his interest in her as a woman. She'd never enjoyed the attention quite so much or reciprocated the pulse-pounding need. Never wanted a man in her bed and inside her body the way she desired Rick now.

Kendall was impulsive, but this time she'd thought things through. She smiled at Rick. "Lead the way."

Raina glanced around at the familiar birdhouse decor adorning the walls and the people she called friends talking among themselves. Meanwhile she remained in this chair. Alone. "Darnit," she muttered.

She hated sitting still while life went on around her. Right under her nose, Rick dragged Kendall out of Norman's, obviously anxious to be alone. Looks like they didn't need Raina's interference or matchmaking. So why was she faking a heart condition, a charade that left her unable to mingle and be in the center of things?

"Anything wrong?" Eric joined her, pulling up a chair.

"It's about time you worked your way back here," Raina grumbled. Eric wasn't just her beau, but the town doctor. To her frustration, he'd stopped to talk to each friend and patient, while Raina who waited in the back of the room had to come last. She'd wanted to run up to him and capture his attention, but she couldn't, not without calling attention to herself and the vitality she was unable to express.

He let out a hearty laugh. "Feeling constrained by your antics? I told you no good could come out of pretending to be ill."

"Spoken as my doctor or as . . ." her voice trailed off. She wasn't sure how to finish the sentence.

"Spoken by someone who cares about you."

His words warmed her heart, capturing the same thing she felt for him. Reaching out, she placed her hand over his and studied him, once again struck by his distinguished appearance. His salt and pepper hair and weathered features gave him a ruggedly handsome look and made him stand out among Yorkshire Falls's single older men. For the first time in years, Raina's heart beat faster at the sight of a man and she wanted the freedom to act on her feelings.

"Isn't it time to end the charade?" he asked.

"I've been thinking that myself." Because of all the emotions rioting through Raina, guilt was paramount. Guilt over deceiving her sons and allowing them to worry about her for no real reason. Although, she reminded herself, her supposed illness had brought Roman and Charlotte together.

Then there was her middle child. Rick's prospects, which just last week had seemed hopeless, now blossomed with possibility. Raina had given every eligible female she could think of a nudge in her middle son's direction, but no sparks had resulted. Until Kendall arrived in town.

Yet they'd hooked up without Raina's matchmaking. "Maybe you're right." She sighed. "I could confess . . ."

"And we could start more openly dating instead of sneaking around," Eric said.

"You have no idea how wonderful that sounds."

"Then do something about it." His words sounded like a dare.

"I'll have to find the right time." Would there ever be a right time to tell her sons she'd betrayed them?

"They love you. They'll forgive you," Eric said, reading her mind.

"I hope so." But she wasn't as sure.

"Would you come over later tonight? I rented some DVDs."

She met his warm gaze, enjoying his interest. "I'd love to. Pick me up so my car isn't seen parked outside your house?" She tapped her fingers restlessly against the table, unable to believe she was plotting like a teenager who'd been forbidden to go out with her boyfriend. But as a woman recently diagnosed with a weak heart, she had no business driving to Eric's and remaining there for a good part of the night.

"I'll pick you up anywhere." He leaned over and brushed a soft kiss against her cheek. "But why don't I just take you home from here and drive you back later?"

"Sounds like a good idea. I'll just tell Chase he's off duty."

"And that puts me on call." Eric grinned. "I like the idea."

Raina smiled, the pleasure overwhelming. If Rick and Kendall were feeling as warm and fuzzy as she felt, Eric was right. It was time to confess because they didn't need her help at all.

Rick held Kendall's hand in a heated caress. She stepped into his apartment and immediately felt surrounded by his essence. With every inhale, she took in his masculine scent, stirring her already aroused senses.

He tossed his keys on the counter. The jingling sound along with the slam of the door and twist of the lock lent an erotic edge of anticipation to the night, serving as a prelude of what was to come.

He turned to face her. "There's no place like home."

Only a small light burned from the back hall, giving her a glimpse, and as she glanced around, the dark wood and barely there decor reminded her so much of Rick.

"So what do you think?" he asked, a wry tilt to his sexy lips.

"This place is very you."

"Tonight it's going to be *us*." His voice came out a low growl, curling her insides with a hunger long denied.

He reached for her, drawing her into his arms for a slow, seductive kiss that quickly turned wanton. The hours they'd spent in Norman's served to build the urgency between them and as he thrust his tongue into her open, waiting mouth, Kendall knew he was as hungry and desperate as she. For someone whose world was spiraling out of control, the notion that she wasn't alone was strangely reassuring.

By the time he broke the kiss and led her into his bedroom, she was burning with need. She told herself she was starting an affair but was more afraid the feelings arcing between them indicated something much deeper. Something she had no business contemplating now or ever.

He came up behind her and she turned to see

he'd already pulled off his shirt, leaving him dressed in a pair of jeans, the button already undone. His chest was tanned and muscular and as her gaze settled on the sprinkling of hair and his dark nipples, her own breasts hardened in response.

"The whole time we were in Norman's, I couldn't wait to get you alone."

"I know what you mean." She grinned. "I felt the same way."

His dark gaze bore into hers. "You didn't help matters, pressing to stay and talk to Charlotte."

"Part of me wanted to be polite. Another part needed to talk business." She grabbed hold of the scalloped edging of her lace shirt and teased him by slowly lifting her top. "You made me realize both could wait." Before she lost her nerve, she pulled the shirt up and over her head, letting it fall to the floor in a discarded heap. "Pleasure's much more important," she said, stepping forward and letting her bare chest, covered only by a wisp of a camisole, rub against his.

"I agree." He grasped on to her shoulders and his thumbs caressed her flesh with circular strokes. His body picked up a similar rhythm and through the soft silk, his hips swayed and his chest undulated against her. "Feel what you do to me."

"I do." Beaded and sensitive, her nipples rasped against the fabric, even the thin sheath too much of a barrier when she wanted only skin against skin.

"That's not all." He gyrated his hips in a circular motion, letting the building swell of his erection pulse and settle against her stomach. The sensual pull shook Kendall to her core, physically reaching out to her feminine mound, and emotionally touching the depths of her soul. She pressed her lower body tightly against him, both wanting to feel his hard body come alive and needing to feel more in an attempt to block any emotional feelings building inside her.

He groaned and eased her aside of him. Words were unnecessary as they undressed quickly, the frenzy to feel skin against skin consuming them both. Rick lifted her and lay her down on his bed, and as he came down on top of her, she took refuge in the sizzling body contact that felt so good. She sighed in pleasure, then realized the sound echoed between them.

Without warning, he sat up, his large body towering over her and his thighs straddling her stomach as he studied her intently. "I've never wanted another woman the way I want you."

Her heart flipped at the admission. "I feel the same way." Honesty compelled her to speak even as she warned herself against getting too attached to the man or the moment.

"I sure as hell hope not." He burst out laughing.

Kendall did a mental rewind and realized

what her words implied. A burning heat rose to her cheeks but she appreciated the sudden lightening of the mood. Intensity wouldn't do either of them any good right now. "I mean I've never felt this way about another man."

He ran a tender hand down her cheek. "I'm damn glad."

Emboldened, she smiled. "Then prove it."

"I intend to." He reached over and opened the night-stand drawer, pulling out a condom, then paused. "Kendall . . ."

"Yes?"

"I keep these out of habit, because Chase told both Roman and I that if we were ever unprepared, we weren't just disrespecting ourselves, but the woman we were with."

Kendall felt a rush of emotion as she realized the strong familial bond shared by the Chandlers, a bond she'd never experienced with anyone before. Except maybe her aunt, but that time had been too brief and the good memories often too painful to remember in light of the void that remained afterward.

"For a man of few words, your brother chooses them wisely." She returned her thoughts to Rick.

Rick nodded. "It's the journalist in him. But that's not my point."

"Then what is?"

A tight muscle pulled at his cheek. "I keep these here but I've never used them." He took out the entire box and dumped them on the mattress beside them. "Eleven plus this one makes twelve." He held the plastic wrapper in his hand.

He didn't have to say any more or tell her what his words and actions meant. He'd never brought a woman to his bed before and he wanted her to know it. There'd been plenty of women, Kendall was certain. Just none here. She swallowed hard.

Instead of reacting, she chose to keep the moment light. "So how many do you think we can use in one night?"

He studied her for an intense second, one in which she was afraid he'd call her hand or push for entry into emotions she didn't want to share.

Instead he grinned, shrugging off the serious moment. "Why don't we find out?" She watched as he took care of protection quickly, then splayed his hands across her thighs. His strong, weathered skin contrasted with her whiter flesh, making his virility and masculinity that much more intense.

He eased her legs open wide with his palms, nudging the head of his penis inside her and she gasped. Hard yet soft, hot yet tender, his body slipped into hers, opening her, consuming her. Kendall sucked in a breath, amazed at the intensity of the feelings this one simple act aroused. But nothing about Rick Chandler or her feelings for him were simple.

Before she could think further, he thrust inside her, filling her completely. Desire took over, kindling the fire he'd already lit and sucking her into a vortex of anticipation and heady sensation.

"Rick." Without planning or thought, she called out his name and his eyes darkened with heat and need.

Buried as deep as possible, their bodies joined, one impossible to distinguish from the next, he suddenly stopped, holding himself back. His arms shook with the force of his restraint.

"You stopped," she murmured. "Why?"

He leaned so his forehead touched hers. "How is it I feel like I've been waiting forever when we really just met?"

Kendall wished she knew. She opened her mouth to answer and was rewarded with a kiss instead. A hot, demanding, openmouthed kiss that told her exactly where they were headed. They didn't need foreplay. Foreplay had been every moment between them since the first time they'd met.

He trailed his tongue across her cheek until his mouth reached her ear. "I want you hot and ready," he said in a rough, husky voice that turned her on even more.

"I am."

"I know." He slid out of her then, letting her feel every hard ridge of his desire, then thrust back inside, revealing every slick inch of his straining erection to her waiting body.

Each teasing thrust tested her restraint and

brought her closer to the brink, closer to climax. Rocking with him, her hips jerked upward, taking him deeper inside, making him a part of her until the whirlwind that had taken hold the day they met caught up with them, bringing Kendall up, up, up and over into hot, sweet, blessed oblivion.

As reality and sensation returned, Kendall knew she'd changed forever, and not just because she'd made love with Rick. But because tonight he'd done the one thing no one in her life ever had — he'd taken the time to show her he cared. Not just once, and not just with his body, but with his heart and soul.

Keep it light. With one glance, Rick could look at Kendall and see the internal struggle going on inside her. He understood since he felt it too. Sex was supposed to be simple.

This thing with Kendall was not.

But for both of their sakes, he'd do as her beautiful eyes pleaded. "We've used two condoms," he said. "Want to make it three? Or should I take pity on you and let you get some sleep?"

She laughed, relaxed, and curled up beside him. "Why do I think you're using reverse psychology and trying to lay the blame on me when you're the one who needs a rest?"

He collapsed against the sheets, spent. "Caught in the act."

"Okay I admit it too. You wore me out."

"Guess that leaves us time to talk."

She turned her head toward him. "About?"

He shrugged. He honestly didn't care. Anything he learned about her was a bonus. Anything that explained her unique personality — what made her a wanderer yet still crave love even if she didn't know or acknowledge it. He knew. He'd seen it tonight.

Seen the gratitude in her eyes when he'd mentioned the party and once there, watched how despite her wariness she'd absorbed the warmth and friendliness like a sponge absorbed water. Damned if he hadn't been drawn to that vulnerable side of her as much as he was drawn to the sexy woman in the tight leather pants.

"I want to know what makes Kendall Sutton tick. What are your goals, your dreams? What's your plan and I don't mean cleaning the house, but after you move on? Is more modeling in your future?" He forced the words out as if they meant nothing to him. Unfortunately he was coming to realize they did.

She shook her head. "No. I only did that as a means to an end. Vanity isn't my thing which I'm sure you realize after watching me walk around with pink hair." She laughed and he felt the vibration straight through his body. "But I do design jewelry and —"

"You do?"

"Why so surprised?" She leaned up on her elbow and stared at him. "What do you think I did for a living?"

The comforter dipped, revealing her bare breasts, and for a second Rick couldn't think at all.

Catching him in the act, Kendall pulled up the covers. "Behave yourself and answer."

"Well, I knew you modeled. I'm not sure I thought beyond that."

"Aah. Okay. I only used my looks." Her lips tipped upward in a grin, showing him those dimples he adored.

Rick knew she was teasing him and was grateful for the sudden letdown of her guard. "You're beautiful. Why not take advantage of your assets?"

"Nothing's wrong as long as you don't assume those are the only assets I've got."

"Would I ever be so shallow?" He splayed his hand across her stomach, then moved his palm upward and cupped her full breast in his hand. "I know you've got many more assets."

She sighed, obviously enjoying his touch. "Name them."

"Huh?"

"Name those assets you say I've got. Prove you're not just using that Chandler charm to get into my bed."

"Correct me if I'm wrong but you're already in *my* bed."

She let out a long-suffering sigh. "Okay, using that charm to get into my pants — so to speak."

"Again, correct me if I'm mistaken but I've

already been there." At the thought, his groin hardened and he rolled on top of her, pinning her beneath him.

"Yes but if you want to be there again, you'll list those so-called attributes of mine." She met his gaze and grinned.

Laughter and pure enjoyment bubbled up inside him. When was the last time he'd enjoyed a woman in bed, her personality not her body? "I have a hunch you're avoiding discussing you and your future plans, but I'll humor you for now."

"Go for it."

He planned to. "First off, you're beautiful. Count it as an attribute or not, but you are. Second, you're bright."

"And you know this by what? My getting stranded by the side of the road in a wedding dress, Mr. Charmer?" Her eyes glittered with amusement and desire. She was enjoying their easy banter as much as he.

"You're warm and compassionate and before you ask, I know this by how you act with my meddling mother, my family and friends."

"So you like me, huh?"

His groin pulsed against her soft body in response. "Yeah," he said in a husky growl. "I do. Now quit evading questions and tell me what I want to know." No matter how much he wanted to be inside her now, he needed her to confide in him more. He needed to know his growing feelings weren't one-sided and cementing that emotional connection was a start.

For years he'd told himself he refused to get emotionally involved with a woman, believed he was denying himself the ability to get hurt again. But the truth was, Rick didn't have any control over what he did or didn't feel. He never had. Since meeting Kendall, he felt like he'd been mowed down and damned if he didn't need her to feel the same way. Though he doubted bonding would make him feel any better when she drove off in her little red car, he couldn't control the compulsion to learn more.

So while she tried to keep her plans to herself, Rick figured if he got her to reveal them, it would be like giving a part of herself. Something his ex-wife had never done, he realized now. And something he needed from Kendall.

With his legs, he pushed her thighs aside and nudged his erection between her moist, feminine heat. "Now talk."

"Police interrogation at its finest." Her voice grew deep with wanting. "I figured I'd go west to Arizona. Sedona. Someplace artistic where I can learn more about design, and where I can perhaps make a name for myself by selling my work." She sighed and the admission seemed to cost her. As if by revealing her innermost dream, she risked it not coming true.

And though he knew he'd hurt when she was gone, he responded to her need now. "If you want something badly enough, I'm sure you'll make those dreams come true. After all, how long do you really think it'll take us to get the old house in selling condition?" He encouraged her to leave even though his heart betrayed him now by wanting her to stay.

"Working together we'll finish it in no time."

Rick figured he imagined the wistful note in her voice. Obviously he was destined to pick women who chose to leave. For Kendall, anywhere U.S.A. would be preferable to staying in Yorkshire Falls. Well, hell, he didn't want a serious relationship anyway, wasn't that what he'd always told himself? And until Kendall, he'd believed it.

"I'll make sure you get to Arizona, Kendall." He stared into her glistening eyes and thrust deep inside her. Her damp heat contracted around him and she let out a soft moan of need, bringing him to the edge in a matter of seconds. "But until the day you leave, you're mine."

CHAPTER SIX

Kendall walked into Norman's the next morning trying to act like she hadn't spent the entire night in Rick Chandler's bed. But her body still tingled with the aftereffects of making love to him and the memories lodged deep in her heart.

She caught sight of Charlotte sitting in a back booth, pencil tucked behind her ear as she perused magazines, catalogues, and brochures. With her raven-dark hair and green eyes, Charlotte was the epitome of exotic and Kendall could see how Roman, the traveler, as Rick had described him to her last night, had fallen for her and chosen to settle down.

"Hi." Kendall dropped her purse on the inside of the booth and slid in across from Charlotte.

"Hi yourself." She closed the magazine she was reading and pushed it aside. "Just keeping up on the industry," she explained. "So welcome to town."

Kendall smiled at the other woman's warmth. "Thank you," she said and settled in more comfortably.

Charlotte narrowed her gaze, studying her. Finally a smile tilted her red lips. "You're glowing."

"And you don't pull any punches." But Kendall's instincts told her to trust Rick's sister-in-law and she leaned across the table. "I suppose I am."

Charlotte laughed. "It's the Chandler charm. Once they turn it your way, you're a goner."

Maybe so, Kendall thought. But she was out of here soon regardless and Charlotte ought to know the truth. "We're only temporary," she said softly. "Rick needs a woman to divert the masses."

"Ah, yes. Raina's army of bachelorettes." Charlotte shook her head. "I almost feel sorry for Rick."

"Because he's got legions of women flocking after him? That's not really a hardship," Kendall said wryly. But she knew that was jealousy speaking and Rick hated being bombarded by the unwanted attention.

"Legions is going too far. But there are enough to give him a swelled head. I'll agree to that."

"And he hates it."

"You know him well already." Charlotte sobered, her eyes wide and serious. "You're a wonderful person to go along with his plan. Roman told me all about it."

"Rick told him?" What else had Rick shared with Roman, Kendall wondered.

Charlotte shrugged. "There isn't much the brothers don't share." Those green eyes studied her as if she could read Kendall's mind. "So what do you want for breakfast?" Charlotte asked at last and slid a menu across the table.

Kendall grabbed the trifold paper, grateful for the subject change and the ability to dive into food and not her psyche. "Pancakes and coffee for me."

"Sounds good. Izzy?" Charlotte called to the robust woman Kendall had met last night.

"What can I get you two women?" Isabelle paused by the table, pen and pad in hand.

Charlotte repeated their orders, changing only her own drink to orange juice.

Izzy grinned. "I love women who aren't afraid to eat." She scribbled something on the paper, collected the menus, and strode off toward the kitchen.

Charlotte folded her hands in front of her. "Now back to something I want to discuss with you. Pam mentioned that you design jewelry."

Kendall nodded, grateful and touched Pam would take the initiative on her behalf. "I have a portfolio —"

"Do you have samples of your work?" They spoke at the same time.

Kendall laughed and reached into her bag to pull out a loose-leaf, photographic diary of her work. "I have samples at home, but since I wanted to talk to you anyway, I brought this along."

While Charlotte flipped through the laminated pages, Kendall explained her proposal. "I was hoping you'd consider taking my designs into your shop. Being completely honest here, I'm in a bind." She bit down on her lower lip, hating to admit her problems yet knowing she had no choice. "I was modeling in New York to help pay for my aunt's nursing home care, but her last days involved round-the-clock nurses and the expenses added up. Then I came here expecting to be able to sell Aunt Crystal's house to help, and I discover it's completely run-down. I'm spending money instead of making any. But I don't expect you to take these on out of pity or any sort of obligation to Rick. I'd just like you to decide if you think we can work out an arrangement that will benefit us both."

"You do beautiful work." Charlotte traced her finger over some of the photos of intricate wire designs. "I can honestly say I wouldn't take in something that would jeopardize the quality of the merchandise I carry. Not only do I think these will sell, but I think we'll make a nice profit. I need to see them in person of course, but I doubt that will change a thing, except maybe to convince me to buy one for myself."

Charlotte smiled and the fist that had tightened around Kendall's heart from the moment she'd seen Crystal's dilapidated house finally eased. "I can't tell you how much I appreciate this."

"Hey, don't thank me. You're obviously talented and this arrangement is good business. I

148

have a glass case by the register in the front of the store. I can display them there and you and I can work out a percentage split."

"Wonderful."

Izzy arrived, plates in hand. Charlotte handed back Kendall's book and she tucked it safely back into her bag, then she slid her business card across the table. "My cell phone's on here so you can reach me at your convenience," she told Charlotte.

"Sounds good."

Izzy placed their food down in front of them and the aroma of pancakes filled the air. Kendall's stomach grumbled. She hadn't realized how hungry she was. But Charlotte glanced down at the food and paled slightly. "You know what, Izzy? I changed my mind. Make it a decaf tea and some dry toast, please. I'm really sorry."

"Are you okay?" Kendall asked.

"Depends on your definition of okay," Charlotte muttered. "I'm fine, really. Just not a breakfast person but your order sounded so good, I figured I'd give it a shot."

"No problem, honey," Izzy said, then leaned closer. "Samson's outside. I'll just pack him up a bag and not tell Norman. Those two don't always hit it off."

"Thanks so much. Charge me, okay?" Charlotte said.

Izzy waved a hand.

"Who's Samson?" Kendall asked when Izzy had walked away.

"The town eccentric," Charlotte explained. "He really doesn't have any family or friends. He may or may not have money, no one knows but he seems to need the handout. I let him do favors for me so he doesn't feel like he's taking charity. I think he's more misunderstood than anything."

Kendall nodded. She glanced at Charlotte, still concerned at her odd reaction to the food but with the plate taken away from her, the other woman looked better. "We had our share of people like that in New York City. Difference is, no one seems to look twice. It's sad."

"D.C. too. Thank goodness Yorkshire Falls is different. More compassionate. At least some people are." Charlotte glanced at Kendall's plate and inhaled deep. "You go on and eat before it gets cold. I'll just talk business until mine gets here if you don't mind?"

"Well . . ."

"Eat," Charlotte insisted. "And listen." She grinned. "Something for you to keep in mind. I've made some contacts in Washington, D.C., and I'm considering opening up a boutique there. If your designs sell here, would you be interested in taking your work to the city?"

Kendall's heart began to beat faster in her chest. "Are you kidding? I'd love the opportunity. Thank you." She'd thought starting in Arizona would give her a more solid résumé and background. Never had she considered starting in a big metropolitan city first, but Charlotte was offering her that chance.

Kendall had come to Yorkshire Falls with no expectations except to sell the house and be gone. In less than a week she'd gotten herself a lover in name as well as fact, more than one friend, a sense of family, and the beginning of a stable career. If Kendall didn't know better she'd think she was settling down.

Raina glanced at the timer on her treadmill, then slowed her pace. Less than five minutes left for her brisk daily walk, something she looked forward to more than ever now that her so-called illness limited her activity. But as she looked out the window, she noticed a car pull up to the curb and her youngest son climbed out.

"Darn." Roman had the worst timing. She yanked the safety plug out of the treadmill and dove to the couch, covering herself with a blanket. Picking up a magazine, she made sure she had the telephone close by. Her phone served as an intercom and she could instruct Roman to come in without having to get the door herself. All in the name of the charade, she thought.

To her surprise, no doorbell rang but instead she heard Roman call out. "Mom?"

He'd obviously let himself in which surprised her since all three of her boys normally rang the bell before coming inside, even if they used their key instead of making her walk to the door. "I'm in the basement," she called back.

His hard footsteps pounded down the long flight of stairs to the finished basement, a room that had served as a playroom when the boys were young, and a large TV room as time went on.

He crossed the room and stopped in front of the couch. "Hi there."

She let her gaze travel over her son. Marriage definitely agreed with him, she thought, pleased. "Hello, Roman. Where's your lovely bride?"

His blue eyes sparkled at the mention of his wife. "She's having breakfast with Kendall."

"And you came to see your mother." She clapped her hands together. "You're such a good son."

"Why would you walk down the steps just so you could lie down in the basement? There's a perfectly good television in the den on the main floor of the house," he said, ignoring her compliment. "It can't be good for your heart to go up and down the steps for no good reason."

"Well . . ." She hadn't anticipated or thought through an answer to that particular question. Her sons believed she'd been told to take it easy. They believed she walked the stairs from her bedroom to the main level with the kitchen just once a day. The basement *should* be off-limits for someone with a weak heart.

He reached out a hand to her forehead, his own brow crinkling with what she thought was concern, but his next words canceled out that emotion.

"You're flushed and out of breath. I wonder why that is?" Roman lowered himself to the couch until he shared a cushion with her. "You're also sweating like you've run a marathon, Mom."

His journalistic instincts had obviously found something amiss and kicked in. Darn her youngest for being so perceptive.

"I'm perspiring, women don't sweat," she shot back, then caught herself and realized she'd agreed with his assessment. Not a good idea when she couldn't afford to condemn herself in any way. She needed to get herself out of this predicament.

Then when she and her boys were together in one room, she had to confess. She couldn't keep this up. It wasn't good for her heart, she thought wryly. "Nonsense, Roman. I'm not sweating, I'm just warm under this blanket, that's all."

"I'd be warm too if I'd been running on the treadmill, then dove off and covered myself with a wool blanket so I wouldn't get caught." His lips turned upward in a semi-grin.

She didn't care if he seemed amused, she didn't like his accusation and her heart picked up rhythm. "Caught doing what?"

"Cornered and you still won't give up on your own." He patted her hand. "Okay, I'll spell it out for you. You've been faking your heart condition so you can manipulate Chase, Rick, and myself to do your bidding and get you grandchildren. All you need to do now is admit I'm right."

She sucked in a startled breath. Not that she thought she was such a master manipulator — though she believed she'd done a darn good acting job so far. But she'd obviously been too overconfident. She'd never once considered that her sons might catch on.

"I'll take it your silence means yes? I'm right?" He squeezed her hand lightly.

Raina sighed. "Yes," she admitted, unable to meet his gaze. "How did you figure it out?"

He rolled his eyes as if the answer were obvious. "I'm a journalist. I know how to spot signs most people would ignore. Add to that I lived with you a few months back, when this supposed condition started. Tea, Maalox, and prescription antacids — a sure sign of indigestion. Plus you hit the stairs like a sprinter when you thought I wasn't around. It wasn't hard to put things together. Especially once I found your exercise clothes in the washing machine."

She forced herself to meet his gaze. "You don't sound angry." Although his eyes, his father's eyes, condemned her.

"Let's just say I've had a while to get used to the truth."

"But you haven't told your brothers." He couldn't have since they were still tiptoeing around her like she might break at any second, whispering in concern when they thought she wasn't paying attention.

"Not yet."

She heard the definitive tone of that word yet and knew her charade days were numbered. "Why haven't you filled them in?"

He ran a hand through his hair. "Stupidity?"

She covered his arm with her palm. "You have to understand my reasons — and know I'm sorry I went to such extremes."

"You didn't feel bad enough to have come clean on your own. Dammit, Mom." He shook his head, his frustration and anger finally coming through. "And the hell of it is I know you'd do it again if you had to, right? For some reason you just can't let us live our own lives."

A lump rose to her throat, the guilt she'd been suffering from for so long overcoming any justification she might have offered. "If you're so angry, why haven't you told Rick and Chase? Tell them and be done with it already."

He let out a frustrated groan. "Like it's that easy? At first I was in complete shock. Then after Charlotte and I got married, I figured what the hell. Let Rick go next and maybe he'll end up as happy as I am."

Raina clucked her tongue, not buying that particular excuse. "That's giving this charade some credit. And when you realized what I'd done I'm certain you were furious. You wouldn't have withheld this kind of information from your brothers just so they could find a woman and end up happy."

She knew her youngest, knew the bond all her boys shared. Roman might want his brothers to share his happiness but he wouldn't condone her antics to achieve that goal.

"You're right, that's giving you credit. And maybe you *did* help bring me together with Charlotte but I also believe in fate. We'd have found our way back to each other anyway. It wasn't just because you'd cornered your sons into picking a sacrificial lamb to give you a grandchild."

She cringed. "It wasn't just because I wanted a grandchild. I want you all to experience the love and happiness I shared with your father. I want to know you'll have more than empty apartments and empty lives when I'm gone."

But she still remembered how she'd felt on discovering her sons had employed a coin toss. *Loser* would give up his bachelorhood and freedom to marry and give their sick mother a grandchild. Roman lost — and ended up the winner. She didn't think he'd appreciate the reminder. "So you don't want to give me credit. Then why not tell Rick or Chase?" she asked again, certain her youngest was dodging the issue and she couldn't imagine why.

"I have my reasons." He didn't meet her gaze.

"Now who's hiding something," she asked, but decided not to force things. She hadn't earned his trust or the reprieve he'd given her by keeping her secret. "Why tell me you know the truth now?" she asked instead.

"Because of Rick. When you called to say he wanted to gather family and friends and you asked if we could make a beeline home, I figured he'd found the right woman. And I wanted to make sure you didn't meddle in his life the way you did in mine." This time he did lock his eyes with hers. "Let Rick and Kendall make their own way. Or else."

"Or else you'll tell. Roman, sweetheart, you should know I was planning on giving up anyway. Rick found Kendall on his own and it's getting hard to keep up the charade. Even Eric —"

"No." Roman spoke in a firm, no-nonsense voice. "You will not tell Rick or Chase now."

She blinked, utterly and completely shocked. "Why not? I thought that's what you'd want."

"I considered that option, believe me." He leaned an arm over her, propping his hand on the sofa and leaning close enough to press a kiss on her cheek. "I love you and I've been observing your relationship with Dr. Fallon. I realize you're having a hell of a time mixing a personal life with your charade."

She sighed. Her youngest had always been astute.

"Eric's a good man and I couldn't be happier you're finally moving on with your life."

She nodded, knowing Roman's past inability to stay home in Yorkshire Falls or commit to a woman had a lot to do with that very issue. "But?"

"But if you admit your scheme now, just when Rick's found a woman he obviously cares about, you'll give him a reason to back off. With his past and after Jillian, it's a miracle he's looking at Kendall Sutton the way he is. And if you turn around now and show him women can say one thing and do another, if he sees your manipulation, he might decide women aren't worth the effort." Roman shook his head. "Much as I wouldn't mind you confessing and suffering the consequences, Rick deserves the chance to be happy. Like you said," Roman muttered, obviously disgusted at giving her notions any credit whatsoever.

Raina didn't like it but Roman was right. Rick probably was on shaky emotional ground and didn't need an excuse to give in to his fears and push him away from Kendall. "I'll keep quiet."

Even though her silence assured her relationship with Eric would continue to be rather difficult and strained, she deserved the trials she suffered now. Roman rewarded her with a huge hug and she squeezed her youngest back. Raina had made her bed, so to speak. She smoothed the heavy covers over her legs. She'd just have to lie in it.

Kendall decided to spend the hours after breakfast with Charlotte cleaning out the closets in the guest house as another way of insuring a sale. Make the storage room look big and enticing, she thought.

She'd no sooner changed into her cleaning outfit than the doorbell rang and the front door swung open wide and Pearl entered without invitation.

"Why you're just like a native, leaving your door open to the neighbors." The older woman walked inside, a foil-wrapped package in her hand.

"Hi, Pearl." Though she should feel imposed upon, instead Kendall realized she was genuinely happy to have company. Another odd sensation for someone who'd always lived alone. "Come on in and sit down." She waved inside.

Kendall had already taken the slipcovers and drop cloths off the furniture and Rick had finished the walls in the entry and living area. The smell of fresh paint added to the cleanliness and appeal.

Pearl joined her in the family room. "Take this. My special brownies for a special girl. You remind me so much of your aunt." She smiled and the weathered lines in her cheeks seemed much less apparent.

"That's such a sweet compliment." Kendall accepted the home-baked treat, the smell of chocolate making her stomach rumble.

"Get us something to drink and we can indulge, women-style," Pearl said, shamelessly taking over and telling Kendall what to do.

Kendall blushed, knowing she didn't have much to offer. "I've got water," she said and shrugged. Filtered water had always been her drink of choice. Easy and healthy, she'd always thought but the fact that she had nothing to serve Pearl shamed her a bit.

Pearl waved a hand in the air, obviously dismissing the idea too. "That's what I was afraid of." She dug into her purse and came out with a jar of iced-tea mix. "You can't live in the suburbs and not have some good old-fashioned iced tea or lemonade with your dessert. Eldin hates lemons, so I buy iced tea for the man. Gotta keep 'em happy, but you'd know all about that, wouldn't you, what with a virile man like Rick around?" She walked to the kitchen as she spoke, making herself at home and chattering the entire way. "So what's with all the painting going on here?" Pearl asked.

"Well . . ."

"Don't tell me. You and Rick are planning on moving in here after all. I told Eldin so, but he said no, you'd stayed at Rick's apartment last night and this old guest house wasn't your style, with you coming from the city and all."

Kendall blinked. She didn't know what shocked her more, Pearl's pronouncement that apparently everyone seemed to know where she'd spent the night or the speed and consistency with which she spoke. With Pearl and her mouth in residence, Kendall didn't have to worry about taking part in the conversation.

Still, she needed to make sure anything repeated was either accurate or helpful to Rick and his cause. "I'm sure you realize by now Rick and I aren't married."

"Yet." Pearl popped a chocolate piece of brownie into her mouth, then washed it down with the iced tea she'd made, sliding Kendall's glass toward her at the same time.

With a sigh, Kendall shut herself up with a brownie and a sip of the sweet, delicious drink. She was coming to understand what Rick meant when he said not to bother correcting people's inaccurate assumptions. In such a small community, they believed what they wanted to, evidence or assertion to the contrary be damned. She was shocked to discover she didn't mind, rather she enjoyed Pearl's stubborn rosy view.

"Well, I'm fixing this place up and I'd like to start on the main house too." On another visit to Pearl's during the week, Kendall had discovered that though the outside was run-down, the only inside problem seemed to be the paint job. She had no desire to insult Eldin by criticizing his skills or suggesting they redo the walls. There were other ways to refresh a house for resale.

"Really? Like what kind of fixing?" Pearl asked.

Kendall didn't mind answering the what. It was the whys she didn't want to get into yet. Why cause Pearl concern over being displaced before Kendall had the chance to look into other relocation options for the older couple? It was the least she could do for Aunt Crystal's friends. "I thought I'd buy some flowers, Rick said he'd mow the lawn and power-wash the exterior," she began to explain.

"You are such a sweetheart." Pearl lurched over and pulled Kendall into a huge hug. "Why, Eldin and I will be living in splendor in no time. You know we couldn't afford to do those kinds of fixings on our own. You're not just as pretty as your aunt, but as sweet too. And of course Eldin and I will help in any way we can." She sat back down, beaming with happiness and pleasure.

Kendall didn't know what to say. How could she destroy Pearl's illusions and scare her into thinking she'd be displaced, yet how could she let her believe she and Eldin could remain in her aunt's house? Kendall massaged the sudden pulsing in her right temple.

"I've got to go tell Eldin!" Pearl grabbed her purse. "Keep the brownies and the plate." The older woman's excitement was tangible.

Kendall groaned.

"Oh, don't worry. I'll come back another time for our chat."

Pearl misinterpreted yet again and Kendall didn't correct her. For one thing she'd already learned the futility and for another Pearl hadn't given her the chance. She ran off as fast as she could, leaving Kendall speechless, alone with the plate of brownies.

She glanced around and shrugged, then peeled the foil off the treat and began to drown her problems in chocolate.

Hours after Pearl's excited departure, the kitchen sparkled inside and out. After practically inhaling the entire plate of brownies, Kendall decided to work off the calories. By the time she finished, anyone who inspected the deepest corner of the cabinets would find nothing but cleanliness and empty space. The closets came next and all were empty anyway except the walk-in in the entryway. By the time she'd tackled that project, Kendall had enough junk accumulated for a garage sale.

Exhausted but still ambitious, she got to work on her bedroom. Since she'd asked Brian to include her bedding and other items in the shipment from New York, from dresser top to inside the closet, the small bedroom now had a homey, lived-in feel. Stepping back, Kendall walked from room to room, admiring the huge improvements.

She'd taken out the day's frustration on something constructive, but she felt guilty that the reason she wanted to fix up the house was so she could sell — right out from under Pearl and Eldin.

Guilt swelled up inside her. "Darnit." That's what Kendall got for letting herself grow fond of people. But how could she help it? These were her aunt's friends and she liked them, as much as she enjoyed it here in her aunt's house. But the time would soon come when she walked away.

Not wanting to dwell on leaving yet, Kendall decided to think productively. She glanced at her watch, then tried phoning her sister. Once again, no answer. Either she was out of her room or the little twerp was screening her calls which was the most likely scenario. Other than the brief phone call the other day, Hannah hadn't returned Kendall's gazillion messages.

She rolled her tense shoulders and tried to relax. At least she knew that her sister was safely at school right now. There wasn't anything Kendall could do about Hannah's situation for the time being. But there was plenty she could do about her own.

Rick hadn't been far from her mind all day. His husky voice, his lean, hard body, and the tender way he'd made love to her came back to her at odd, vulnerable moments during the day. She'd find herself zoning out and when she came back to reality, she'd have a dust rag in hand but her body would be tingling as if Rick's lips or mouth had been roaming over her sensitive skin. Even now she trembled at the memory of his hands gliding along her naked body and wanted a repeat of the event.

His shift would end soon and she knew exactly how to entice him after a long day. After a quick shower, she picked up the phone and called Chase for a little more insight into Rick, the man. What was his favorite food? Music? The basics in life. Armed with answers, she headed to his apartment.

As she'd seen firsthand, he was a man who worried about everyone yet rarely thought about himself. She intended to turn the tables on him. Tonight she planned to take care of him for a change.

Rick dragged himself up the back stairs to his apartment. Exhaustion warred with hunger and he didn't know how he'd find the energy to find something to eat in his refrigerator. He'd have stopped downstairs for a bite, but at Norman's conversation was as much a staple as food and Rick wasn't in the mood for talking. Not after his last few days. Working a ten-hour shift, having the impromptu family party at Norman's, and then spending the night with Kendall only to wake up and haul another ten-hour shift had wiped him out.

Grateful for the solitude, he let himself into his apartment and tossed the keys on the counter.

"Well, no one can say you aren't a creature of habit."

He recognized that soft voice and didn't give a damn that his solitude had just disappeared. "Kendall?"

"That's me." She called to him from inside, beyond the hallway.

He walked into the living area to find her sitting on one of his bar stools at the kitchen pass-through area. She looked casually sexy in white fitted leggings and a black tank top, a glass of wine in her hand and a sultry look in her eyes.

His body, which had been begging for sleep seconds earlier, awakened with a roar. "How'd you get in?"

She laughed. "Ever the cop. Forget, *I'm glad to see you, Kendall* and go right for the interrogation. But to put your overworked mind at ease, I spoke to Chase and when I explained what I had in mind, he confessed to having an emergency key. He let me in and here I am." She spread her arms wide, gesturing around the apartment.

For the first time, Rick noticed the pizza box on the counter and the delicious Italian aroma that surrounded him. She'd obviously gone to a lot of trouble on his behalf and the knowledge helped to lift his lingering weariness.

He stepped forward and leaned an elbow on the counter so they were face-to-face. "Did I mention I'm glad to see you?"

She shook her head with a smile showing off her dimples.

"Well, I am." He'd inched closer and as he spoke, he moved his mouth over hers, tasting the fruity wine and tasting *her*. But unfortunately, his stomach chose that moment to growl loud and clear.

She laughed and moved back, breaking the physical connection. "I take it you're hungry?"

A naughty grin tipped her lips.

"Hell yes. I'm hungry." For more than just food, though he knew he'd have to eat first if he wanted the stamina to devour later.

"I brought you pepperoni pizza."

He raised an eyebrow, surprised. "My favorite. I take it that's what you had to discuss with Chase?"

"Among other things." She served him a cheesy slice of pizza, then walked to the kitchen and returned with a bottle of his favorite beer, popped the top, handing him the bottle. "To . . ." She paused.

"Us."

"Tonight," she said at the same time he spoke.

"To us tonight." He grinned and clinked their glasses together.

She pushed a plate toward him and patted the stool beside hers. "Come eat. You must be running on empty by now."

Her concern warmed him in places long forgotten, reminding him of dreams he thought he'd given up on, of having someone to come home to at night, and maybe even a family of his own one day. Dreams Kendall had already told him she wouldn't, couldn't make come true.

Yet this skittish woman brought those very hopes back to life anyway. It was that skittishness he had to nurture and he had to admit her presence here now was a good sign. "So what have you been doing with yourself during the day?" Keeping things light seemed to be his renewed mantra with Kendall.

"I had a business breakfast with Charlotte." She took another sip of wine.

"Aren't you going to eat?"

She blushed, red staining her cheeks. "I already did. A full plate of Pearl's brownies, but that's another story," she said, laughing.

"And one I want to hear. But first, what did you accomplish with Charlotte?" he asked, then took a welcome bite of pizza.

"She's going to take my jewelry in to sell." Pride and pleasure tinged her voice. "On consignment."

"That's amazing! So we're celebrating tonight too." Her work was obviously important to her, for reasons Rick sensed went beyond her financial needs.

Kendall nodded. "I guess we are celebrating but I hadn't thought of it that way. I wanted tonight to be about you."

Gratitude flowed through him. "Well, indulge my curiosity. That's the same as catering to me. So tell me about your jewelry."

She frowned at his obvious attempt to put a wrench in her plans. "I'd rather hear about what *you* do."

He laughed. "Okay, I'll humor you. Me first."

She glanced down and realized he'd finished one slice and she put a second on his plate.

He wiped his mouth with a napkin. "My day

was typical. The usual paperwork, patrol, questioning, and some training at the high school."

"What kind of training?"

"DARE training for the teachers. Drug Abuse Resistance Education." He explained the acronyms she'd heard but never knew exactly what they stood far. "I'm the DARE officer at the school."

"Mmm. Lucky kids getting to learn under you. Something tells me a good-looking guy like you definitely holds at least female interest," she said jokingly.

"Kendall," he said, warning her. Though he joked about many things, DARE wasn't one of them.

"I'm serious. It's so important to keep kids aware. I hope they're doing half as good a job at my sister's boarding school as I'm sure you're doing. And with teenage girls' minds turning toward the opposite sex, if you *do* hold their interest, who cares if the reason is your looks? They'll *listen* to you and you've accomplished a huge goal for those kids, their parents, and for society."

She spoke passionately about a subject close to his heart and her words dispelled his earlier misgivings. Rick could have kicked himself for thinking she'd belittle something so important. He knew her better. That she could relate to him on this level proved something his gut already knew. They were good for one another in many ways.

"What about the guys in the program?" she asked. "How do you keep their interest?"

"It's not as easy. But based on your description, getting the girls' attention has to help. They want to be where the action is." He laughed, amazed her perspective made enough sense that he now planned to use it in the future.

"So what was today's meeting about?"

"Since it's summer we're working on teacher training for September."

"Did it go well?" She leaned forward, resting her chin on her hands.

"As well as it could with Lisa Burton there," he muttered.

"Lisa." Kendall said the name with obvious dislike.

"You've met her?" Rick asked, wary. Who knows what the jealous teacher had done or said to Kendall, Rick's supposed girlfriend. He caught himself, realizing that Kendall was no longer his pretend anything.

She was real. Incredibly, beautifully real.

Kendall sighed. "I didn't meet her exactly. She was one of the women at the hair salon who pretty much snubbed me. Not that I care."

He could read the lie in her eyes. She'd been hurt and he couldn't believe how badly he wanted to not just protect her but take away any slight or pain. "Lisa's not worth worrying about. Just a jealous woman who doesn't know how to take no for an answer."

"*She's* one of the ones after you?"

He almost said they were all after him, that's how overwhelming the barrage had been. But true to his plan, now that the town thought he was with Kendall, no one had ambushed him in days. "If Lisa bothers you, let me know."

Kendall raised an eyebrow. "So you can what? Arrest her for rudeness? Please." She waved away his protective concern. "Honestly I've been to many new towns. Not everyone likes everyone and that's the way life is. I can handle her. But if she puts so much as a hand on *you,* then I can't be held accountable for my actions." She grinned and finished the last of her wine.

"Possessive thing, aren't you?" He tapped the tip of her nose with his finger.

"What's mine is mine." She shrugged easily.

The wine had obviously relaxed her defenses and though she spoke jokingly, there was a hint of seriousness in her tone that pleased Rick. To his never-ending surprise when it came to Kendall, he didn't mind being claimed.

"Finished?" she asked.

He glanced down, once again shocked he'd eaten not just his second slice but a third without being aware. The conversation and company were too stimulating for him to concentrate on food.

"I sure am. I'm stuffed." He started to rise, but her hand on his shoulder stopped him.

"You worked all day. I've got the cleaning.

171

Finish your beer and relax." She gathered the paper plates and her empty wineglass and headed into the kitchen.

Because of the open pass-through area between the kitchen and the family room where his bar stools were, Rick was able to continue conversation — and watch Kendall while she worked. She had an amazing body and her outfit outlined every curve, arousing his baser male instincts despite the earlier exhaustion.

Though he couldn't tear his gaze away from her narrow hips and firm behind — he was male after all — her heart and inner spirit interested him most right now. "So tell me about your jewelry."

She'd tossed the paper plates and wrapped the extra slices. "Refrigerator or freezer for these?" she asked him.

"Refrigerator. I'll live on those tomorrow."

"Okay. I have two different styles of jewelry," she said as she got back to work. "I hope to learn newer techniques in Arizona especially working with turquoise, but right now, I do wire jewelry with beading. I also have another idea but I haven't tried it out yet. I only have sketches and I'd have to show you —" She obviously and deliberately cut herself off. "That was silly. You wouldn't be interested in female jewelry."

In a heartbeat he stood and strode into the kitchen, catching her between the counter and his body. "I wouldn't presume to know what interests me, if I were you."

She licked her lips. "Why's that?"

"Because you might miss out on something amazing if you do. Now I might not be interested in women's jewelry, that's true. But when it comes to something that you've created, that's a different story."

A unique-looking choker that resembled a lace collar lay wrapped around her neck. He lifted the piece and fingered some of the small and intricate beads in his hand. He studied the piece and craftsmanship with awe. Kendall had talent to say the least and Rick was certain Charlotte had seen it or she wouldn't have agreed to take the pieces into her beloved shop.

"This is beautiful," Rick said. "And so are you." He unhooked the necklace from behind and lay it on the counter beside him, then leaned forward and placed his lips on the soft skin where the choker had once been.

He inhaled her fragrant scent and his groin pulsed with aching need. Not ready to assuage that particular desire, he worked on arousing Kendall first instead. He ran his tongue along the slightly red line left by the jewelry, soothing her flesh, and if her soft moan was any indication, accomplishing his goal.

"Rick."

Her husky voice worked on his already sensitive nerve endings and the bedroom in the small apartment seemed too far away.

"Rick, wait."

He groaned and stepped back. "What's wrong?"

"Tonight's not about satisfying me and I can tell that's where you're headed. Not that I mind. I'd love it in fact, but I promised myself this would be *your* night." She lifted her hands and cupped his face. "You earned it." She placed a soft kiss on his mouth. "You deserve it." She slid her tongue across his lips as her thumbs caressed his jaw. "And I want nothing more than to give back to you this time. *That* would satisfy me even more."

"Mmm. Okay."

"Good. Now you've had a long shift. Go relax in the bedroom while I clean up." While she spoke, she massaged his shoulders, showing him exactly what she had in mind.

She'd put a great deal of thought into this evening and he had no doubt there'd be much more to come than simply a massage of his aching muscles.

"It'd be faster if I helped."

"I'd be happier if you didn't. Now go," she said, her tone lowering.

No one had ever spoken to him in such a gentle, heated voice. No one had touched him with such special care. And no one had ever put his needs before their own. Kendall had. She obviously had her own agenda. She wanted to be in charge of this evening, wanted to give to him for a change.

He couldn't say he minded.

"I'll be in soon. I promise. I just don't want to leave a mess in here." She gestured toward the bedroom. "Go on."

"You never mentioned you were so bossy." He grinned as he took a step back.

"That's because you never asked." She shot him a wink and turned back to working on the cleanup.

He watched her in his kitchen for a moment before he headed for the bedroom and stretched out on top of the bed. As soon as he relaxed into the mattress, his body remembered how exhausted he'd been earlier. He couldn't be more grateful Kendall had surprised him, that she was here with him now.

He wanted nothing more than to have her beside him in his bed. And his heart settled in his throat as he recalled how unlikely it was that she'd remain here for very long.

CHAPTER SEVEN

Kendall tossed the beer bottle into Rick's recycling bin and after towel-drying the wineglass, she replaced it in the cabinet from which she'd taken it earlier. Because this night was for him, she didn't want to take any chances of leaving a mess he'd end up having to clean later. The kitchen spotless, she shut the lights and headed inside.

A dim flickering light greeted her and she knew he'd had the bedroom TV on while he awaited her. Her heart pounded in her chest in anticipation of the night ahead. But when she stepped into the room, she discovered that in the brief time she'd finished in the kitchen, Rick had fallen asleep. He lay on top of the covers, his sneakers still on, testament to his exhaustion. She smiled and walked up beside him, sitting on the edge of the bed.

In sleep his features relaxed. Stress- and exhaustion-free, he looked even more incredibly sexy. She ran a hand down his cheek and he turned into her palm. With the warm, intimate gesture of trust, her insides curled with need, want, and desire, but she admitted a hefty dose of emotion was involved too.

Just the fact that she'd decided to come over here tonight and take care of Rick told her she felt more than just lust. But she refused to panic. After all she'd been through, she intended to adhere to a *here and now* mantra. Moments like this in her life had been too rare.

She lay down and curled into Rick, letting his body heat seep through her skin and warm her inside and out. Security was something else sadly lacking in her life and with this man, she felt not only desired, but cared for in a meaningful way. No reason not to take it all in while it lasted.

She yawned just as his arm came around her and pulled her into him, her backside pressing insistently against an erection she felt certain he wasn't even aware he had. She smiled knowing that when he awoke, she'd take care of that problem for him as well as any other things that needed soothing.

Warmth seeped through Kendall's body as a strong hand slipped between her legs and found its way beneath her clothing to her private, feminine folds. She was slick with moisture, ready for him to thrust inside her and make love to her. But apparently he had other plans because his skillful hands and fingers alternated between a soft, teasing glide with one finger, and an insistent rotation of his palm against her feminine mound. Working magic, he brought her closer and closer to the brink of orgasm.

Her breathing came in shallow gasps as the incredible sensations bombarded and pounded at her body. She jerked her hips forward in a futile attempt to take him deeper into her body. The waves built higher and higher until they took over and she cried out loud at the same moment she finally, blessedly toppled over the precipice in the most explosive orgasm she'd ever had.

Kendall woke in damp heat, Rick's arms around her waist and his hand — the source of that exquisite pleasure — resting against her body. She writhed against him, convulsions still wracking her with warm, explosive sensations until she collapsed in his embrace. He pulled her close, pressing a tender kiss against her neck that brought a lump to her throat.

"You don't play fair." She snuggled even deeper into him.

His deep chuckle reverberated through her. "You weren't complaining."

"I was asleep."

"Then that must have been some dream you had because you screamed my name."

She rolled to her side so she could see his face. "You rat." But she grinned. "I remember reading somewhere that orgasms that occur during a dream are stronger and more pleasurable than those that occur while you're awake."

He propped himself up on his elbow and gazed down at her. "And is it true?" A self-satisfied smile tipped the edges of his mouth.

It had been an incredible experience and he knew it, the arrogant man. Kendall decided it was time to turn the tables on him. "Absolutely true." Sort of, she mentally amended. Every orgasm she'd had at his hands or with him inside her had been incredible. She stretched languorously, her body still sensitized from arousal and need.

A frown replaced his earlier smile.

"What's wrong?"

"Stronger and more pleasurable while you're asleep, huh? I think I'm just going to have to outdo myself while you're awake."

She felt his wandering hand and stopped his movement by clamping down on his wrist. "First, you already outdid yourself, and second, this night is supposed to be about *you*. Why do you find it so difficult to give up that control?"

Even as she asked the question, she realized she was getting deeper into his psyche and what made him tick. His need to protect obviously went way back and she wanted to know more.

"Are you sure you want to know? The answer might take a while."

"I'm sure."

He shrugged and eased against the pillow, obviously accepting that they were going to talk awhile first. "You already know my father died when I was fifteen. I saw Chase take over. He made sure the paper kept running and gave Mom one less thing to worry about during that awful time."

"I'm sorry." She squeezed his hand and snuggled back into him, more to give him com-

179

fort than for herself.

"That's life I guess. But don't feel bad for Chase because he's never regretted his decisions. And don't feel bad for me. I've had a good time of it so far. A few bumps in the road but nothing I couldn't handle."

She didn't buy his cavalier assessment of his past but she wasn't about to argue, not while he was opening up to her.

"It was Mom who worried us all," he continued. "And taking care of her became our jobs."

"Raina seems pretty independent to me."

"She is now." He glanced up at the ceiling. "Maybe she always was, but as the three men of the house, we all thought it was our duty to look out for her."

Kendall nodded. All three Chandler brothers were amazing men. Any woman would be lucky to land one of them. She shivered and got back to business. "And then? How'd looking out for your mother translate into police work?"

He glanced out of the corner of his eye. "You're awfully curious tonight."

"Humor me." She didn't want to admit that she craved the closeness they'd begun to share. "Why law enforcement?"

"Doesn't every boy want to be a cop?"

"Maybe but not all of them actually grow up and live the dream."

He smiled. "Good way of looking at it. Chase made sure Roman and I had the chance to live our dreams. Roman's were simpler. He'd always wanted to follow in Dad's footsteps, only he wanted to take his show on the road. I wasn't so sure, but Chase made certain we both went to college before making any lifelong decisions."

She sighed. "You're so lucky to have family that cares that much about you."

He squeezed her closer, as if sensing the sensitive and painful nature of the topic. "You've met my mother. There are obviously pros and cons to my kind of close family," he said, wryly. "I wasn't into reporting the news but we all worked the paper after school, regardless. I hated it and after I'd ditched one too many assignments, Chase stuck me with Chief Ellis. He figured if I had to report on him hauling the juvenile delinquents into jail, I'd straighten out. As usual, in his know-it-all way, big brother was right. I found my calling."

Kendall laughed. "He sounds more like big daddy than big brother."

"Only when we were watching. Chase had his own social life when he could squeeze it in. I can't prove it, but I'm sure of it anyway. But he did make certain we all walked the straight and narrow, which except for Roman's foray into women's underwear wasn't all that hard."

"What!?!"

Rick grinned. "Roman played the ultimate prank. When he was sixteen he stole a girl's underwear. I believe you met the victim. Terri Whitehall."

"That priss?" Remembering the starched collared, prim woman, Kendall laughed harder. "So that explains why he was blamed for the panty thefts this past spring." The Chandler brother seemed to be the stuff of town lore and Kendall had heard many stories during her excursions to the General Store for food or housecleaning supplies.

Rick nodded. "No way it could have been Roman. Mom made him pay for his crime way back when. He had to hand wash his boxers and hang them out to dry on a clothesline on the front lawn. The girls came to watch and laugh. Cured him forever."

She rolled her eyes. "You Chandlers were a handful, weren't you?"

"Spirited, Mom called it. Chase just said we were a pain in the ass." Rick chuckled, knowing that despite all the ups and downs of being a Chandler, he was damn lucky as Kendall had said.

She obviously hadn't been as fortunate. "Tell me about your parents," he said.

"Tell me about your marriage," she countered.

He sucked in a deep breath. No way would he discuss his ex-wife with Kendall. Jillian was his past. He'd put her behind him long ago.

But if that was true, then why didn't he want to confide in Kendall now, a taunting voice asked. Because to bring up that pain might force him to raise more barriers against

Kendall, to protect himself from being hurt worse than when Jillian had chosen another man and life over him. Kendall had already made the decision to leave and Rick had no intention of dredging up past feelings that would cause him to shut her out. Until she left, he wanted nothing keeping them apart.

He flipped over and pinned her on her back, her arms against the mattress. "I'm skilled in the art of interrogation," he said with a grin. "Do you really think you can deter me?" It wasn't lost on him that his groin had settled between her legs, his desire obvious despite the barrier of clothes.

She let out a forced sigh that came out sounding more like an aroused moan. "Well, if you're going to use torture tactics, I suppose I have no choice but to talk," she said in a breathless, husky voice.

He was glad he affected her but it didn't change what he needed and for now that was information. For all her independence, by her own admission Kendall never had a stable family life. As an adult, she was obviously still running from something. At least that was Rick's take on things. Maybe if he understood the *what* he could work on changing her views. He didn't hold out hope but he had to try.

Rick Chandler never gave up without a fight. "I want to know how their absence affected you," he said, speaking of her parents.

"It didn't."

But she shifted her gaze away from his, making her words the self-protective lie he'd already suspected. "Kendall?" He released his grasp on one of her hands and turned her chin so she had no choice but to face him. "I suspect it was a lonely childhood."

"I had family," she said, sounding way too defensive.

"What's the longest you lived with any one of your relatives?"

"Two years, maybe three. I had a lot of family to choose between," she said too lightly.

He opted not to ask her why none offered stability by asking to stay with them permanently. His goal was for them to grow closer, not to cause her pain.

She let out a sigh. "I think isolationism must be the family motto. My mother has two sisters and a brother, my father has a brother. Each did their duty. None wanted a child that wasn't theirs permanently underfoot."

She surprised him by digging into the topic he'd opted not to touch. Realizing how difficult it must be to reach inside herself and open up, he remained silent and let her reveal more on her own.

"Except for Aunt Crystal." Kendall's eyes lit up at the memory of her most beloved relative. "That was the best time. I was ten and I don't remember all that much but a lot of love. And cookies." She smiled, a warm, tender glow on her cheeks. "Even after I left because the ar-

184

thritis hit her hands first and she knew she wouldn't be able to take care of a young child, she wrote every week . . . or I thought she wrote. I realized later she dictated the letters to a friend."

"The point is she cared."

Kendall nodded, then swallowed hard. A lone tear dripped down her cheek.

He hadn't wanted to dredge up painful memories, but he'd accomplished his goal. She'd let him in. He wiped the drop of moisture off her cheek with his thumb, then sealed his lips over hers. As usual the kiss ignited the burning desire to be inside her but more than physical need, Rick wanted to show her he cared. To make her feel special and let her know she was wanted in so many different ways. He undressed her slowly, appraising her with his eyes and worshiping her with his hands. He got rid of his own clothes in quick succession and grabbed for the foil packet in his drawer.

"We're working our way through the box," she said, obviously pleased.

"That's the plan."

He'd no sooner ripped open the package than Kendall snatched it from his hand. "Let me."

And while he watched, she did as she'd promised earlier — she took care of him — sheathing his hard erection with trembling hands. Then she lay back on the bed and opened her legs, waiting for him. Knowing she wanted him as badly as he desired her was a huge turn-on, one that humbled him in many ways. The sight stole his breath.

He moved on top of her, thrusting fast. She was moist and wet, contracting around him, taking him deeper and deeper inside. She wrapped her legs around his waist and suctioned him completely into her. Their skin was slick with sweat, their bodies rocking in unison, not fast and frenzied, but a slower coming together, a meaningful joining of two people who'd bared not just their bodies but their souls.

Rick thought he'd long since understood the distinction between having sex and making love. But as he surged one last time, taking them both over the edge, he finally comprehended that distinction, in a way he'd never experienced before.

Minutes later, the aftershocks still shaking him, his breathing still rough, he settled beneath the covers with Kendall in his arms. A sense of peace and rightness settled over him, along with one of imminent doom.

"I was supposed to take care of you tonight," she whispered as her eyelids drifted shut.

He forced a laugh. "You did."

"I'm glad." Her drowsy voice wrapped around his heart.

He held her in silence and waited until her breaths came in slow, shallow succession before shutting his eyes. He could easily get used to this, but unlike the dream of becoming a cop, this one that involved Kendall was much more futile.

A high-pitched ringing woke Kendall from a deep, luxurious sleep. She didn't want to be bothered, not when she was cocooned in such delicious warmth, but a hand on her arm was shaking her, giving her no choice but to open her eyes.

"Kendall. It's the phone in your purse," Rick said.

She groaned and buried her head in the pillow before rolling over and out of bed. Air-conditioning hit her bare skin and she shivered. She dug through her bag, pulled out her phone, and glanced at the incoming number. She didn't recognize anything but the Vermont area code. Hannah, she thought and realized the cold air on her naked body was the least of her problems.

She pressed the green button, hoping she hadn't missed the call. "Hannah? Hannah, are you still there?"

"Of course I'm still here. Vermont's the other end of the world. I can't travel far without money or a car." Her sister's annoyed voice sounded over the phone lines.

"That's not what I meant." Kendall ran a hand through her morning-messy hair. "We need to talk."

"Yeah we do."

Kendall narrowed her gaze. Hannah had

been avoiding her phone calls for days and now she was suddenly being agreeable? "What's going on?"

"Like you care."

Kendall ignored that comment. "I spoke to Mr. Vancouver —"

"He hates me."

"Apparently you're giving him good reason." Her sister snorted.

"He said you're on probation."

"Uh, not anymore."

Kendall blinked. "You're off probation? How'd you manage that? Did you apologize or —"

"I left."

"What do you mean you left?" Kendall shrieked and Rick jumped out of bed, coming up behind her and leading her back so she could sit down on the mattress. "Where are you? And how are you?" She willed herself not to panic. Yet.

"What do you think I mean? I left. It's not like they wanted me there anyway. I'm sure I saved him the job of kicking me out."

"Kicking you out?" Though Mr. Vancouver had intimated such consequences were possible, Kendall had thought for sure he'd sit down with Hannah and her parents, or Hannah and Kendall, and talk first. And she'd never thought her sister would do anything to lead to such drastic consequences.

"Would you quit repeating everything I say?

It's no big deal. This school sucks."

"Watch your mouth."

"Don't tell me what to do. You're not my mother."

Kendall cringed at Hannah's nasty tone. What happened to her sweet sister and what had caused her to run from school? "Look, I happen to be the only adult relative listed on your emergency card at school. That gives me some rights. And the first right I've got is to get a straight answer." To the most important question, Kendall thought. "How are you?"

"Like you care," Hannah shot back with that snotty tone again.

"I do."

"Whatever. I'm fine and I'm at the bus station near school. I need a ticket and I need to know where you are. Between Mom, Dad, and you, it's like having no relatives at all."

Hannah's words were like a knife in Kendall's heart. She'd lived the very life Hannah just described and it hadn't been fun, nor filled with warm, fuzzy moments. Their parents had chosen boarding school for Hannah as a means of providing more stability than Kendall had had. But could stability replace family, a chiding voice inside Kendall asked. "Hannah —"

"Don't get all mushy on me. Just get me out of here, okay?"

Kendall blinked. Her sister's animosity and hurt obviously ran deep. And Kendall hadn't even realized it existed. She'd been so caught up in caring for Aunt Crystal and dealing with her own problems, she'd merely assumed Hannah was safe and happy in boarding school. An assumption that would obviously cost her now.

But first, she needed to get Hannah home. As if either of them had a home. Kendall glanced at her watch. It was eight A.M. already. She rubbed at her eyes. "Give me the information about where you are and I'll call and buy a bus ticket. You have your ID on you?" She gestured to Rick for a pencil and paper.

"Yeah."

Rick handed her the things she'd asked for. "Thanks," she mouthed at him. "Go ahead, Hannah." Kendall scribbled down the Vermont bus terminal name and area code, then asked and got the pay phone number. "I'll make the arrangements and there'll be a ticket waiting for you. I'll meet you on the other end."

"Whatever."

Kendall saw past the bravado to the scared girl alone at a bus station, or perhaps Kendall just needed to believe her sister wasn't as hardened and uncaring as she sounded. After all, she'd been in touch with Hannah lately and she'd sounded fine. *But when was the last time you really made time to listen to her,* that same accusing voice asked. Not wanting to face the answers or the guilt, Kendall turned her attention to the here and now. "Be careful, Hannah."

"I'm not going back to that place." Hannah's

voice cracked and Kendall knew she hadn't imagined it this time.

Kendall swallowed over the lump in her throat. "We'll talk when you get here, okay?"

"Just promise me you won't send me back there."

She'd have to reach her parents somehow, but no child should have to stay where they were that unhappy. "I promise."

A loud exhale of relief sounded over the other end of the phone.

"I'll call Mr. Vancouver and explain you're on your way to me. I don't want him calling the police or reporting you missing."

"Don't take anything he says too seriously. The cue ball —"

"That would be Mr. Vancouver?" Kendall hazarded a guess.

Hannah snorted in reply. "He has no sense of humor."

"I wouldn't either if you were calling me a cue ball," Kendall said wryly. She wasn't sure she wanted to hear Hannah's latest prank either.

"I only did it to his face once."

She shook her head, realizing she had her work cut out for her when Hannah arrived. "Let me go buy the ticket. I want you here safe and sound. Stand by the pay phone. I'll call you back with the details."

Kendall spent the next five minutes on the phone, purchasing the ticket, making certain the clerk would watch out for Hannah until she got on the bus, and then she called her sister back.

Finally, she hung up the phone and turned to Rick. "She's on a 10:45. I have to pick her up in Harrington at 2:55 this afternoon."

"What happened?" Rick eased the cell phone out of her hand and placed it on the nightstand.

Kendall ran a shaking hand through her hair, then began to pace. "I can't believe this."

"Come sit down." He patted the mattress where they'd made love and then slept in a blissful state of oblivion — while her sister was so unhappy.

And Kendall hadn't a clue. Hadn't seen it coming. She shook her head, her thoughts reeling. "Hannah must be distraught. I mean how could she just leave school? How could she do something as stupid as arrive at a bus station, no real destination in mind. Who does something that impulsive?"

Rick winced. "Excuse me for stating the obvious, but you do."

Kendall opened her mouth to argue, then realized she couldn't. "Okay, so it runs in the family. But do you know what can happen to a fourteen-year-old girl alone at a bus terminal?" She shuddered to think about it. "That clerk better watch out for her."

Rick picked up the paper she'd written her notes on earlier, then grabbed for the phone and dialed. "Hello?"

"What are you —"

He held a hand up to silence her. "This is Officer Rick Chandler from the Yorkshire Falls Police Department. Yorkshire Falls, New York. You have a minor child there named Hannah Sutton?" He waited for an answer, then nodded at Kendall. "Good. I'd appreciate it if you made certain she got on the proper bus and wasn't bothered by strangers while she waits. I can give you my badge number for an ID if you need —" He remained silent again, listening. "Won't be necessary? Thank you. I appreciate that. Bye." He set the phone back down and grinned at her.

"Can you do that?"

He shrugged. "I just did. Feel better?"

"Much." She came back to bed then and treated him to a grateful hug. "Thank you. I can't tell you how much that meant to me."

Rick couldn't tell her how much she'd come to mean to him. Not without scaring her off. "I'll go with you to get her."

"Don't you have to work?"

"I can get someone to switch shifts."

Warmth filled her gaze. "I really appreciate that. You know for all my talk about loving my sister, we haven't lived together since I was eighteen. I don't know what to do with a teenager. And an angry one at that." She shivered at the obviously overwhelming sense of responsibility. "How can I get through to her?"

"She called you, didn't she? You two will come to terms."

Kendall shook her head. "I'm sure I wasn't her first choice but she didn't have anyone else to call. I got the distinct impression she doesn't think I care much. I do, but I'm beginning to understand — I've given her reason to believe what she does." She hung her head, obviously not proud of herself.

He tipped her chin upward. "Kendall, you're her sister, not her parent. You were living through your own problems. You're here for her now. That's all that counts."

He ran a soothing hand over her bare back, savoring the feel of her skin. The closeness they'd shared had been a moment out of time. Reality had intruded in the form of a fourteen-year-old girl. Rick felt sorry for both Kendall and Hannah. He hated losing the alone time he'd planned to share with Kendall, but he'd be here for her and help her through this rough patch.

She gave him a shaky smile. "Thanks. I guess I'll have to try to locate my parents, *if* they can be found, which is unlikely. They're on an excursion in Africa somewhere."

"No cell phones there, huh?"

"No. Which means any decisions regarding Hannah are my responsibility." She sighed. "And I promised her no more Vermont Acres, so I'll have to feel her out and see what kind of school she'd be happy in come fall."

"Sounds like a good plan. I mean you wouldn't want to tie yourself down to anyone or anything."

She stiffened her spine and glared at him. "What's that supposed to mean?"

Rick shook his head. "Nothing." Damn his big mouth. "It's just that staying in Yorkshire Falls is another possible solution to Hannah's problem."

"Oh, no." She shook her head. "No. New York City was my last permanent gig for a while." She glanced away as she spoke, unable to meet his gaze.

Because she was fighting her urge to stay? He hoped so. Because sometime during the night, despite his good intentions, he'd fallen hard for Kendall Sutton. Oh, hell. He'd fallen from the minute he'd seen her in her wedding dress on the side of the road.

With her sister's arrival, Rick was given the chance to convince Kendall that Yorkshire Falls was her home and the small town provided the perfect place to put Hannah in school and settle down. *In his dreams.*

Well, he'd damn well better begin rebuilding those walls if he wanted to walk away with his heart intact.

Kendall thought teenagers were supposed to chatter nonstop. But the silence in the car was deafening. As soon as Hannah had walked off the bus and sidestepped her attempted hug,

Kendall knew she was in trouble. When Hannah had looked past Kendall to Rick's uniformed presence, Kendall realized she'd made a huge mistake bringing him along for this first meeting.

"What's with the cop?" her sister had asked, complete and utter disdain in her voice.

"He's not a cop, he's my . . ." Kendall's voice had trailed off. Rick was a cop, just not here because of anything Hannah had done. And Kendall had no idea how to categorize her relationship with Rick to herself let alone to her fourteen-year-old sister. She settled on what she thought was a benign term. "Boyfriend."

"Oh, gross."

"Speaking of gross, just what did you do to your hair?"

Hannah grabbed one of the purple kinked strands. "Cool, huh?"

Biting her tongue hadn't been easy but Kendall managed. She couldn't afford to alienate her sister even more. Now they all drove back to Yorkshire Falls in silence except Hannah's incessant cracking of her gum.

"So what's there to do in this town?"

Kendall turned toward Hannah and faced Rick while he drove. "Rick? You'd know more than me."

He glanced over, one hand on the wheel. "The kids like Norman's and there's an old movie theater, and there's the town pool during the day."

Hannah rolled her eyes. "See what happens when you ask a cop for hangout places? I might as well stay home."

"Thank you would be more appropriate than complaining," Kendall said. "Actually I was hoping I could teach you some beading or if that doesn't interest you, I thought we could do some sketching together."

Hannah merely glanced at her warily, as if she didn't trust Kendall's word that she wanted to do anything with her.

Well, Kendall would just have to convince her. "I've seen your artwork and I know you've got talent."

"Whatever."

Hannah's words sounded indifferent but her gaze clung to Kendall, giving Kendall hope that all her sister needed was time and patience before she came around.

"As soon as you make some friends you'll be fine," Rick assured Hannah. "I'd be happy to introduce you to some kids your age."

Kendall shot him a grateful glance.

"As long as they aren't geeks," Hannah said and sat back in her seat, arms folded over her extremely cropped top. After commenting on her sister's hair, Kendall clamped her mouth shut on the subject of her clothes. But there was no doubt her sister looked like a Britney Spears, Christina Aguilera wanna-be.

Rick pulled up to the house and parked. "This is it."

Hannah sat up and grabbed the headrest of Kendall's seat so she could get a better look out the front window. "Aunt Crystal lived here?"

"Before she had to move to a nursing home."

"It's huge."

Her sister's eyes opened wide, giving Kendall a glimpse of the young girl she remembered, not the angry teen she'd retrieved from the bus depot. "We're in the guest house in the back." Kendall hoped the news wouldn't burst her sister's spontaneous excitement.

"A guest house? Cool!" She jerked open the back car door but turned before climbing out. "Who's in the main house?"

Before Kendall could answer, Pearl and Eldin came down the driveway to greet them, Pearl in all her housecoat glory and Eldin in his splattered painter's overalls and cap.

"You've got to be kidding me?" Hannah rose out of the car and stared just as Pearl began a quicker walk down the drive.

"Oh, Eldin, look," Pearl said, pointing to Hannah. "Crystal's other niece."

She grabbed Hannah in a huge hug, then pulled her back for a good look. Kendall glanced at Rick and winced while Rick just shook his head and groaned.

"I hope Hannah watches her mouth," Kendall muttered.

"Don't get your hopes up, sweetheart." He yanked the keys out of the ignition. "I'm not sure which one of them needs rescuing but we'd better get out there."

Kendall nodded but grabbed his sleeve first. "Rick?"

He turned.

Just his smile lent her a shoulder she hadn't realized she needed, which made her next words that much harder. "I know you didn't sign on for this so if you want to bail now I wouldn't blame you."

"We have a bargain, don't we? I'm not one to dishonor an agreement, so you're stuck with me."

Her stomach cramped at his words. When had she reverted to a mere bargain in his eyes? After last night, she'd thought much more existed between them.

But you pushed him away, didn't you? a voice in her head asked. Recalling her reaction to his idea of her staying in town, she realized he had every reason to keep his distance now and to protect himself. From her. She didn't blame him any more than she liked his sudden shift in attitude.

But whatever his reasons, he was here with her now and had promised to stay. She wouldn't ask for anything else when she wouldn't give anything more in return.

She forced a grin. "Okay, well, you had your chance. I won't offer you an out again." Reaching for his hand, she held on tight, needing him more than she cared to admit.

"No problem." His gaze met hers and lingered.

Seizing the opportunity, she leaned over and captured his mouth in a kiss. Meant to reassure who, she wondered. Herself? Or him? Before she could figure out the answer, Hannah screamed.

Breaking apart, Kendall and Rick exited the car and came around to where Hannah and Pearl stood.

"What's wrong?" Kendall asked.

"Other than the fact that she smells like mothballs and she hugged me?"

"Hannah!" Kendall yelled, mortified.

"It's not mothballs, it's violet sachet," Pearl said, unaffected. "And I told her I'm so glad she's here. She's skinny and obviously hasn't been eating well at school. I have a plate of brownies cooling now."

Interest flickered in Hannah's eyes and Kendall saw her fighting not to show her desire for the food and warmth Pearl offered.

Pearl leaned closer to Kendall and in her stage whisper spoke in Kendall's ear. "You really should get her a bra. She's young and they're perky but she really ought to wear a brassiere."

Hannah started to speak and Rick put a warning hand over her mouth. "Not now."

Pearl turned to Hannah just as Rick released her. "I'll go get those brownies and bring them over, okay?" Without waiting for an answer, she took off for the house.

"I'm Eldin," the older man said, sticking out

his hand toward Hannah. "And Pearl means well."

Hannah stared until Rick gently nudged her arm with his elbow. Taking the hint, Hannah shook his hand quickly, then dropped it again. She was probably afraid he'd grab her into a bear hug like Pearl had done. Instead Eldin shook once and dropped Hannah's hand. Satisfied, he nodded and started back up the driveway, more slowly than his significant other, probably because of his bad back.

Warmth filled Kendall as she'd watched Rick not just taking charge with Hannah, but handling her well. Kendall was merely in a state of complete shock. One she'd have to get over and quickly.

"Bye, Eldin," Hannah called toward the older man, surprising Kendall.

Maybe she'd be okay here after all, Kendall thought.

Then Hannah turned back to face her sister. "No way am I living in this hick town with your cop boyfriend and two old people. And the old lady stares at my chest." She folded her arms tight. "That's sick." She narrowed her gaze, then stormed off in the direction of the guest house.

Kendall looked at Rick and sighed. "She's a joy."

He laughed. "She's a teenager. I've seen worse."

"God help me." Kendall rolled her eyes heavenward. "Her hair's fluorescent purple."

He grinned. "Yours was pink."

"Would you stop mentioning all the similarities?" The truth was enough to drive Kendall mad.

He glanced at his watch. "Much as I hate to leave you on your own, I have to get to work."

"You're probably relieved."

"Kendall, Kendall." His gaze met hers. She saw the conflict in his eyes as he fought the attraction for a second before, with a groan, he reached out and cupped his hand around the back of her neck, bringing her within kissing distance. "What am I going to do with you?"

His breath was warm and a hint of spearmint teased her senses, making her wish he'd kiss her already. "I don't know. What did you have in mind?"

"Convincing you I'm a good guy would be a start. Making you believe in sticking around would be an even better ending," he admitted with obvious reluctance.

Before she could respond, he sealed his lips over hers, initiating a kiss. He tasted more delicious than she'd imagined as his tongue swirled inside her mouth.

"Mmm." The moan came out without permission but she wouldn't call it back even if she could because his body shook in reaction and he pulled her closer.

"Oh, gag me."

Kendall jumped back to see Hannah, her expression set in a grimace, glaring at her and Rick.

"Pardon me for interrupting but the house is locked. Just how did you expect me to get in?" she asked.

Kendall raised an eyebrow Rick's way. Apparently the honeymoon was over and reality had set in — in all its teenage glory.

Kendall changed into her favorite sleepwear, a matching tank and shorts set, yawned, and crawled into her bed. She'd barely been living with a teenager for a few hours and exhaustion had already set in. Hannah hadn't come out of the room she'd appropriated as her own, not even for dinner, and Kendall figured she had only herself to blame. She'd not only made the guest room livable, she'd made certain to stop in town today for another air-conditioning unit for her sister. She couldn't even count on the heat to drive Hannah into civilized company. But even a teenager couldn't stay in her room forever. Tomorrow Kendall would force her sister to sit down and talk.

Kendall's eyes drifted shut. Since coming to Yorkshire Falls, she'd gotten into a routine of sorts. She'd turn the air on early and close her door until the room chilled like the Arctic, then she'd shut the unit at bedtime and the refrigeration would last until about midnight when she'd begin the routine again. In silence now, she listened to the sound of quiet, so different from the New York City hustle and bustle she'd heard for the last couple of years. The birds chirping and the peace had grown on her. She'd actually begun to take comfort from expected sounds of . . . nothing. So when the unusual noise of a car motor broke the stillness of the night, sounding close as if in her own backyard, Kendall bolted upright in bed.

She had the distinct sense something was wrong and an even stronger hunch what that something was. Running to the window, she yanked up the old shade in time to see her red car pulling out of the driveway onto the street.

"Dammit, Hannah." Fear streaked through Kendall and without thinking twice, she grabbed for the phone. Kendall had never been great at memorization and she still hadn't committed Rick's various phone numbers to memory so she dialed 911 and was connected to the Yorkshire Falls Police Department. "Officer Rick Chandler, please. It's an emergency."

She tapped her fingers against the nightstand while she waited.

"Officer Chandler speaking."

Rick's voice instilled some form of comfort. "Rick, it's Kendall. Hannah took my car. She's only fourteen. I don't know if she can drive and I don't want her in an accident or causing an accident and I don't know where she'd go. I mean she doesn't know anyplace or anyone in this town." Kendall ran a frustrated hand through her hair. "*I* don't know anyone or anyplace in this town. Well, I know more people than Hannah knows but —"

"Kendall, stop!" Rick's stern voice halted her rambling.

"Sorry." She blinked and was startled to realize a tear dripped down her cheek. "I'm sorry. She locked herself in her room for the night. I figured she'd stay there. I never thought to lock up the car keys. I mean she's fourteen."

"I'll take care of it, okay?"

She sniffed and nodded, realizing he'd hung up before she could answer him anyway. Which was fine. She needed him out looking for Hannah, not consoling her. And when he returned her sister home safe, Kendall would absolutely throttle her.

Then first thing tomorrow, she'd head to the bookstore or library for a How-To book on raising teenage hellions.

CHAPTER EIGHT

Rick had just signed off duty when Kendall's 911 call came in. Though he'd decided to wall off his emotions where Kendall was concerned, he'd never planned to maintain a physical distance. He enjoyed and cared for her too much.

He drove around town, not in his police cruiser but in his civilian car, looking for Kendall's familiar red Jetta. Though he didn't know Hannah well, he recognized an angry kid when he saw one and in the course of DARE, Rick had seen plenty. No way would he let Hannah and Kendall drift so far apart it was too late to mend the rift.

At a loss for any specific area to find Hannah, he started along First Avenue and when he came up empty there, he extended his search to the streets nearer to Edgemont, where Hannah had begun. The elementary school was located a block and a half from Crystal's, now Kendall's house, and he wasn't surprised when he pulled into the parking lot and saw the lone red car parked diagonally between two spots.

He pulled up beside the Jetta and got out. The only concession to his being a cop was the flashlight he took from the glove compartment. Flicking the light switch on, he swung his arm around, illuminating areas around the school property. He stopped when he saw movement down the hill by the swings. Apparently there was still plenty of child in Hannah after all, and it was the needy child to whom Rick planned to appeal. He wanted her to give her big sister a chance.

As he walked down the grassy mound toward the swing set, he inhaled deeply. The smell of cut grass and dew surrounded him, bringing back memories of his time at this school and he grinned at the pleasant reminder before getting down to business.

"Hi, Hannah," he called out, not wanting her to panic and think she was being approached by a stranger. Not that she'd consider Rick a best friend or confidant, but at least she was safe with him.

"What do you want?"

He shone the light between them. "I think that'd be obvious. I want to bring you home."

"Why do you care?" She didn't slow her swinging, her legs pumped back and forth like a young, carefree girl.

But Rick had a hunch it'd been ages since she felt either young or carefree. "Because I'm a friend of the family and your sister's worried about you. So worried she called me."

She snorted at him, kicking her feet into the dirt and halting her movement. "More like she's worried I'll crash her car."

"She never mentioned the car, Hannah. She could have reported it stolen, then I'd be forced to take you in." And considering she'd been driving without a license, driving underage and illegally, he ought to take her in anyway.

"But she did call the cops."

He shook his head. "She called *me*." He emphasized the distinction. "She trusts me and you should too." He sat himself in the neighboring swing beside her.

Hannah turned to glance at him, narrowing her gaze. "I'm only fourteen. Aren't you going to arrest me for driving without a license?" she asked, obviously testing him.

Despite the defiance in her young voice, Rick caught the hint of fear there too. It was the fear he could relate to, the fear that made him want to hug and reassure her, but he couldn't. Only her sister could do that.

Instead he opted to build trust. "I could arrest you but I won't."

"Why not? 'Cause you're doing it with my sister?"

Her nose wrinkled in disgust and he stifled a laugh. "No, because I think Kendall deserves the chance to deal with you first."

"So you two aren't . . ."

"Doing it?" he asked. "I think that your sister and I deserve some privacy as to whatever we are or aren't doing."

"I'll take that as a yes." She sniffed and wiped at her eyes. "Whatever, I don't care. You said you think Kendall deserves to deal with me? What about what I deserve? She'll ship me off to another boarding school first chance she gets."

His heart squeezed at Hannah's statement, not just because he suspected she was right, that was what Kendall planned, but also because the kid was obviously starved for attention. She needed so much more than either he, a trip through jail, or even another boarding school of strangers could provide.

The irony was, Kendall needed the same thing, and as the oldest sibling she had the ability to fix things for them both. If only she'd realize and change her perspective on her transient life. For both Kendall's and Hannah's sakes, Rick hoped Kendall would come around. His needs went without saying.

Kendall, it seemed, was in control of all three of their destinies. "Did she say she was sending you back to boarding school?" he asked.

Hannah shook her head. "She just said she wouldn't send me back to Vermont. Other than that she didn't say squat."

"Because she can't talk to you through a locked door?" he asked, wryly.

"I guess." Despite herself, Hannah smiled for the first time.

And when she did, Rick caught a glimpse of the beauty she'd one day become, just like her sister.

"But she doesn't want me," Hannah said.

"What makes you say that?"

Hannah clamped her mouth shut tight, all

traces of that smile gone.

"Well?"

She glanced up through damp lashes and her heavy bangs. "I just know and so do you."

"I know no such thing." That much he could say with complete certainty. Kendall's worry for her sister, her love and concern, were obvious. Just because she'd never thought to bring Hannah to live with her permanently didn't mean she wouldn't want to.

Kendall had planned to stay a short time and leave. With Hannah around, she'd probably have no choice but to stay through the summer. If so, Rick had another two months with Kendall. Two months for these two to deal with their own pasts and with each other. Kendall, especially, would have to deal with each, if Rick had any hope of her deciding to stay on permanently.

"Why are you being so nice to me?" Hannah's voice interrupted his thoughts. "I mean I have to be cramping your style."

"Excuse me?" He raised an eyebrow.

"You know. You can't . . ." She kicked at the dirt with her black-laced boot. "You can't do it while I'm around."

"No one said we were *doing* anything." He grinned. "And I'm being nice because I think despite this little incident, you're a good kid."

He caught his mistake at the same time Hannah spat, "I'm not a kid."

"Right. You're not. So let's go home and face

the consequences like the adult you are."

She scowled at him.

"Besides, your teeth are chattering." And Kendall was worried sick. "And I happen to know your sister bought some hot chocolate she might be convinced to give you. If you apologize."

"I'll think about it," she muttered. But she stood and began walking toward the parking lot.

"Hannah?"

She turned.

"Keys?" He held out his hand.

With an exaggerated sigh, she slapped them into his palm. "Kendall can get the car tomorrow. In the meantime, mind if I give you some advice?"

"Could I stop you?"

He shook his head and laughed. "Kendall loves you. And I think you should give your sister a chance before pulling another stunt like this or hurling accusations."

"Are you always so full of advice?" she asked.

"Usually. And here's another thought for you. I'm off work tomorrow. Make sure you tell Kendall I'll pick both of you up at nine. The DARE program from the high school is hosting a summer car wash here. I'll bring you over to meet some of the kids."

"Oh, joy." She glared at him.

But through the facade, Rick caught a glimpse of a grateful smile and a flash of gratitude in her eyes. He only hoped she saved some of that goodwill for her older sister. Because Kendall had her work cut out for her when dealing with Hannah.

Selfishly, and just for a second, Rick wondered how that would leave any time for him in Kendall's life now. "Remember, we have a date tomorrow," he reminded Hannah.

"Yeah right."

By the time he drove up to Kendall's house, Rick knew she must be frantic. His hunch proved right when Hannah stomped up the driveway and Kendall flung open the door and pulled her sister into a huge hug of obvious relief.

To Rick's frustration and dismay, Hannah didn't return the gesture. Her arms remained stiff at her sides.

"I was worried sick," Kendall said, stepping back. "You could have gotten yourself killed or killed someone else." Her voice shook as she spoke.

"Well I didn't."

Rick stood behind Hannah, folded his arms over his chest, and waited. When the young girl remained stubbornly silent, he decided to step in. "Anything else?" he asked Hannah.

"I'm sorry," she said begrudgingly.

Kendall sighed. "I want to believe you. And we're going to have to set some ground rules, but if you promise not to do anything like this again, talking can wait and you can get some sleep."

"I'm not grounded?" Hannah asked warily.

"Not this time."

In Kendall's eyes, he saw her struggle to remain stern yet somehow let her sister know she cared.

"You're not going to send me away?" Hannah bit down on her lip, looking more like that lost child than the defiant kid.

Once again Rick had a hunch they'd just been given access to the place where Hannah's deepest fears resided, and Kendall must have sensed that too. Her eyebrows knit tightly and tension pulled at her jaw. "I'm here for the summer and so are you," Kendall said.

Rick cringed. Kendall's words might be the best she could come up with at the moment, but no way would they satisfy Hannah any more than they satisfied him.

Sure enough, the young girl turned and ran for her room. The sound of the door slamming followed soon after. Kendall flinched at the noise before she turned to Rick. "Thank you."

To hell with distance. He held out his arms and she willingly went into them.

"I'm no good as a parent," she said, shoulders shaking.

And she shouldn't have to be. That job rightly belonged to Kendall's mother and father. But then life rarely doled out what was fair. "Don't sell yourself short. I think she just doesn't trust anyone right now."

"Especially me. She's angry and I feel so bad that I let her down."

He smoothed his hand over the back of her hair. "You'll just have to earn her trust."

"How?"

By taking her in and giving her a home, Rick thought. By staying in one place and providing the stability neither of them ever had. But it wasn't his place to tell Kendall what he thought she ought to do. What he wanted her to do. Those were conclusions she'd have to come to on her own.

"Just be there for her." He offered the best advice he could.

She tilted her head back. "And you'll be there for me?" She shook her head. "Forget it. I had no right to ask that."

He tipped her chin upward with his hand. "No can do. You're admitting you need me." And he had a weakness for females in need. Rick knew enough to learn from past mistakes but obviously not enough because he wasn't backing off now. Kendall might leave in the end but he cared for her too much to let her down. "What kind of guy would I be if I turned down your request?"

"A smart one?" She grinned.

"What a way to stroke my ego, sweetheart." He laughed and so did she, melting the ice he wanted to keep around his heart. A little self-protection was in order. "Actually I have a suggestion. A way of keeping our deal intact and giving Hannah some stability at the same time." Once more he fell back on their arrangement. A black and white, unemotional bargain though at the moment he felt anything but detached.

Her brows knitted as she met his gaze. "What did you have in mind?"

"That we keep up the act in front of the town. Play the part of one big happy family, you, me, and Hannah. It'll definitely cement the impression that I'm spoken for." Which he wanted to be, Rick thought. By Kendall only. "And at the same time we'll give Hannah what she needs, a family and two people who care. I'm sure it'll help you reach out to her."

Kendall nodded, eyes wide and hopeful. "That sounds amazing."

"I agree." He stroked her cheek with one fingertip.

How could she not realize this deal was merely a means to an end? With everything in him Rick hoped that by acting the part of a family, Kendall would come to see that the reality wasn't something to fear, rather something to cherish. That together they could create something strong and lasting.

"Thank you for doing this for me," she whispered.

"Don't thank me," he said in a voice too gruff for his liking. He'd do anything for her but she wasn't ready to hear it. Besides, by agreeing to his suggestion, she'd given him something too. He now had the rest of the summer with both Kendall and her sister.

But he was taking a risk. If he'd overestimated Kendall and her ability to give her heart, he was setting himself up for heartache. And this pain, he sensed, would be far worse than any Jillian had inflicted. A smart man would back off as she'd suggested. A risk-taker would stay the course.

Rick Chandler had never run from a challenge, but this time he'd damn well make sure he looked out not just for the woman in his life, but for himself too.

After a restless, sleepless night, Kendall awoke and headed for the kitchen where she found her sister, wide awake, showered and dressed. That is, if anyone could call Hannah's short shorts and midriff-baring top dressed. Kendall was about to ask who'd wear such an outfit when she recalled her own choice of clothing the first day she'd hit town, after she'd changed out of her wedding dress.

It seems Rick had pegged Hannah well. Her sister was more like Kendall than even she'd realized, from the outrageous hair coloring and clothes to the more serious, internal emotional needs. Hannah's outrageous dress and acting out was a means of self-protection. She was running from her feelings, not facing herself. And Kendall knew why. After all, she understood all too well what it felt like to be an unwanted child, and despite her parents' attempts to provide more stability, Hannah was obviously suffering the same anxieties.

Kendall sighed. Understanding Hannah would go a long way toward allowing Kendall to get closer to her baby sister. Reaching out would do more. "Morning, Hannah."

Her sister spun around, carton of orange juice in hand and telltale mustache on her face.

"The glasses are in this cupboard." Kendall opened one of the tall cabinets she'd cleaned the other day. "They aren't a matched set, but they'll do. I cleaned them myself so you don't have to worry about catching anything." She laughed.

Hannah merely shrugged, then accepted the glass.

"You're up early. I figured you'd sleep in after last night."

"Do we have to talk about that now?" Hannah asked.

"I thought I was talking about being up early, not last night. Although we are going to have to lay down some ground rules about living together."

A car horn honked loudly. "That's my ride." Hannah set down the glass she hadn't yet used.

Kendall blinked. "Your ride? You don't know anyone in this town yet."

Hannah met her gaze, staring at her through heavily made-up eyes. Kendall narrowed her stare. Was that liner black or dark lavender? Hard to tell, it was caked on so thick. So was her foundation. Thanks to her modeling days, Kendall knew a thing or two about makeup and maybe after she broke through Hannah's emotional walls, she could chisel through some of that face makeup too.

"Who could possibly be picking you up?" Kendall asked.

"Rick. He said we have a date." Hannah pivoted fast and walked out, slamming the door shut behind her.

"She's testing me," Kendall muttered. "I know she's testing me." A quick glance outside told Kendall that Rick was indeed waiting for Hannah. Score one for her sister, not that Kendall was the least bit concerned. Whatever Rick had planned, he must have forgotten to mention it last night. Since there was no one she trusted more than Rick, she wasn't going to run after Hannah and give her any satisfaction now.

Kendall rubbed her hands over her eyes, then reached to grab a bowl from the cabinet.

"Kendall?" Rick's voice called to her from the entryway.

"In the kitchen." She turned to find him walking into the small room and he wasn't alone.

Hannah walked ahead of him as he prodded her forward the entire time.

"What's going on?" Kendall asked.

"*Someone* was supposed to tell you I'd pick both of you up this morning. And *someone* neglected to mention it," he said.

"And could that *someone* be you?" Kendall asked Rick very sweetly and laughed.

"Depends on your perspective. When I got home last night I realized I'd forgotten to tell you that I'd pick both you and Hannah up this morning. But since I trusted her to relay the message, I figured I wouldn't call and possibly wake both of you up."

The young girl rolled her eyes. "So I forgot. Big deal."

"Pick us up for what?" Kendall asked.

"I told Hannah I'd take her over to the DARE program car wash so she could meet some kids her age and I figured you could pick up your car at the same time." Rick shot Hannah an annoyed glance.

"I *said* I forgot. So sue me."

Kendall folded her arms across her chest, as annoyed as Rick at the games Hannah chose to play. "You forgot. But you didn't forget to tell me you and Rick had a *date* this morning, now did you?"

Rick opened his mouth to speak but when Kendall winked at him from behind Hannah, he quickly shut it again.

"Selective memory?" she asked her sister, not holding back the sarcasm. "You're goading me, Hannah, and I want to know why."

"You don't want me here. The only reason

you're putting up with me in the first place is because I have nowhere else to go. Otherwise you wouldn't think twice about me."

Hannah's comments merely cemented Kendall's earlier impression of her sister as a lonely, abandoned child. Guilt resurfaced, compounded by the notion that Kendall should have thought more about Hannah's life and feelings than she had before.

But Hannah's pain didn't excuse her rudeness and Kendall drew a calming breath before answering. "Tell you what. You two go to the car wash. Introduce Hannah to some kids. I'll shower and get myself together. Tonight we'll talk and I'll set the record straight. Got it?" she asked.

Hannah turned away, as if she meant to ignore her. "Talk to the hand," she muttered.

"How long's the car wash?" Kendall asked Rick through gritted teeth.

"All day. Izzy and Norman are providing lunch for the kids."

"Great! I think Hannah could benefit from some good old-fashioned work. I'll see both of you at Norman's at five."

"I can't wash cars all day!" Hannah cried, spinning around and giving Kendall the opportunity to talk to her face-to-face. "I mean, my nails will break and I'll get dishpan hands."

"Better you washing cars than me washing out that sarcastic, obnoxious, *forgetful* mouth," Kendall snapped back. "That's ground rule number one. You treat me with respect and I'll do the same. See you at dinner." Taking her cue from Hannah, Kendall turned and walked out, her only concession to politeness the fact that she didn't slam a door behind her.

Kendall walked to the school to pick up her car. Then she planned to head home, load the trunk, and meet with Charlotte at her store. But first she decided to snoop. Without bothering Rick or Hannah, she watched their interaction; Hannah hung out with the kids whom she'd obviously clicked with and Rick acted the part of the parental guide he probably didn't realize he'd become.

For a man who claimed to not want marriage or kids, he'd make one hell of a father. The thought brought a lump to her throat. Upon viewing his stern caring with her sister last night, Kendall had developed an even greater respect for him as a man. Seeing him now with the teenagers and realizing how well liked he was in his community, how could she not fall a little bit in love with him?

She wrapped her hands around her bare forearms and shivered. So many unanswered problems and questions, she thought. She didn't know what to do for her sister, didn't know why Hannah had decided to focus her anger on Kendall and not their parents. She didn't even know how to go about finding the right school or getting her sister to go back once she had.

And mostly Kendall didn't know what her feelings for Rick meant, for herself or the solitary future she'd always envisioned.

She'd always been impulsive, hence the constant movement. Being able to pick up and go from place to place on a whim gave Kendall an odd sense of security. No one and nothing could ever trap her. If things got too suffocating, she moved on. And though she'd never made a huge success for herself, perhaps because she'd never stayed in one place long enough, she had managed to get by financially, occasionally taking sales jobs in crafts stores where she could learn by reading, watching, and listening. She planned to do the same in Sedona while learning new aspects of her craft. But Arizona wasn't the draw it had once been. She didn't think of the place with nearly the longing she once had.

Because now she had obligations. For a woman who'd never put down roots, she now had plenty of ties to this small town. She owned a house and was responsible for the occupants who didn't pay rent but whom she feared displacing. She had a small business ready to begin in Charlotte's Attic and the possibility of working further with Rick's sister-in-law in D.C. She had an emotionally needy sister who had nowhere to go and no one to rely on but Kendall. And she had a relationship with a special guy.

One who played the role of bachelor but

who'd spoken of her staying beyond the summer and withdrawn when she'd balked at the idea. He'd obviously been hurt badly by one woman who'd left him and knowing Kendall planned to do the same, he'd reerected the walls he'd built on day one. She hated the barriers between them as much as she understood the need.

And she didn't know what she was going to do. About anything. Frustration and fear filled her until she squeezed her hands into tight fists, fighting back tears. Then she drew a deep breath. She might not have a plan, but she was an independent fighter. She'd figure this out. Somehow.

She squinted into the sunlight as one of the kids sprayed a healthy dose of water on Officer Rick, as she'd noticed he was called. He dumped a bucket of water in retaliation and the shouts of glee echoed in the air. Hannah was in the middle of the fray and Kendall couldn't help but smile.

For all the problems surrounding her, for now, while she was in Yorkshire Falls, life was better than it had been in a long while. Better than it had ever been.

And the thought scared the living daylights out of her.

Hours later, Kendall sat in Charlotte's Attic, feeling as if she'd been friends with Charlotte and her manager, Beth Hansen, forever. The women were open and outgoing and their discussions included girl stuff and resulted in the kind of female bonding Kendall had missed out on as a teen.

She was catching up big time now. She knew more details about Roman and Charlotte, and Beth and her boyfriend Thomas, than she'd imagined being privy to.

Having a hunch she'd be next up, Kendall deliberately kept the subject on Beth. "So how long have you and Thomas been dating?" Kendall asked.

"About four months now," Charlotte answered for Beth. "Anyone want more lunch?" She pointed to the large Greek salad the women had brought in from Norman's next door. A salad Kendall and Beth devoured and Charlotte picked at.

Because Kendall had arrived right around lunchtime, they'd insisted she join them and hadn't taken no for an answer. Now an hour later, though they hadn't gotten to business, Kendall was glad to have been included in their female bonding.

"None for me. I've had enough," Beth said.

"Same here." Kendall rose and started gathering up the paper plates.

Charlotte picked up the soda cans and a water bottle. "You don't need to do that."

"Sure I do." Since they wouldn't let her pay, the least she could do was help clean.

Charlotte shrugged. "I suppose if you're

going to end up with Rick, then you'd better get used to cleaning."

"I'm not —"

"You should see the messes Roman used to leave," Charlotte said as she walked toward the back room with the garbage in her hand.

Kendall followed, tossing out the plates and plastic forks.

"Until you trained him better, right?" Beth laughed. "Is Rick at least marginally better at keeping a place clean, Kendall?"

Recalling his neat apartment, Kendall nodded. "Must be the disciplined cop in him."

"Either that or he had Wanda in to clean." Charlotte laughed. "I hooked him up with my housekeeper when he took over my lease."

"And he needs it. Rick's not exactly the neatest person around," Beth said.

"And Beth would know. She and Rick have been friends for a long time." Charlotte walked side by side with Kendall as they returned to where Beth was wiping down the small table where they'd eaten. "Right, Beth?" Charlotte asked.

"Right. Unlike those other ridiculous women who throw themselves at him, I know a good friend when I see one. Not long ago I was getting over a broken engagement and Rick gave me a shoulder to lean on." Beth met Kendall's gaze and held it, convincing Kendall of her sincerity.

With both her words and her actions, Beth

epitomized what was good in Yorkshire Falls and she'd made Kendall feel like she was an honest friend, not someone out to provoke her jealousy. "Rick's good at the shoulder bit. His initials should have been S.O.S." Kendall laughed.

"There was a time that protective streak of his got him in trouble," Beth said.

Charlotte shrugged. "Jillian was an idiot."

"Right," Beth said. "She never should have married Rick in the first place. No good could come of it. She knew Rick always had a thing for her and — Oops. Sorry, Kendall." Beth blushed. "Sometimes I talk too much."

Kendall shook her head, too fascinated by the information. "No, that's okay. Insight into a man's good."

"But it wasn't meant to make you feel bad or worry. Jillian's so far in Rick's past it isn't funny."

Kendall hoped so. Because just hearing that he'd had feelings for his ex-wife was like a sharp knife gutting at Kendall's insides. But she didn't intend to share that information with her female cohorts. "You really don't need to convince me of anything. Rick and I have an arrangement —" As the words came out of her mouth, they felt bitter on her tongue.

Not just because she owed Rick and needed to uphold her end of their bargain but because she'd begun to feel proprietary about him despite her words to the contrary. *Uh-oh.*

Charlotte burst out laughing, startling her.

"What's so funny?" Kendall asked.

"I'm not sure if it's your expression or your insistence that there's nothing serious between yourself and Rick. But whatever you say, okay. Let's talk business."

"Sounds good to me." Relieved to be off the subject of Rick, Kendall pulled out a travel case she used to show her designs and opened it on the table. "This is my wire jewelry. In my experience it appeals to a variety of women. What's your minimum age demographic?"

"Early twenties," Beth said. "Some mothers bring their younger daughters in, but most take them to Kmart or the mall in Albany."

"Want to change that?" Kendall asked. "When I was in New York I didn't have the connections to get my jewelry into the trendy boutiques but I was able to sell on campus at some of the colleges and the students loved the matched sets. Take a look."

She pulled out a tray of thin choker necklaces made of glass beads imported from West Africa, along with matching dangling earrings. "These sold well."

"They're different," Beth murmured, approval in her voice.

"What are these?" Charlotte pointed to a black silk string hanging out from beneath the drawer.

Kendall lifted the drawer. "This is something new I'm trying. Knotted silk string necklaces."

"I adore them." Charlotte studied the pieces in question. "And yes I think the kids will love them." She snapped her fingers. "Oh, and I know the perfect place to debut them. There's a sidewalk sale this weekend. I'll check with Chase and see if he can alter the ad we took in *The Gazette*. Add information about Kendall's jewelry. What's your business's name?"

"Kendall's Krafts."

Charlotte grinned. "Love the alliteration. And I'm sure we can make this work for us both!"

Charlotte's voice rose in anticipation, creating an excitement that even Kendall couldn't quite squelch. "You should know, I can't afford much but I'm more than willing to contribute to the cost of the ad." Kendall couldn't afford her offer but she considered it an investment in her future.

Charlotte waved a hand in the air. "Nonsense. First off, he doesn't act it but Chase is a real softie when it comes to family. And I know both Raina and Chase consider you family. Because of Crystal," she rushed to clarify. But her grin told Kendall she was also thinking of Rick. "Don't tell anyone though. It's one of the perks us Chandlers get."

Us Chandlers. Kendall shivered at the notion, liking being included in that moniker way too much.

"Okay, so on to commission," Charlotte said, unaware of the turmoil her words caused inside Kendall.

Kendall took a minute to think. When it came to setting a percentage for commission, she always factored in the cost of her goods, labor and overhead, along with the pricing of other competitors in the market. In this case, she seemed to be the only one in the small town offering her kind of wares which was a huge benefit.

She grabbed a sheet of paper, planning to write down a fair price she fully expected Charlotte to haggle downward, but one which Kendall could still live with. Instead, Charlotte scribbled a number first and passed the paper across the table.

Kendall glanced down. The amount Charlotte offered was a higher amount than what Kendall had had in mind. She crinkled her nose, wanting to argue. She had no doubt Charlotte's generosity stemmed in most part from Kendall's relationship with Rick, something she didn't want to take advantage of. But much as she hated to admit it, she wasn't in the financial position to argue herself down — not when Charlotte's offer was more than fair to them both.

Kendall grinned, relief flowing through her. "You've got yourself a deal. Now. Did you know you have just six seconds to catch a potential customer's eye?" Excited, she dove right into the next part of her proposal.

"That's one lesson of retail I had to learn quickly, especially in this town." Charlotte laughed. "What are you getting at?"

Kendall drew a deep breath for courage. She never took the initiative once she'd released her goods for sale within a retail store. In most agreements, the artist held ownership rights but had no say in the display or how the items would be sold or marketed. After careful research and a trial and error approach, Kendall had learned the rules well. But something about Charlotte's enthusiasm inspired confidence and a surge of creative ideas.

Nothing ventured, nothing gained, Kendall thought. If she wanted Charlotte to take her in when she opened in D.C., she needed to prove herself here and now, in a smaller market. "I'm suggesting that you use the necklaces on your mannequins. Change your window display to catch people's eyes and add the necklaces to match and accessorize."

"Hmm. Good idea," Beth whispered to Charlotte.

"Thanks," Kendall said.

"Anything else?" Charlotte asked, eyes alight with approval.

Kendall shrugged. "Just that red and yellow are the most eye-catching colors. Any chance you can work with that?" Kendall asked, pushing one step further in her quest to make her mark on Charlotte and this town. A quest to cement her career — something she'd never expected on her impulsive trip to Yorkshire Falls.

"Charlotte can work with anything that makes a profit. Just look at those handmade crocheted panties in the corner display. She designs and creates them herself." Beth couldn't hide her pride in her friend and boss.

"I certainly do," Charlotte said. "And I certainly will work with anything Kendall suggests. She's got as good an eye as you, Beth. Now, much as I hate to cut this fun meeting short, I need to see my husband."

"It's only been . . ." Beth glanced at her watch. "What? Three hours?" She laughed. "Newlyweds," she said, rolling her eyes.

Charlotte didn't even break a blush. "Oh, and you aren't seeing Thomas the minute we close for the night?"

Beth laughed. "I didn't say that."

"You know I envy you two." The words escaped before Kendall was even aware she'd spoken them.

Charlotte tipped her head to one side. "How so?" she asked, sounding truly interested.

In the short time Kendall had known Charlotte, she'd come to like her a great deal and she couldn't help but be honest with her now. "You and Beth go way back. You even read each other's thoughts like sisters." She caught the wistful note in her voice but couldn't recall it. "You make me feel like I've known you two forever." Yet Kendall was still on the outside just as she always had been.

And then Charlotte pulled her into a warm

embrace, bulldozing any remaining barriers. "That's the great thing about this town. You come here or you come back here and you automatically become one of us."

"And we're impossible to get rid of." Beth laughed from behind her.

To Kendall's surprise she didn't mind and a lump rose to her throat. She hugged Charlotte in return, then the other woman stepped back.

"And now I'm off to meet my husband." Charlotte fairly glowed. "You two work out the rest of the details." With a wave, she was off and after twenty more minutes with Beth, so was Kendall.

She stepped out of Charlotte's Attic and into the bright late-afternoon sun. She still had plenty of time to kill before she had to meet up with Rick and the teenager from another world, she thought wryly.

With a little luck, maybe an afternoon with kids her own age would help Hannah's disposition. Make her happier and easier to talk to. Although Kendall still had no idea what to say in order to ease things between them, she looked forward to seeing her sister and hoped the drive home would provide inspiration. Briefcase in hand, she started for the car she'd parked down the street.

"Hey, sweetheart. Can I interest you in an afternoon of lovin'?" Rick's familiar voice whispered from behind.

She turned to see him, one shoulder propped

against the windowpane. "What are you doing here?" she asked, thrilled to see him. Thrilled to note he'd sought her out.

"Five hours of twenty teenagers is about all I can take in one sitting. I've been officially relieved. And don't worry about Hannah. I've got Jonesy, a good friend and officer, bringing her to meet you at Norman's around five. See? All bases covered."

"I'm sure she's thrilled with the personal escort."

He shrugged. "Actually she was too busy to realize she had a personal, uniformed escort." He chuckled. "Now are you going to keep talking or are you going to come over here and put me out of my misery?"

She stepped forward without hesitation. He met her halfway, grabbing her by the wrist and pulling her into the alley behind the bank of stores that led to his apartment. Next thing she knew she was in his arms, his mouth hot and insistent on hers.

She'd missed him. She hadn't realized how badly until now. Until she'd heard his voice, inhaled the masculine, arousing scent of his cologne, and felt his lips devouring hers like he couldn't possibly get enough. He stroked her cheek with his knuckles and groaned, pressing his hard body against hers, crushing her back to the wall, and she didn't care because he felt so good.

She eased into him, letting her waist mold to

his, feeling his desire for her hard and ready through the barrier of clothing, making her feel more wanted and desired than any woman had a right to feel.

He broke the kiss first and his eyes met hers, desire and heat mingling in his gaze. "It's been too damn long."

"I know." Her breath came in shallow gasps, her words breathless and difficult.

"Then let's get upstairs."

His sexy grin, meant for her alone, filled her with turbulent emotion she couldn't afford to decipher or feel, not after the overwhelming sense of belonging she'd just found with his family and friends. A meaningless fling would have been easier to handle.

Nothing about Rick was simple. He was tenderness and desire all wrapped up in one delectable but dangerous package. Dangerous to peace of mind, her easygoing life, and to her heart.

But right now she didn't care. She'd missed him, she needed him, and they only had this short stretch of time alone before reality intruded in the form of one rebellious teen.

"What are you waiting for?" she asked him. "Take me upstairs and make love to me."

CHAPTER NINE

After a day at a car wash with two dozen teens, Rick needed adult company. He'd needed Kendall's company. The hours spent under the sun had left him hot and the days he'd just spent on duty and without Kendall had left him burning with unslaked need. Self-protection obviously only went so far, he thought wryly.

Her hand in his, Rick walked into his apartment, slamming the door closed behind them.

"We've gone from having all the time we want to having to squeeze in time when a child isn't around. Now I know how new parents must feel," Kendall said, then her eyes opened wide as she obviously realized the direction her words had taken.

"But look how exciting your life has become."

She relaxed her shoulders. That was part of his resolution. To keep things between them light and easy. A summer fling, as they'd agreed upon.

"I like excitement." Her eyes glittered with desire and that same need echoed inside him, evidenced by his rapidly beating heart.

She devoured him with her gaze and his pulse picked up rhythm. Other women had admired him before. As a single guy in a small town, he was more than used to feminine attention, especially since his mother's campaign for a grandchild had begun. But Kendall looked at him differently and he liked the way her single-minded focus made him feel.

"You're wet," she said, obviously just noticing that his T-shirt stuck to his skin.

"Teenagers with buckets and a hose will do that to you." He pulled at the damp cotton material. "The kids had a mind of their own."

"You're wonderful with them." She bit down on her lip, then admitted, "I was watching you."

His heart skipped a beat. "I didn't see you."

"That's because I didn't want you to know I was there."

"Aah, spying on me, were you?"

She shrugged. "I was curious about Hannah and how she'd fit in. And I was curious about you. What your days are like. What you're like when you're not with me." She shook out her adorably shaggy hair. "But don't let it go to your head," she said on an embarrassed laugh.

"As if I've got a vain bone in my body." He grinned, brushing the fact off as she obviously wanted him to do. But privately he was thrilled she'd bothered. Oh, hell, he was just plain happy with any display of interest she offered because it meant she gave thought to him when they were apart, and Lord knew he'd thought about her plenty.

She stepped forward, bracing her hands on

his forearms. "I think we should get you out of those wet clothes." She licked her lips in obvious anticipation, then ran her palms over his shoulders and down his arms before moving those arousing hands to his chest.

"You won't get any argument out of me, sweetheart."

She played with the bottom of his shirt, teasing him by lifting the edge slowly, making certain her fingers grazed his skin with an erotic, hot touch.

A torrent of desire rushed through him, hard and strong. He wanted her in a way that surpassed sexual need. Not even her hellion sister or her self-imposed end-of-the-summer deadline could deter or deflect his actions now. Though that fact should give him pause, he had her alone and damned if he'd let anything get in the way.

"I want this shirt off you," she murmured.

"Then do it." He raised his arms over his head, giving her the control she'd once said he refused to give up. He'd give up more than that for her, Rick thought, damning himself at the same time.

He met her gaze as she lifted his shirt, then helped her toss it onto the floor. Her fingers raked over his chest, then she paused to bend and place a warm kiss against his fevered skin. Another touch of that mouth and he might not make it to the bedroom. Sensation shot through him and he sucked in a sharp breath.

"Sounds like I hit the right spot."

"At this point any spot you hit would be the right one," he said wryly. "But much as I'm enjoying, I've been outside all day and I could use a shower first."

A teasing smile lifted the corners of her mouth. "I wouldn't mind taking another one."

He shook his head and laughed. "Oh, baby, you sure know how to tempt a man."

She met his gaze. "Only you." As if to prove her point, her fingers went next to the button on his jeans.

Who was he to argue? Once again he gave her free rein, gritting his teeth as her palms grazed first his thighs, and clenching his fists when she paused, running her hand over his hard length on her quest to divest him of all clothing. She had her own agenda, her own time schedule, and he didn't mind. Her hands on his body was foreplay of the most intense and erotic kind and he could enjoy the sensation all day.

Shutting his eyes, he leaned back against the wall and gave himself up to her ministrations. Blood rushed through his veins and to other parts of his body and when he heard ringing the first time, he thought the sound was in his head.

And then her hand stilled and he recognized the noise as the telephone. "Dammit." He forced his eyelids open.

"You'd better get it. It could be important."

Kendall sighed and gestured toward the phone on the wall.

He yanked up his pants, leaving only the button open, and grabbed the phone. "This better be good."

Kendall raised an eyebrow at his frustrated greeting and he winked at her.

"Rick, it's Lisa Burton."

He exhaled an aggravated groan. Lisa had annoyed the hell out of him at the DARE car wash. His taken status hadn't deterred her this afternoon and now this phone call. "This isn't a good time."

"I wouldn't call if it wasn't important."

"Well, I'd have assumed a 911 call was important too." His patience for games had run out. Maybe it was pure male frustration talking or maybe now that he knew which woman interested him, he wished women like Lisa would accept and back off.

"I'm calling as a teaching professional. I have a young girl here named Hannah who says she's your responsibility."

At her words, Rick refocused. "You're with Hannah? What's wrong?"

Kendall came up to him in an instant, placing her hand on his shoulder. "Is Hannah okay?" she asked him.

"She's fine," Lisa told Rick.

"Then what's she doing with you? I left her with Jonesy." Not with the one woman he didn't want any kind of connection with.

"He had to leave. Right after you left he got a call from his wife. I didn't think it would be a big deal to watch over another teenager, so I told him I'd keep an eye out. I figured it was no big deal and it wasn't . . . until Dr. Nowicki arrived."

Uh-oh. Rick ran a hand through his hair. "What did Hannah say to the principal?" he asked, resigned.

Kendall groaned aloud, burying her face in her hands. "Oh, no. What'd she do now?"

Rick wrapped a hand around Kendall's waist. "Your sister's fine," he whispered in Kendall's ear.

"Oh, your girlfriend is with you? Figures." Lisa sniffed, obviously offended. "Maybe Hannah has a right to act out. It seems her sister can't be bothered with her. And you snuck off first chance you got to be with your new *lady friend.*" Lisa choked over the words, as if it galled her to admit she'd lost not just the battle but the war for Rick's attention. "You left the poor girl alone in a strange town. It's no wonder she's looking for attention."

Rick generally wouldn't put much stock in Lisa's obviously biased, jealous assessment of Hannah's situation as it pertained to himself and Kendall. After all, when he'd left Hannah, she'd bonded with two very nice girls and she'd been happy — which had been his goal in taking her to the car wash.

But considering he had taken off to be alone

with Kendall, he felt guilty despite the fact that he'd believed Hannah was settled and cared for. And he was sure Kendall wouldn't be any more pleased than he was.

Before dealing with their feelings though, they had to pick up Hannah. "Are you still at the elementary school?" he asked Lisa.

"Actually I brought her to Norman's. She said she needed to meet you there."

"Thank you, Lisa." He swallowed his pride. "I didn't mean to snap earlier. We'll be right down to get her." He hung up the phone and turned to Kendall.

"What'd she do?" She cringed as if afraid to ask.

"Lisa didn't say. But she's downstairs waiting for us now. You can ask her yourself."

"Why don't you stay here and take your shower. I'll talk to Hannah and you can meet us whenever you're ready." She paused. "Or not. Like I said, Hannah isn't your problem."

He shook his head. He didn't think she was backing off, just trying to be fair to him, to give him an out — before he took one himself. "You go on and I'll be down in ten minutes, dry and ready to help out, okay?"

She nodded. "If you're sure."

Her hesitant voice told him she wasn't. That no matter how many times he told her he wasn't going anywhere, she was waiting for him to do just that. Rick didn't miss the irony. *He* wasn't the one leaving. "Read my lips." He grasped her face in his hand. "I'm sure." He brushed a kiss over her lips. "Now go."

She shot him a smile and ran out the door. The sound of her footsteps followed, growing fainter, farther away. Just like Kendall.

Like Jillian before her.

Rick paced the floor of his apartment in the town where he'd always lived. He tried to distinguish Kendall's situation from Jillian's, to put himself in Kendall's place. Never having had two parents she could rely on. Moving from home to home, family to family, never having people she could call her own, including close friends. And then coming to a town where most people were what they seemed. Where friendship was offered with no strings and all the trappings of stability were dangled before her. Seemingly just out of reach — if only because she was afraid to reach for what she'd never had.

Hell, he'd had it all, grown up with a loving family, had married, then divorced, and *he* was afraid to reach out completely and be hurt again. How could he blame Kendall for her inability to do the same?

Kendall walked into Norman's and immediately spotted Hannah sitting in a booth with Lisa Burton. Upon walking up to them, Kendall met her sister's defiant gaze but instead of starting an argument in front of the other woman, Kendall decided to work on tact and diplomacy.

She glanced at Lisa first. "Thank you so

much for bringing Hannah here."

"It wasn't like I had a choice, Ms. Sutton. She was unchaperoned and she'd already dumped a bucket of water over the principal."

Kendall winced.

"I couldn't leave her alone to cause more trouble and it wasn't like *you* were anywhere to be found."

Kendall narrowed her gaze. She'd only heard Rick's side of the phone conversation, not Lisa's, and she had no idea why his friend Jonesy had taken off. But Kendall assumed he had good reason and had made sure Hannah was cared for. Recalling Rick's words the other day, she could only assume jealousy was causing Lisa's behavior and Kendall refused to give the other woman the satisfaction of showing her emotions.

"Hey, don't blame my sister, miss." Hannah spoke up before Kendall could formulate a neutral reply.

Kendall blinked in shock. Hannah had actually stuck up for her. Even her sister's rudeness couldn't prevent the accompanying tug of pride and caring rushing through Kendall as a result. And though Hannah's smart mouth as well as the water-dumping incident called for a scolding, Kendall didn't want to destroy any small inroad in their burgeoning relationship by reprimanding her in front of a teacher, especially Lisa Burton.

"Hannah," Kendall began tentatively, but her

sister ignored her, still glaring at Lisa through eyes lined with dark makeup but smudged from a long day in the sun.

"I heard you tell Officer Rick you'd love to do him *any* favor he might need," Hannah said to Lisa.

Kendall didn't miss Hannah's emphasis on the word *any* or the implication the word implied. Nor did Hannah if the *ick* expression on her face was any indication.

"Eavesdropping's impolite," Lisa said in a haughty teacherlike tone.

"Then why'd I see you doing it all day? Everywhere Rick was, you were. Everyone he talked to, you listened in on. What's up with that?" Hannah folded her arms across her chest, waiting for an answer.

A bright flush stained Lisa's cheeks. "It's obvious she needs adult supervision," Lisa said despite her embarrassment.

Kendall didn't know who was worse, Lisa or Hannah, but she had to put a stop to this now before it degenerated. And Lisa called herself a teacher? The example she set was pathetic.

"Well, like I said, thank you for bringing Hannah home." Kendall smiled at Lisa through gritted teeth, then turned to her sister. "Hannah, Izzy's holding a table for us in the back. Let's go."

To Kendall's surprise, her sister slid out of the booth without argument and stood beside her.

"Rick's taken," Hannah hissed at Lisa, then stormed off toward the back of Norman's.

Kendall shook her head. Apparently more than one Sutton girl had a thing for Rick Chandler.

"The child's rude," Lisa said.

Kendall shrugged. "That may be, but she's also right." Catty or not, she couldn't help but let Lisa know where things stood. Coming from an intimate rendezvous with the man, Kendall's possessiveness regarding Rick was at an all-time high. So was her protective streak, and after hearing of Rick's past from Charlotte, Kendall felt certain a woman like Lisa was the last thing Rick needed.

"You're both rude and I'm certain the Chandlers will see it soon enough." Lisa grabbed for her purse and started for the door.

"Thanks again for bringing my sister home," Kendall called out to Lisa's retreating back. She smiled and waved for the audience of patrons at Norman's.

Kendall met up with Hannah at a small table in the back and sat down, folding her hands in front of her. Where to begin, she wondered.

"Don't read anything into me sticking up for you. I just don't like that woman hanging all over Rick." As usual Hannah beat her to the punch.

Kendall decided to ignore her sister's protestation. Hannah *had* stuck up for her and Kendall planned to take advantage. "I don't like it either but Rick's a grown man and an expert at fending off women. He doesn't need either one of us doing it for him." Seeing an opportunity to bond with her sister, Kendall leaned forward in her seat. "But it was fun putting Lisa in her place, wasn't it?"

Hannah nodded warily, a slight smile working its way onto her face. "He needs us to look out for him."

"But I'm sure he'd appreciate it if you took a more, shall we say, subtle approach."

"Maybe I'll think about it."

Kendall figured it was as much of a concession as she was likely to get.

"Where's Rick?" Hannah asked.

Obviously her sister had a thing for the middle Chandler, something Kendall could well understand. "Showering I think. He'll be down in a few minutes. Hannah, about the principal . . ."

"I swear it was an accident." Hannah held up her hands in her own defense. "I was getting one guy back for squirting my shirt and he was quick enough to duck first. It's not my fault Dr. Nowicki is short enough to be a target."

At Hannah's age, it seemed nothing was ever her fault.

"Well, look who's here!"

Kendall turned to see Raina and the town doctor walk up to their table, saving Hannah from a be-more-careful-next-time lecture. "Hi, Raina, Dr. Fallon."

246

"Eric," he said. "No formality here."

Kendall smiled. "Eric. I'd like to introduce you to my sister Hannah," Kendall said, along with a silent prayer for Hannah's polite behavior. "Hannah, this is Rick's mother and Dr. Eric Fallon." She added the Rick connection for extra luck in gaining her sister's goodwill.

"Nice to meet you." Hannah graced the older couple with a genuine smile.

Raina walked over and shook Hannah's hand. "Same here. You're a beauty, young lady."

To Kendall's surprise, Hannah blushed.

"I need to talk to you, Kendall, and since your sister is here, I can use her help too." Raina glanced at Eric. "Give me five minutes would you?"

"Anything for you. But you need to sit down and rest."

Raina shot him a glare, narrowing her gaze. She obviously disliked being told what to do.

"Your heart," Eric reminded her, tapping his chest.

The older woman flushed and nodded, but Kendall focused on Eric. Was it her imagination or was there a sarcastic bent to his voice? She shook her head. Not possible. "Raina, Eric, please join us." Kendall gestured to empty chairs.

After the older couple seated themselves, Raina launched right into her request. "I've planned a surprise party for Rick's birthday. Or should I say I'm delegating plans for a surprise party, since my daily activities are limited."

"It's Rick's birthday?" Kendall asked. "When?" He'd never mentioned a thing. And she wondered why she was insulted he'd kept something so basic from her.

"Well, duh," Hannah chimed in. "Tomorrow. That Lisa woman —"

"Ms. Burton," Kendall corrected.

"That Ms. Burton woman said she had the *p-u-u-rfect* gift in mind." Hannah shuddered in complete and utter revulsion.

Kendall sighed. Some women never gave up.

"Can you imagine what she wants to do to him?" Hannah asked, horrified. "Kendall, you have to keep her away from Rick."

"Oh, I do so enjoy young people." Raina laughed. "Hannah's right. We need to keep Lisa away. I realize I might have encouraged her — before you came to town, you understand," she said to Kendall. "But I never knew she was so persistent. In my day, once a woman had been turned down, she had more pride than to keep at it."

"I thought men asked women out in the olden days," Hannah chimed in.

"Oh, Lord. Hannah —"

Eric's booming laugh cut off anything Kendall might have added. "You're right, young lady. In the olden days, most women were more demure and passive and let a man do the bidding. But then as now, *some* women were more brazen and had a mind of their own." His smile grew wider as his gaze drifted to Raina, the caring and affection between them obvious.

An unfamiliar knot twisted tight in Kendall's chest.

"So Mrs. Chandler's got her own mind?" Hannah perched her chin in her hand and focused on Eric.

"I think we should get back to Rick's birthday discussion before he shows up," Kendall said. Before Hannah got completely irreverent.

"Good idea. But don't worry." Raina leaned closer to Hannah. "You and I can finish this discussion another time." She patted Hannah's hand. And Hannah didn't pull away.

Would wonders never cease, Kendall thought. The key to her sister's heart seemed to revolve around the Chandlers.

"At any rate, I'm going to ask Rick to bring the two of you to dinner tomorrow night. Izzy and Norman said they'd do the catering and cleaning, so that's set. I don't have to lift a finger. You two will bring the guest of honor and I've already made phone calls, the only thing I can do to arrange Rick's various surprises."

"What surprises?" Kendall and Hannah asked at the same time.

"I want to do a version of *This Is Your Life*. Let Rick's childhood memories come to him." She clapped her hands. "It's going to be such fun."

"What's going to be such fun?" Rick arrived and in typical cop fashion didn't miss the conversation or the opportunity to interrogate.

"Well, your birthday dinner, of course." Raina didn't miss a beat.

"Your mother invited me and Kendall to dinner tomorrow. Isn't that cool?" Hannah asked Rick.

From the flicker of aggravation and something more in his eyes, Kendall had the sense "cool" was the last thing Rick thought this birthday celebration would be. And poor man, he thought it would just be family. Wait until he realized what his mother had in store.

Recovering quickly, he walked over to Hannah's chair. "It's Da Bomb," he said and ruffled her still purple hair with his hand.

Kendall wondered what she'd have to do to get her sister to rinse out the dye and go au naturel again. But when Hannah giggled over Rick's attempt at teenage slang, Kendall realized there was something more important in life than how her sister chose to look. And that was how she felt inside. When Rick was around, Hannah's laughter was easy and carefree, like the happy kid she ought to be. Kendall's heart felt like it blossomed inside her chest.

"You're such a Poindexter." Hannah rolled her eyes as she poked fun at Rick, bringing Kendall's concentration back to the conversation at hand.

Raina and Eric looked at Rick expectantly, obviously waiting for a translation.

"A nerd," he explained. "Working with teenagers has expanded my vocabulary." He grinned.

Hannah laughed again and over her head Rick caught and held Kendall's gaze. Warmth translated between them along with an electric reminder of just how intimate they'd been before the telephone rang in his apartment earlier.

Now his hair was damp from his recent shower and he hadn't shaved, the razor stubble she'd felt against her cheek earlier adding a sensual edge to her reaction to his ruggedly sexy appearance. *Later.* He seemed to transmit the thought with his darkened eyes. And oh how she wanted to be with him, Kendall thought.

But with a birthday bash to get him to and her sister who adored him, Kendall wondered how they'd find the time to pick up where they left off.

The morning after Raina informed them of Rick's last-minute party, Kendall paced the floor of her attic workspace while Hannah cracked her gum and shot down every suggestion Kendall made for Rick's birthday gift. They needed to create something by late this afternoon before they picked up Rick for what he thought was a family dinner at his mother's.

In her brief time in Yorkshire Falls, Kendall

had grown to know Rick well, his expressions and what went on inside his head. And though she didn't know why, she was certain he wouldn't be pleased with tonight's event. She'd debated warning him ahead of time, then decided she had no right to come between mother and son or betray Raina's confidence and surprise.

Kendall concentrated on his gift instead. She and Hannah had agreed to make a joint present, something special for Rick that no one else would possibly come up with. They'd been back and forth with ideas since late last night. With no success.

"Cuff links?" Kendall offered as another suggestion.

Hannah rolled her eyes. "Yeah like he's gonna use those in his T-shirts."

"Tie clip?"

"Puhleeze." She folded her arms across her chest. "What are you trying to do? Turn him into a dork?"

Kendall groaned and tossed her hands in the air. "Okay, I give up. What would *you* like to make for Rick?" So far the only other thing they'd agreed upon was the fact that they'd create his birthday surprise instead of purchasing an impersonal store-bought item. Short on cash and credit, Kendall had been relieved Hannah had gone along with the idea.

"Well since you finally asked, I think we should make him a necklace. Not a pansy kind but a cool kind. Leather braided maybe." Hannah walked around the bridge table, searching through Kendall's plastic containers with assorted varieties of stones and beads. "Hey, what are these?" She picked up a handful of round beads.

"Hematite rondelles."

"Geez. How about using my language?"

Kendall laughed. "They're rounded flat beads. Shiny and blue-black in color. All of which you can see by looking at them. The technical term for the mineral used in making the jewelry is hematite and rondelle describes the shape. That's where the name hematite rondelles comes from."

Hannah stared at her wide-eyed, a hint of interest flickering across her features. Perhaps they'd found a topic that could help them bond, Kendall thought. She'd love to teach Hannah all she knew about beads and jewelry making and she'd be happy to learn what she could from Hannah's fresh, young perspective. She'd start by giving her sister a confidence boost.

Kendall held out her hand for some of the beads and Hannah transferred them to her palm. She fingered the smooth, lustrous stones and held them up to the window light. "Strung together they'd have a masculine look." She glanced at Hannah. "You've got an eye for this, you know."

Her sister blushed red. "Okay, these are way

cool. Rick gets a necklace of hemorrhoids."

"Hematite, you wise guy."

Hannah giggled. "Whatever. We'll use these."

"I know which bead would break up the solid black look." Kendall sorted through her sterling tube beads and pulled out her favorite. "Check this one out. It's handcrafted on the outside of the tubing. Every twenty-fifth or so hematite bead, we add one of these for contrast."

"Let's get started." Hannah rubbed her hands together and pulled up a chair to the work area.

Kendall was thrilled to see her sister animated and interested in something so close to her own heart. "Why don't you pull out the nicest-looking hematites and I'll get the wire ready."

Half an hour later, they were still at it, Hannah absorbed in choosing flawless beads and asking all sorts of questions while she worked. For the first time since her arrival, Kendall felt as though Hannah had let down her guard, enabling Kendall to do the same. The sense of family and bonding she'd always missed in her life surfaced now and it was all Kendall could do not to pull her sibling into a huge hug and spoil everything.

"So how'd you get into this?" Hannah asked.

"Aah. Well, with all the moving around I did, I didn't have many toys or things. But when I lived with Aunt Crystal, she taught me how to string macaroni as a way of making jewelry. We'd use all different kinds of pasta and put hooks on them. Then we'd paint. Aunt Crystal worked with real beads and things until her arthritis hit her hands. I guess you could say jewelry making runs in the family."

"She probably made old lady stuff," Hannah said in the snotty tone that had been noticeably absent the entire morning.

Kendall narrowed her gaze. "Crystal had talent." She glanced over at Hannah's choices in beads. "And so do you."

"Right. Like it's so hard to pick black beads." Hannah scooped up a handful and tossed them all together, mixing all the beads and undoing the meticulous work she'd already accomplished. "Here you go. All done."

"Oh, Hannah, why?" Looking at the mess, Kendall's heart squeezed tight. "You did such an amazing job and now you combined them all again." Hours of her sister's work, undone for no good reason.

Or was there an explanation Kendall just didn't know about? If so, Hannah didn't appear inclined to elaborate. She sat with her jaw clenched tight leaving Kendall with no choice but to replay their conversation in her head. Her sister's attitude had changed the second Kendall mentioned Aunt Crystal but she didn't understand why Hannah would be angry or envious of an older relative she'd never even met.

"Hannah," Kendall began tentatively. "Are

you jealous of Crystal? Of my time with her?"

"Why would I be jealous just because you had time for her and not me?"

"That's not how it was." Kendall reached for Hannah, but her sister twisted her body out of reach.

"I don't want to talk about it."

And the mutinous set of her jaw told Kendall she wasn't kidding. She exhaled hard, knowing she needed a subject change and fast if she wanted a return to the bonding they'd begun to share. "Do you like making jewelry?" Kendall asked.

Hannah shrugged. "It's OK."

But recalling how the young girl had eyed the assortment of beads, Kendall figured it was more than just okay. "You know, I used to do pasta jewelry everywhere I went. From home to home. Wherever I lived, no one minded me keeping busy by creating necklaces. It kept me quiet and out of their hair till I moved on." Kendall shrugged, good memories mixed along with the bad. "Stability's the one thing you had that I didn't." Maybe she could get Hannah to see the positives in her life.

"Big deal. Staying in the same place, year after year. No family around. Friends come and go depending on their family situations. It's not as hot as you think." Hannah's overglossed lips set in a pout.

Obviously Kendall wasn't getting through to her sister. "Well . . ."

"Ladies, where are you?" Pearl's voice carried from downstairs. The sound of her muffled footsteps quickly followed as she tread up the stairs and joined them in the attic.

They were no longer alone and Kendall lost the opportunity to talk to her sister and maybe, somehow fix things for Hannah, herself, and their too-fragile relationship.

Rick couldn't help but notice the tension was thick when Kendall picked him up and drove them all to his mother's house for dinner. He didn't know what had happened between the sisters earlier but obviously both were upset and neither had much to say to each other.

They had plenty to say to him. At least Kendall did. "So when were you going to mention it was your birthday?" she asked him and not for the first time.

"Yeah, even Lisa Burton knew. You should have seen Kendall's face when she heard that Lisa knew and she didn't." Hannah spoke gleefully from the seat behind them.

"Sit back and be quiet," Rick and Kendall snapped at the same time. Hannah was deliberately baiting Kendall, trying to get on her nerves, and he had to admit, she was doing a damn good job of irritating him too. Or maybe it was just the date that was getting to him.

"Touchy subject?" Hannah asked, before surprisingly doing what she was told and curling up into the corner of the car.

Rick groaned. The kid had a point in more ways than she knew. His birthday was definitely a touchy subject. He acknowledged the date and put up with his mother's family celebrations. But he didn't choose to make a big deal about it. Because his birthday also happened to mark his wedding anniversary to Jillian, an occasion he'd rather forget than remember.

Kendall pulled up in front of Raina's and Hannah bolted out of the car. As Rick started to do the same, Kendall put a hand on his arm, stopping him.

He turned toward her.

"You should have told me," she said, no doubt about what she was referring to.

"It was no big deal."

But the hurt in her soft eyes told him a different story. He hadn't deliberately hidden the information, he'd just refused to acknowledge it to anyone, including himself. But he didn't think she'd accept or appreciate the distinction any more than he felt like getting into the specifics of why he'd kept quiet. Kendall and her plans, her eventual departure, reminded him too much of a painful past he had no desire to repeat.

In the wake of his silence, she exhaled hard. "Let's go. Your mother's waiting." She got out of the car, slamming the door behind her, leaving him with the distinct feeling that by virtue of his silence, he'd betrayed something precious and important.

CHAPTER TEN

"Surprise!"

Rick jumped back, startled at the crowd of people waiting for him inside his mother's house, and as he glanced around, he realized he'd been ambushed. A goddamn surprise party, he thought. He'd rather be alone on this night as had been his ritual for years. And his mother knew better than to gather a crowd.

He loved people but this was the one particular time he preferred his own company. Being surrounded by the very folks who'd probably committed this date to memory wasn't his idea of a fun night. Kendall's hand unexpectedly came to rest on his shoulder in a show of support. A nice surprise considering how hurt she'd been earlier. He figured she still expected some answers but he appreciated her insight and presence beside him anyway.

"Happy birthday." His mother slowly walked up to him and kissed his cheek.

Knowing stress was no good for her heart and she'd gone to a lot of trouble for him, he forced a smile. He'd deal with her later when they no longer had an audience.

"You shouldn't have," he said through clenched teeth.

"Nonsense. It's not every day my middle son turns thirty-five."

"Start the show!" Norman called from the crowd.

A round of steady clapping quickly followed along with the steady chant of "Show, show, show . . ."

"What show?" Rick asked warily over the continuous chanting noise.

He glanced around, noticing Roman and Charlotte stood beside Chase holding up the back wall. All three shrugged almost in unison. Obviously they didn't plan to take credit for Raina's insanity.

"I'm really in the dark too," Kendall whispered. Like his brothers, apparently Kendall didn't want to shoulder blame or responsibility. She was his mother's co-conspirator only in that she'd brought him here.

A loud whistle halted the chanting for a brief minute before it started up again.

"Okay, simmer down." Raina gestured with her hands, indicating everyone should be quiet.

Rick shot her a concerned glance and she quickly lowered herself into the nearest chair.

That seemed to silence the unruly crowd.

"Now you all know I'm not up to running things," she said softly. "So I hired an emcee." She crooked a finger at Rick and he leaned closer. "I tried to get your brothers for the job but they refused."

"I owe them," he muttered.

"Well, let's get started," Raina suggested.

"Then we can eat!" said someone from the back of the crowd.

Rick narrowed his gaze at the sound of the distinctive voice and looked around for the loner. "Samson, is that you?"

Rick didn't see the older man right away but he was a master at blending into the crowd. The duck man, as the children called Samson Humphrey, spent his days hanging out in the park by Norman's, ignored most people, and looked homeless but wasn't. He also was the panty thief culprit though no one except Rick, Charlotte, and Roman knew that. Turning out in a large crowd wasn't the old man's style. Unless . . .

"Of course it's him. He wouldn't miss a free Norman's chicken sandwich," Norman said.

"Damn right," Samson called out, confirming Rick's suspicion. "But if you used that honey mustard, froufrou stuff, I'm not eating."

Norman growled from low in his throat. "Why you ungrateful . . ."

Before Rick could step in, Raina clapped her hands, probably to stop the mayhem before it started. Then without warning, an entourage walked down the stairs.

"This is your life, Rick Chandler," Big Al, the retired high school baseball coach, said through his booming cordless microphone, seeming not to care that they were inside the house.

Rick watched in disbelief as his past seemed

261

to parade before him. An eclectic mix of his old teachers, coaches, and friends formed a circle in his mother's living room.

His stomach cramped. "This can't be happening."

"Of course it can." His mother's glee matched his sense of impending doom.

With Kendall by his side and Hannah giggling from the sidelines he found himself pushed through the throng of people. Finally he was given a front row seat, surrounded by his mother, his brothers, Charlotte, Kendall, and Hannah. The rest of the guests crowded in around them.

"Let the fun begin."

Rick winced at the booming sound. Big Al obviously thought he was back at the football field.

"Mrs. Pearson, recently retired from Yorkshire Falls Middle School, had Rick in her kindergarten class. Take it away, Mrs. Pearson." Al handed his microphone to the petite, gray-haired woman to his right.

"Testing. Testing." She held the thing close to her lips and emitted a high-pitched squeak that had the room cringing and groaning loud. "Sorry. It's been ages since I've used one of these suckers. I mean things. Once I retired I let my language run free." She laughed. "Anyway, let's continue."

"Please don't," Rick called out.

"Don't be a sissy, little brother. You can

handle it." Chase folded his arms across his chest and grinned.

Damned if Rick wouldn't get him back on his birthday.

"Rick was an imaginative boy." Mrs. Pearson spoke in her best teacher tone. "And from the beginning he knew how to draw a crowd. Quite the little entrepreneur too. Why I remember one playground hour when I noticed all the kids — mostly girls — lined up behind him."

"Rick always was a charmer," Raina said.

Rick shook his head, feeling a flush rise to his cheeks. Wasn't he too old for his mother to make him blush? Obviously not. Shit.

"Now, now, no interruptions," Mrs. Pearson said, but she had a smile on her face, enjoying her return to the spotlight, no matter how brief. "So it turns out that young Rick had gone to the doctor for a checkup earlier in the week. Doc Little, you all remember him from before he passed on?"

There was a murmur of assent and "God rest his soul" from around the room.

"Well, it seems Doc Little told Rick his ears were so clean he could see all the way to China. Rick, being a smart boy, lined up the kids and was collecting pennies — from anyone who wanted to see what China looked like firsthand."

The guests cheered for Mrs. Pearson as she passed the microphone to Ms. Nichol, another elementary school teacher, who resembled Lucille Ball.

"I hope they're not going to go grade by grade," Rick said.

"Oh, no. Just the highlights," Raina reassured him with a pat on the hand.

"Swell."

Kendall laughed and the *This Is Your Life* show continued. Rick endured a not-so terrible story from the still redheaded Ms. Nichol, a reminder of his middle school hijinks from another teacher, and embarrassing high school tales about how Coach had caught him making out with girls behind the bleachers.

He had to hand it to his mother. She'd managed to lighten the night and even make him forget what this date stood for, at least for a little while. Catching her knowing smile, he knew she'd planned this on purpose. Before he could decide whether that was a good thing, Kendall grabbed his hand. Warm and soft, her skin slid against his, reminding him of how much he'd missed being with her.

Leaning over, she whispered in his ear, "I'm getting more information out of this show than I have out of you."

"I've never excluded you." When it came to Kendall, he'd felt more, given more of himself than ever before. And on the heels of the anniversary of his biggest disaster, it scared him.

Kendall scared him. Not an easy thing to admit. So no, Rick thought, except for that one memory that touched a nerve because Kendall, like Jillian, would leave, he hadn't excluded

Kendall at all. If anything she'd gotten too close.

Before Kendall could reply, his mother spoke into the microphone. "As you all know, I have the best boys. Even if they haven't given me a grandchild yet." Behind her, Eric cleared his throat, obviously not pleased she was using a public forum to air this particular grievance.

Neither was Rick. Difference was, he'd grown used to her complaint. His mother met his gaze and patted his cheek. "But seriously I have wonderful sons. They take care of me in my time of need." Her hand came to rest on her chest.

And her gaze darted to a point far away — like a suspect with something to hide. But that thought didn't make one bit of sense.

"So," Raina continued, jarring his thoughts, "it's a pleasure for me to pass on my favorite story about my middle son."

"Can I leave now?" Rick asked wryly.

"Only if you want to be hauled back and shackled with your own cuffs," someone yelled out.

Kendall smothered a laugh but a loud hiccup came out instead.

"Okay, okay. Get on with it," Rick said.

He put an arm around his mother's shoulder, grateful she cared enough to make his birthday something special and grateful she was still around to celebrate with him. *Still around.* The thought chilled him. So did the one request

265

Raina had in life that went unfulfilled.

Grandchildren. Something he'd almost given her back when he'd married Jillian. Raina, bless her generous heart, had welcomed and planned for Jillian's baby as if it were Chandler flesh and blood. Unlike Jillian's parents who'd disowned her, Raina took Jillian into her heart. And just like Rick, Raina had had her heart broken. But she'd never once looked back, not even when discussing her desire for grandchildren. Never blamed him, or forced the issue when he didn't want to talk about it. Because she was his mother and she loved him unconditionally. Yet here they were many, many years later and Raina still didn't have the grandchild she desired. Not even from Roman, who'd married a few months ago.

Grandchildren, he thought again and his gaze drifted to Kendall.

"Well, my story dates back to when Rick was three." Raina's voice and his childhood memories brought a welcome respite from the thoughts stirred up by this birthday cum anniversary.

"I thought we were all the way past his high school days," Roman said.

Like Rick, he obviously knew where their mother was headed and it wasn't pretty. Rick shot his youngest brother a grateful look though they both knew Raina wouldn't be deterred. They were right.

She ignored Roman and continued, twisting

in her seat, facing the crowd for maximum impact. "Guess what my adorable child wanted to be for Halloween?"

"I take it it wasn't something as basic as a ghost or goblin?" Kendall leaned into him, her breasts heavy against his arm.

He swallowed a groan, then shook his head. "Just listen."

"Chase, Rick, and I were in the car when Rick announced he wanted to be a fairy godmother for Halloween."

The crowd erupted in hoots of laughter and applause. That damn heat worked its way back to his cheeks. Dammit, he was getting too old for this. But he couldn't help but laugh at the story, as did Kendall. She laughed hard, not stopping even when Rick poked an elbow lightly in her ribs.

"I'm sorry," she said between gulps of air. "I just can't imagine it."

He rolled his eyes. "Me neither, but she swears it's true."

"Oh, yeah?" A sexy grin tipped her lips as she met his gaze and a heavy beat of sensual awareness pulsed between them. Completely inappropriate considering how much company surrounded them but altogether right just the same.

"Tell us more about the fairy," a voice sounding like Samson called from the crowd.

Rick shook his head. There was nothing to do but grin and bear it. With Kendall keeping him hot and his thoughts occupied with taking her to bed, he could handle anything.

"Well since you asked . . ." Raina chuckled. "Rick's grandmother had read him Cinderella and he'd taken a shine to the fairy who granted any wish. I knew darn well John would enroll him in military preschool if there were such a thing, so I swore him to complete secrecy and promised him packs of baseball cards if he never told his father."

A round of applause followed. Rick exhaled a sigh, amazed that his younger antics amused these people and touched that they'd all shown up on his behalf.

"Okay, show's over." Eric took the microphone from Raina's hands. "My . . . patient . . . needs her rest. There's Norman's best food on the island in the kitchen. Make yourselves at home. Eat, drink, and be merry." He raised a glass to Rick. "Happy birthday, son."

Rick blinked, unsure he'd heard the man correctly, thinking he'd meant *son* more as a warm term than a literal statement. But a glance into his eyes and Rick knew — that word held a wealth of meaning, for both his mother and for him. On the subject of Raina, Eric Fallon had nothing to worry about. Rick, like all her sons, wished Raina health and happiness. She'd found the latter with Eric. After twenty lonely years, Eric had given her something special and Rick felt he owed the man for that.

Though he didn't have a glass, he met Eric's

gaze and gave him an approving nod. One full of man-to-man understanding. Rick hadn't had a father in years, but if anyone deserved his mother, Eric did.

Rick stepped forward to shake the other man's hand, then turned to Raina. "I love you, Mom."

"I love you too. And, Rick —" Something suspiciously like moisture had pooled in her eyes.

"What is it?"

She opened her mouth, then closed it again before gesturing over to where Kendall stood. "Just that she's waiting. And I know you care for her. That look in your eyes? You didn't even have that around Jillian."

"Well, at least I know the outcome ahead of time. Now don't you have to rest?" Though she didn't look quite as tired as he'd expected she would. With a weak heart, something worse than a heart condition as she'd explained to them months earlier, she tired easily and was at serious health risk. But she certainly didn't look at risk now.

"You know no such thing," Raina said, referring to Kendall. "When you want something badly enough, you have to go for it." She patted his cheek. "Think about it. Now Eric's right. I need my rest." She took hold of the older man's arm. "He said I could stay the night at his house so the party could continue here. He even offered to let me sleep in his bed." A

269

bright blush spread across her cheeks. "I mean borrow his bed while he sleeps on the couch while the party goes on till all hours here." She turned pleading eyes on Eric. "Get me out of here before I make a fool of myself."

"Already happened, sweetheart." Eric shook his head and laughed. "But your wish is my command. Let's go before you do get yourself in trouble. Make that more trouble. Don't worry, I'll take good care of her, Rick."

"I have no doubt you will." Rick inclined his head, giving his subtle blessing, then watched as the older couple worked their way through the crowd and out the door.

What a night and it wasn't half over. Kendall still looked busy with her sister, so Rick headed for the soft drinks on the side table in the corner. Pouring himself a cola, he raised his glass and hummed. "Happy Birthday to me, happy birthday to me. Happy birthday . . ."

"Always sing to yourself?" Kendall came up behind him, snaking her arms around his waist.

Her chest pressed against his back and her warmth seeped inside him, softening his heart yet hardening his body to the point of burning need.

He laughed. "Caught in the act."

"I loved that story about the fairy god-mother."

"You and everyone else in the room," he muttered.

"Had for a pack of baseball cards." She pivoted around so she was facing him, her arms still tight around his waist. "I didn't know you could be bought, Officer Chandler," she said in a husky voice.

"Those were the good old days. And it wasn't the cards, it was the gum."

"I thought you said you didn't remember the incident?"

She lifted her brows, causing a wrinkle of skin between them, and his desire to kiss her grew stronger. "I don't remember. But assuming it's true and not a figment of my mother's overactive imagination, I was all of three years old. What do you think held greater appeal, the cards or the gum?"

She threw her head back and laughed. "Good point. And one that tells me you can be bribed."

"Into felonies now are we?"

She set her lips in a pout that incited his already aroused hunger. "No, actually I'm into you."

A low growl came from his throat. "Now that I like."

Kendall forced a smile. She didn't know how well he'd like it if he realized what was going on in her head. After a night of insight into Rick's past, she'd discovered how much she didn't know about him. How much she wanted to know. When she'd told him earlier that she was getting more information out of the show than out of him, she hadn't been kidding. He hadn't told her about his birthday. Hadn't mentioned it at all.

Rick Chandler, an open, lively, talkative man, had kept silent. And she hated it. He knew more about her life than she did about his. Until tonight she hadn't realized how purposefully he'd acted.

The show had piqued her curiosity about Rick and it was time she found out how much this man was willing to reveal. "So back to bribery. Do you mean to tell me there's *nothing* I could offer that would entice you to reveal hidden secrets?"

Despite the party and the crowds, his gaze settled on hers, hot and with complete understanding in the darkened depths. "Oh, I'm sure there's something you can offer that would make me throw my principles to hell and back." He never broke eye contact, mesmerizing her, tantalizing her with his heated stare.

"Are you sure you won't jeopardize your job?"

"Something tells me it'd be worth it. What are you offering in exchange for information?" He leaned closer.

His breath was warm on her cheeks, her body on fire with want and desire. But he still hadn't promised to talk. Hadn't said he'd reveal what she wanted to know. His life. His past. His marriage. He'd so obviously perfected the art of keeping his distance while giving the perception of closeness at the same time, she wondered if he knew how to act differently. To open up and risk being hurt.

Did she?

She shivered beneath his gaze, knowing that until now, his distance had been enough. Probably because distance had been safer for her as well. Still was. So why fight it, she wondered. Why push him for information?

Without warning, the microphone shrieked again and a female voice intruded on the crowded party, and on Rick and Kendall's hot exchange. "I wanted to wait until Raina left before finishing up the last of Rick's surprises for the evening."

"What's going on?" Kendall turned around for a better look and Rick stiffened beside her.

"Lisa," he muttered. "Dammit, I'll be right back."

"Oh, no. Not without me." Kendall wanted to hear this exchange firsthand. She followed Rick through the crowd.

Unfortunately, Lisa continued talking. "*This Is Your Life, Rick Chandler* wouldn't be complete without a summary of his later years. I notice no one mentioned Jillian Frank."

Silence descended upon the room. Rick came up beside the other woman. "Give me the microphone and stop embarrassing yourself."

She lowered the instrument but didn't release her grasp. "I'm a schoolteacher. Very little embarrasses me." She then raised the mike and spoke again. "I just wanted to wish Rick a happy anniversary too."

Kendall sucked in a deep breath. "What?" She hadn't meant to speak out loud but she was obviously discovering why Rick hadn't mentioned his birthday to her earlier. The day was too painful. Her heart clenched, twisting with a pain of her own.

Hannah came up to Lisa. "You are so pathetic."

Kendall knew things could unravel fast from here. Apparently so did Rick because his gaze searched out Roman's, and seconds later Roman and Charlotte herded a grumbling Hannah away from Lisa.

"We'll keep her for the night," Charlotte called over her shoulder as they guided the young girl out the door. Hannah complained until the door closed behind them.

Kendall exhaled a sigh of relief. One problem down. Another to go, she thought, turning back to Lisa. It didn't escape Kendall's notice that the rest of the town stood eating and drinking and gaping as if they considered Lisa's behavior a part of the evening's entertainment. For them it was.

For Kendall it was an awful revelation and she refused to give Lisa the satisfaction of knowing she'd gotten to her. Not even when Lisa turned back to Kendall.

"You're probably the only one in town who didn't know that Rick's birthday coincides with the day he married his pregnant friend. Not that it matters since she dumped him for the baby's father. But he never got over it. Never got seriously involved again. So don't think you'll be the one to change that —"

Rick grabbed the microphone out of her hand while Chief Ellis walked up to Lisa. "Sorry, Rick," the chief said through a mouthful of food. "I was in the kitchen sampling Izzy's petit fours or I'd have been here sooner. This lady invited?"

"Hell, no," Rick muttered.

"Trespassing, disturbing the peace . . ." Chief Ellis rattled off a list of violations and along with Rick, they propelled Lisa to the door.

Meanwhile Kendall's mind whirled with words she couldn't assign a meaning to. Anniversary. Pregnant. Baby. She'd wanted insight into Rick's mind, his past. She'd just been handed that information in spades. And she'd rather have heard it from him.

Kendall's stomach twisted as she tried to process what being left by a pregnant wife would do to a man like Rick. A man with a strong honor code. A man who'd been willing to marry a pregnant friend. She rubbed her aching temples with her hand. No wonder he steered clear of relationships. No wonder he was wary of women. And no wonder he was probably even more wary of Kendall, because she'd told him from the beginning she was leaving.

"Okay, folks, show's over." Chase clapped his

hands and murmurs of assent rose from the crowd. Then he turned to Rick. "You sure do know how to throw a party."

"If you'll recall, I'm the guest of honor. If it was my choice there wouldn't have been a party." He rubbed the muscles in the back of his neck that had grown tenser by the minute.

"And I now know why that is." Kendall came up beside them. "Why you never mentioned your birthday . . . or your anniversary."

Chase cleared his throat. "Do I see a lovers' quarrel coming on?"

"None of your business," Kendall and Rick replied at the same time.

Chase laughed. "Just like an old married couple. I can remember when Mom used to finish Dad's thoughts."

"We're out of here," Rick said, grabbing Kendall's hand.

"I'm only leaving if you promise to talk to me," she whispered in his ear.

"I'll talk if you'll listen," Rick promised.

Kendall took his words as a challenge. After all she'd heard tonight, she had no doubt listening to him retell his past would be as difficult for her to hear as it had been for him to live.

Rick wasn't much of a talker. For all his joking ways, for all the people he befriended, serious discussion about his life was something he avoided. He'd never realized that particular piece of information about himself before now. But as he led Kendall into his apartment, a sense of claustrophobia overtook him and he broke into a sweat.

He tossed his keys on the counter and inspiration struck. "Come with me."

"Where?" Kendall asked. "I thought we were already here." She gestured around the apartment. "Four walls and the bedroom, which I refuse to enter by the way until we're talked out."

Rick walked to the set of windows leading to the large fire escape and lifted one high enough for even a tall person to bend and get through. He waved his hand outside. "Come join me on the terrace."

"You're kidding?"

"Nope. When Charlotte rented this place, she used the fire escape as a deck of sorts. It's secluded and it seats two." He ducked and stepped outside, then held his hand out to help Kendall do the same.

He waited until she'd settled as comfortably as possible on the hard iron surface and sat, knees bent beside her. "It's not paradise, but it'll do."

"Actually it's pretty close." She lifted her face toward the direction of the warm breeze and let out a contented sigh. "I take it you were feeling claustrophobic inside?"

He stiffened. "What makes you say that?" Mind reading wasn't a game he was familiar with and they'd been in synch twice already tonight. After Chase's married couple crack, it was enough to make him damn uncomfortable.

She met his gaze. "Because I asked you to talk. To open up. And you've gone so far out of your way not to do that, I figured you must be feeling cornered now."

"And you'd know all about feeling cornered?" He hazarded an accurate guess, knowing she'd spent her life running from whatever it was that prevented her from settling in one place.

"Would you stop doing that?" She smacked her hand against the floor in obvious frustration. "Ouch. Dammit." She shook her hand out in front of her.

He lifted her palm and pressed a kiss against her stinging flesh.

She yanked her hand back. "Don't try and distract me. You're too good at turning the tables on me. I'll ask you a question and seconds later I'm spilling my guts instead of you."

He grinned. "What can I say? I'm trained in interrogation tactics."

"Trained in avoidance tactics is more like it," she muttered. "You're the one who's feeling cornered right now, not me."

Rick glanced up at the dark night sky. The time had come to either reveal his innermost pain or walk away from Kendall for good, before she walked away from him. Which she'd probably do anyway. He rubbed his hand along the back of his neck. "Jillian and I knew each other since she moved to town. I was a few years older than her but we became good friends and stayed that way all through high school."

"Just friends?" Kendall asked.

"Yeah, just friends."

"But you wanted more."

He shrugged. "I was a guy. She was a pretty girl. Of course I wanted more." Rick wanted to get through this telling as easily as possible, no emotion or theatrics involved. "I graduated high school and commuted to Albany for college, trained and joined the police force. Jillian was doing the commuting thing too and had finished her third year of college when she came home that summer."

"Pregnant." Kendall lay a hand on his arm and he covered it with his own.

"Four months."

Kendall sighed.

Even if she had forced the story out of him, her presence and support meant a lot to him now. There was no one else he'd rather share his past with than Kendall. No one he'd rather share his future with either. The thought hit with greater impact and force than a bullet and he sucked in a startled breath.

"Are you okay?"

"Fine." *Yeah right.*

"So finish the story," she gently prompted.

He gathered the fortitude from somewhere

deep inside him. He no longer had feelings for Jillian, of that much he was certain. He wasn't dealing with raw emotion or lost love when he told this story now. But he was coping with a loss. One he'd never fully acknowledged before. Because Jillian's leaving represented the end of the life he'd always wanted. The life he'd accepted that he'd never have.

Or thought he'd accepted until he met Kendall. Somehow this wanderer had reignited the desire for family he thought he'd put behind him. Ironically, even as she'd fed the yearning, she couldn't provide the fulfillment.

But Rick couldn't blame Kendall, not when she'd been honest from the beginning. Because she'd been deprived of love, caring, and stability all her life, she thought she didn't have it in her to stay in one place. To trust in someone else's word and deed. Yet she knew just how to provide and evoke all those wonderful feelings in someone else — in Hannah, and in Rick. She was just afraid to reach out and grab those same things for herself.

"Rick?" She said his name tentatively. "If you can't do this —"

"I can." He couldn't force her to stay, but he could confide in her now and still hope she'd come around on her own. Her honesty with him earlier demanded the same truthfulness now. He regrouped to explain. "Jillian had told the father that she was pregnant but he'd just graduated and wasn't ready for commitment."

"Nice of him to inform his sperm of that," Kendall said in disgust.

"I can't argue with you there." He let out a bitter laugh. "She was too far along for an abortion and her parents threw her out of the house. It was a scene out of a television drama, not reality. At least not reality in Yorkshire Falls. But she showed up on my doorstep. I was renting a small apartment near the station in town. She moved in and things progressed from there."

"Uh-uh. That's too stark a description. Too black and white." Kendall leaned against the railing and eyed him skeptically.

She studied him as if she could figure out what he was not only thinking, but feeling. Jillian had known him too, but in a shallow sense. She knew he'd take her in and never let her down. But she didn't understand him nor had she bothered to get inside his head. Her own needs came first, a pattern that continued even after they were married and the panic of uncertainty had passed.

But Kendall was here now, asking about his past, his feelings. She obviously cared about the reasons behind his actions. She wanted his happiness too. In his experience, that quality was rare and he valued her all the more for it. No one had ever known him as well as Rick sensed Kendall already did.

"It wasn't just a hormonal thing, what you felt for Jillian, was it?" Kendall asked.

Her words confirmed his hunch. She knew

him well. Well enough to read his feelings for her? He doubted it, if only because until now he'd hid them, even from himself.

He loved her. And those emotions were out there now for him to recognize, acknowledge, and feel. He wanted her in his future because he loved her. And damned if he knew what he was going to do about it.

As a cop, Rick wasn't a man used to remaining idle and once he came to a realization, action took over. He refused to look back and say he hadn't given his all — to any one person, thing or situation. He stretched his legs out as far as the small, confined area would allow and glanced at Kendall.

A humid breeze ruffled her hair and she'd pursed her lightly glossed lips, giving him time to formulate a reply. But as Kendall sat there so stiff and uptight, waiting to hear how he'd felt about his ex-wife then, she had no clue all he could think about was how he felt for *her* now.

"What makes you so sure that what I felt for Jillian went beyond the need to help a friend?"

Kendall shrugged but he sensed more behind the gesture than a casual dismissal. "You're the proverbial white knight but not even you would give up your life by marrying someone you didn't love. Favors and goodwill only go so far. Even for Rick Chandler," she said wryly. "Don't get me wrong, I believe you'd have helped Jillian out regardless, but for you to have married her you'd have to have cared for her." She drew a deep breath. "Loved her."

Rick raised an eyebrow, surprised she'd brought that word into this fragile conversation. "I cared for Jillian as more than a friend," he acknowledged. "The sexual attraction had always been there. I'd be lying if I said that didn't make the whole marriage thing easier to do."

Kendall stared at him, wide-eyed.

If he had to hazard a guess, he'd say she was holding her breath. He stroked a finger down her soft cheek. "With hindsight, I can say I loved the idea of Jillian. The idea of the life we could have together. The perfect family unit." He shook his head at the memory of how young and naive he'd been. And how messed up his life would have become if the baby's father hadn't come to his senses, he realized now. "Mother, father, baby. Hell, I nearly bought us a dog to make the picture complete."

He turned to Kendall so he was on his knees, towering over her enough to make his point. "I cared enough to convince myself to marry her but I didn't love her."

Was it his imagination or did she just exhale a sigh of relief? He wanted to grin, to kiss those still pursed lips, but he refrained, knowing he had more to say first. "That life I thought was so perfect would have been a noose around my neck. One I'd never be able to get rid of."

Her soft eyes met his. "She was lucky to have you. But you're right. Two people who marry for the wrong reasons will make each other miserable in the end. Still, she never knew how good she had it, did she?"

"Actually, she did. I got a letter that first Christmas. An apology and a thank you all wrapped up in one. She was living the life she wanted and she was happy. That's all I ever wanted for her."

"But you carried the pain around all this time?"

"I carried the idea of losing something around. I never realized until now that Jillian didn't take anything away from me. She gave me back my chance at life." Amazing what talking revealed to a man. Talking to the right person, he amended.

Any barriers he'd built crumbled as if they'd never been. He was a man treading in deep water, yet he had no choice but to take the risk.

"So you no longer regret her leaving?" Kendall asked.

He shook his head. "Hell no." If anything, he wished Jillian well and silently thanked her for taking off. "If she hadn't gone with the baby's father, what the hell would I have done when you stumbled into town?"

Kendall laughed but there was no real humor in the sound. "You'd have taken one look at me in my pink hair and wedding dress, dropped me off at my aunt's house, and run the other way."

"The hell I would have." He let out a low growl.

"Well, you wouldn't have had any need for a pretend lover, that's for sure. And definitely no need for me."

He grasped her face in his hands. Didn't she know how he felt about her? Couldn't she read it in his eyes, hear the words even though he hadn't yet said them aloud?

Or maybe she was just pretending ignorance. He knew her equally well. He knew that if Kendall faced the fact that he loved her or that she might feel the same way, she'd fall into her standard pattern and run.

No way would he let that happen. If he could help it. Sifting through his options, he came up with only one. Keep silent and keep her around. Use a little reverse psychology and back off emotionally. Play the part of Kendall's summer lover and let her be the one to come to her senses on her own.

Rick had just faced his past. Kendall deserved the time and the opportunity to face hers. But if he came on too strong, he'd risk losing her. Hell, he risked losing her either way, but with restraint and patience, at least he stood a chance. They stood a chance.

He definitely had a need for her. He always would. But for now, he'd let her think it was a purely sexual need, while doing his best to supply everything she'd been missing in life, the feeling of family, security, contentment, and love. All the things she unknowingly gave to him.

The things he'd have to get used to doing without again, if he failed and Kendall took her bigmouthed, adorable sister to Arizona, leaving Yorkshire Falls and him behind.

CHAPTER ELEVEN

Kendall glanced outside where the tables were being setup for the day's sidewalk sale. All stores, vendors, and school activities were participating. But if the line in Norman's for coffee didn't move, Kendall would throttle the people ahead of her. She needed caffeine.

"Thank God the sun's out. Can you imagine a sidewalk sale in torrential rain?" Charlotte shuddered. "This is my first year participating but last year I heard they set up those heavy-duty tents and the water poured off the ends . . ." She reached out a hand and shook Kendall's arm. "And you're not listening, are you?"

Kendall blinked and focused on Charlotte's concerned expression. "I'm sorry. What did you say?"

Charlotte laughed. "That's okay. You're preoccupied."

After a night with Rick, Kendall was most definitely preoccupied and in way over her head. Her feelings for Rick continued to grow. Finding out about his past changed things. Knowing he had been married and had almost been a father did something to her deep inside. She didn't want to think of him caring for another woman in that way. And if something like that bothered her, Kendall needed to force herself to think in new and scary directions.

"Did I thank you for taking Hannah last night?" she asked Charlotte, changing the subject. Maybe after a caffeine jolt she'd be ready to embark on that new line of thought.

"Only about three times. She's a genuine joy."

"Are we talking about the same teenager with the big mouth, buttinsky personality, and the chip on her shoulder?" Kendall asked. "And I mean that in the most loving way that only a sister can imagine," she added with a smile.

"Actually we're talking about the polite, discreet, and helpful girl right out there." Charlotte tapped on the glass-plate window, pointing to where Hannah was helping Beth fold and display potential items for sale.

"Well, what alien invaded her body?" But she didn't care so long as her sister was happy. And judging by the wide smile and constant movement of Hannah's mouth, the young girl was thrilled to be chatting with Beth and assisting for the morning.

"I think it has to do with me *not* being her guardian that lets me see another side to her. Remember how you were with your parents?" Charlotte said and immediately clapped her hand over her mouth. "Oh, my God, I'm sorry. I forgot Roman told me you lived with different family members over the years. Geez that was insensitive of me."

Kendall waved away a hand. "Don't be ridiculous. It was a natural thing to say and a completely correct assumption about why Hannah's being difficult with me." She put a comforting hand on Charlotte's arm. "Thank you for trying to help analyze the situation. Insight can only help."

Charlotte inclined her head. "My pleasure then."

"But you should know, I think her good behavior with you has more to do with your being Rick's sister-in-law than anything else."

Her eyes opened wide. "Hannah has a crush on Rick?"

"Not in that way, no. She just idolizes him." Kendall sighed. "Rick seems to be able to reach her when I can't. Honestly I'm grateful someone can."

"I'd say that Rick has a way with all women but that would be too flip for the situation. What Rick has is a way with children. Teens especially. The DARE program is such a huge success in our community thanks to Rick. He continues activities over the summer on his days off because it keeps the kids focused even when school's out. They look up to him."

Kendall nodded. She'd noticed that herself. Obviously when Jillian had taken off, she'd deprived him of the opportunity of being a father. And, oh, what a wonderful father he'd be. To a baby, a toddler, a child, or a teen. She clasped her hands to her chest, then realized where her thoughts were headed. That new and scary direction again. But it was true. Rick would be an exceptional parent to a child of any age.

Still thinking about commitment of any kind wasn't easy for Kendall. She'd never envisioned a lifetime that included forever. Then again, no one had extended an invitation her way either.

"Hannah seems to have responded to Rick like any typical teen," Charlotte said.

Kendall nodded. "That's true. Hannah and Rick clicked from day one." Just like she and Rick had clicked from the second they'd met.

"Hannah's not the only Sutton girl who's fallen for Rick's charms, is she?" Charlotte whispered, in obvious deference to eaves-dropping patrons on line along with them. "I know I'm being presumptuous. But when I was falling for Roman, I had Beth to confide in and I figure that since you're new to town, you don't have someone to talk to. Someone who knows you and Rick. And, well, I wanted to offer an ear." Charlotte blushed red. "If you want one."

Kendall opened her mouth to speak but words failed her. Charlotte's gesture, so warm, compassionate, and thoughtful, took Kendall off guard. "I'm not falling for Rick." The standard words came automatically but so did her heart's immediate denial.

Charlotte raised an eyebrow in obvious disbelief. A half smile formed on her lips. "Sorry, Kendall, but I'm not buying the story. Try saving it for someone who hasn't been in your shoes already. Same shoes, different brother." Charlotte tapped her feet against the floor, pausing in her rhythm only to take a few steps forward in line. "You can deny it for as long as you want. Seconds, minutes, days, or years. It doesn't matter. One day your feelings for Rick will catch up with you. Just like my feelings for Roman caught up with me."

Kendall wasn't sure whether to be outraged Charlotte had read and intruded upon her private thoughts or be appreciative she'd cared enough to give her the warning. When it came to feelings, Kendall had always kept her emotions inside and dealt with them on her own.

Necessity had driven her to solitude at a young age. Habit and constant moves prevented her from sharing things with others as she grew older. Now Charlotte offered Kendall the chance to confide in another woman. More importantly, Charlotte offered a chance at the kind of genuine friendship Kendall had never had.

Charlotte couldn't begin to imagine the importance of her offer. Gut instinct told Kendall that Charlotte's warmth came easily and without thought, whereas Kendall's desire to accept came with more difficulty. Although the lonely little girl inside her heart was dying to reach out and accept the gesture of friendship, fear prevented her from doing so.

Gathering herself, she met Charlotte's patient gaze. "You're presuming you and I are alike. We aren't." They couldn't be.

Because anytime Kendall had allowed herself to get close to someone — her aunt, her parents, another kid in a new town — as soon as she let herself accept that sense of security, the blanket was ripped off and Kendall was left alone. And that was the crux of her fear, she realized for the first time. The basis of her need to run. People she loved, people she cared for, left her.

Her parents had abandoned her. In her own way, Aunt Crystal had done the same, first when she'd had to send Kendall away and later in death. In Kendall's experience, one rooted in childhood, she always lost those she loved most. Kendall's life and the people in it were a series of drive-bys. Her biggest fear was getting close to the people in Yorkshire Falls, to Rick and his warm, loving family, and then losing them.

Charlotte shrugged. "Okay, we aren't alike. If you say so."

"I do. From what I understand you wanted to stay in Yorkshire Falls. I plan to leave." But what if she didn't? What if she stayed here, a small voice in her head asked. Kendall shivered and shook off the notion. She'd never wanted to put down roots in one place. Never had a sense of belonging. Surely she couldn't belong in Yorkshire Falls.

"What else makes us different?" Charlotte asked with a grin, obviously amused by Kendall's assessment.

Kendall had a hunch she didn't need her inner self giving a voice to her deepest desires. She had Charlotte to do it for her. "Well, you weren't adverse to getting married. I'm as far from that mind-set as you can imagine."

If that's true, then why were you evaluating Rick's potential as a parent, that small voice in Kendall's head asked. Darn this small town and Rick's warm family and friends. Damn them for showing her all she'd missed out on in life. All she could have if she weren't afraid to grasp what life may or may not offer.

Charlotte stared, as if she knew the war going on in Kendall's mind and was giving her time to fight the battle before interrupting. Then she cleared her throat. "I guess I was wrong. Considering all you just said, you and Rick are really the opposite of myself and Roman. I mean for starters, Roman was the wanderer, not me."

"I suppose," Kendall murmured, unsure whose side she fell on now. Why did she have the feeling that unsettling her had been Charlotte's intent all along?

The other woman shook her head and laughed. "Well, if I'm presuming anything about you now, it's that you're human. And humans are complicated. They don't always know their own minds though they think they do."

"Do you have a degree in psychology?" Kendall grinned.

"No, just one in observation. Case in point. I *thought* I wanted to stay in Yorkshire Falls because staying represented security. Turns out security for me can be defined in many different ways. And any way that includes Roman works just fine for me." Charlotte shrugged. "Maybe you just think you want to keep moving from place to place. Or maybe not." She shook her dark hair out behind her. "Come to think of it, you're right. I shouldn't presume to know anything about you. But if you ever need a friend or an ear, I promise to listen and not preach next time. Deal?"

She held out a hand and Kendall grasped it. "Deal," she said, her head whirling with Charlotte's words and the game of Devil's Advocate her own mind played.

"Next. What can I get you two ladies," Norman asked, saving Kendall from having to think through the meaning in what she'd just heard.

"Orange juice for me. A frozen Chai Tea for Beth and . . ." She glanced at Kendall, waving a hand, indicating she should take her turn.

Beth's drink sounded interesting. "I'll try anything once. Does Chai have caffeine?" she asked.

Norman nodded. "Enough to perk you up, missy."

Kendall laughed. "Then a Chai Tea for me and a large O.J. for Hannah."

"Two Chais and two O.J.s," Norman repeated. "Anything else?"

"Nope." Charlotte insisted on footing the bill

against Kendall's arguments and moments later they were back out on the heated street and the sidewalk sale began in earnest. Charlotte's handmade crocheted panties were a hit along with Kendall's jewelry. After an hour, the wire jewelry had sold phenomenally well and Charlotte had collected deposits and a list from people who'd requested specific color schemes or ID bracelets and necklaces.

"I never expected this kind of volume," Kendall said in awe.

"Hey, when you're good, you're good." Beth gave her an earnest smile. "Welcome aboard, Kendall."

Warmth fluttered inside her chest and the most she could manage was a smile in return. She glanced across the street and noticed her sister bouncing around with a group of nice-looking girls. Hannah too seemed part of a crowd here in Yorkshire Falls.

What ifs began circling in Kendall's head once more. What if she settled here? What if she didn't pack her bags and move to Arizona? What if she trusted in herself and in others for the duration?

Kendall shook her head. Twenty-seven years of habits were hard to break on one day. For now she wanted to enjoy the bright sunny day and the sense of belonging without the stress of decision-making or thought. She was grateful when seconds later, Thomas Scalia arrived to flirt with Beth. At least watching the other couple distracted Kendall from her own flights of fancy. As if she could ever really belong anywhere. But *here* felt so right . . .

"Ms. Sutton?"

Kendall turned at the sound of her name and found herself facing an attractive brunette.

"I'm Grace McKeever," the other woman said. "My daughter's name is Jeanette. Jeannie and your sister have become fast friends." She gestured across the street to where the girls giggled. They congregated in one group while another clique of guys huddled nearby.

Kendall stifled a laugh.

"Jeannie's the one with the dark ponytail. Anyway, I promised her I'd take her and a friend to an afternoon movie in Harrington and then for dinner. We'll probably grab Chinese food and be home later on tonight. I'd love to take Hannah, if it's okay with you."

"That's so sweet of you to offer." Hannah had mentioned Jeannie more than once since the car wash and when Kendall had questioned Rick about her choice of friends, he'd reassured Kendall that the McKeevers were wonderful people. "Of course it's okay. I'd be forever grateful, actually."

"Wonderful. The girls will be thrilled."

As if on cue, Hannah and Jeannie ran over, both talking at once. "Mom, can Hannah sleep over?" Jeannie asked.

"Kendall, I have to get this purple washed out of my hair," Hannah said at the same time.

"And Pam said she had just the solution to do it, and she said she could fit me in now. I don't know what I was thinking, but Greg hates girls with fake hair, so I have to rinse this stuff out. Can I, Kendall, please? And I really want to sleep at Jeannie's house. Did you know that Greg lives next door?" Hannah said, asked, and explained all without taking a breath.

Her sister wanted to rinse out her hair? She liked it here enough to come out from hiding? *Why not,* that small voice asked. *You* did, recalling how she'd rinsed the pink soon after arriving because she'd wanted to be herself. Kendall blinked, startled at the similarities between the sisters. And a positive one this time.

"Well, Kendall?"

Hannah's voice interrupted her thoughts and Kendall glanced at her sister. "Yes, yes, and no."

Her bright eyes opened wide, clearly upset. "That's *so* unfair. Just because I slept at Charlotte's last night doesn't mean I shouldn't be able to sleep out again tonight and I earned money helping Charlotte all morning, so —"

"Whoa." Kendall held up a hand, cutting her sister off. "Yes, you can definitely have the purple washed out of your hair. My treat. Yes, you can sleep at Jeannie's house *if* it's okay with her mother." She paused, an idea hitting her. "Actually, why don't the two of you sleep at our house and give her parents a break after the movies and dinner? And no, I didn't know

Greg lived next door to Jeannie," Kendall finished on a laugh.

Hannah blushed. "Sorry."

"That's okay." At least Hannah was acting like a typical teenager and not an angry young girl. "So what does everyone think?" Kendall asked about the idea of the girls sleeping at her place.

The girls looked first at each other, then at poor Grace McKeever.

"Please, Mom, please can I sleep at Kendall's?" Jeannie tugged on her mother's sleeve. "They're staying in Ms. Sutton's old guest house. Hannah said it's so cool. She has her own room and there's an attic where Kendall set up all her jewelry designs. Hannah said it's awesome. Please?"

Hannah said anything about Kendall or the house was *awesome?* Kendall had to blink back tears. She turned and wiped her eyes, intending to blame the sun if anyone called her on it.

"It's fine with me, girls. We'll stop at the house before we leave for Harrington so you can pack up your things."

"Cool!" The girls shot each other conspiratorial grins, as if they'd accomplished some covert deal.

"Don't forget a blanket or sleeping bag of some kind," Kendall said to Jeannie. "We don't have extra beds and furniture."

"Double cool!" Jeannie said as Grace jotted down her cell and home phone number and

Kendall did the same so they could exchange. Then Grace excused herself to do some more shopping. The girls turned to run back to their crowd of friends, but Hannah pivoted back and leaned across the table, meeting Kendall's gaze.

"Thanks."

The appreciation in Hannah's eyes told Kendall more than anything her sister could possibly say. "My pleasure." Reaching into her jeans pocket, Kendall pulled out spare money and gave it to her sister. "Spend wisely," she joked.

Hannah shoved the bills into her front pocket. "Kendall?"

"Yes?"

Hannah swallowed hard.

"Hannah, come on. They're waiting for us," Jeannie called out.

"I . . . I love you. Bye." Before Kendall could reply, Hannah turned and ran to join her friends.

"I love you too." And this time, a tear really did fall, dripping down her cheek.

As the sidewalk sale drew to a close, so did Rick's shift. He was free to do as he pleased and seeing Kendall pleased him greatly. He caught up with her as she was exiting Charlotte's Attic, a briefcase in hand.

Matching her stride, he fell into step with her. "Hey there."

Her eyes flashed a genuine greeting. "Hi yourself."

"Successful day?" He gestured to the briefcase.

"Amazing. I sold much of what we had out and took special orders for dozens of others." She shook her head in awe. "It's just been great."

"I know how to make it even better."

She paused and turned toward him. "Oh, yeah?" A smile pulled at her lips.

After their serious conversation the night before, he'd deliberately kept things light between them and judging by her welcome now, his tactics were working. Instead of running scared, she was moving closer.

He wanted her closer still. "Did you ever make out at a drive-in movie?" he asked her.

Her lips pulled up in a smile. "Can't say I've had the pleasure, why?"

"Tonight's the annual slide show. It coincides with the sidewalk sale every year. They turn the football field into a makeshift amphitheater and recount town history. It's not the most exciting thing to see but everyone shows up anyway. And I just happen to know a secluded place with the best view. Want to be my date?"

"You're not working?"

"I'm officially off duty and all yours," he said, leaning closer.

"I like the sound of that."

Her voice dropped a husky octave and he

liked that even more. But before he could concentrate on tonight, he had something he needed to discuss with Kendall. "I stopped by my mother's this morning on the way to work."

"All cleaned up from the party?"

He nodded. "Except the stack of gifts left over. I had no idea that everyone who showed up last night brought presents." He felt ridiculous accepting gifts for his birthday and he wished he could return all of them.

All except one. He pulled the collar of his shirt down slightly to reveal the thin black piece Kendall and Hannah had made for him. He wasn't a jewelry kind of guy, but this wasn't a typical piece of jewelry. It was masculine and unobtrusive enough to make him comfortable wearing it. But most importantly, the necklace was a gift from the heart, Kendall's heart.

"You like it?"

The hesitancy in her voice surprised him. When it came to her work, she was confident or so she'd seemed as he'd observed her from afar all afternoon. He hadn't wanted to interrupt or cause her to lose a sale. The more successful she became in Yorkshire Falls, the better for him.

"I like it and you." He stepped closer, bracketing her between him and the brick wall of the nearest building. His body reacted, something she obviously didn't miss because a low moan escaped her throat, turning him on even more. "I need to thank you properly." He treated her to a wicked grin. "After all, my mother raised me to be a gentleman."

"She also raised you to take this sort of thing behind a closed door." Raina's distinctive voice and chuckle broke the seductive spell he'd begun to weave.

"Oh, God." Kendall ducked beneath his arm.

Dammit. He'd wanted Kendall excited and anticipating the evening to come, not distressed and mortified. "Hello, Mother," he said through gritted teeth and stepped aside to let Kendall gather her composure.

"Hello, Rick." Raina smiled. "Kendall."

"I thought you were home resting," Rick said.

"I was. Then Chase wanted to snap a few last-minute photos and I begged him to take me along for a quick trip to see the sale. I haven't missed one yet and didn't intend to this year either."

"And now that you've seen and been seen?"

She rolled her eyes. "I'll go home and rest up for this evening of course."

Rick shot her a you've-got-to-be-kidding look. She was going out again this evening?

"There's nothing unhealthy about sitting on a blanket with a doctor by my side." Raina blushed but squared her shoulders as if daring him to argue that point. "Will you and Hannah be going to the show?" she asked Kendall, obviously turning attention away from herself.

It worked. Instead of his mother's health, he

focused in on Kendall. In his desire to be alone with her, Rick realized he'd forgotten about Hannah.

"Actually Hannah's going to dinner and a movie with a friend." Kendall stepped up beside Rick. "I don't expect them back until around eleven and then they're having a sleepover," Kendall said, obviously recovered from her embarrassment at being caught like two teenagers by his mother.

"Anyone I know?" Raina asked.

"Jeannie McKeever."

Rick breathed a sigh of relief. Grace McKeever was known for having an open house for all her kids' friends. With the girls sleeping there he'd have another night to let Kendall get used to having him around — in her life and hopefully in her heart.

"I'm having both girls sleep over in the guest house tonight. I've never had a sleep-over myself as a child so I thought I'd give Hannah the experience in a place that feels like home to her, you know?" Kendall asked of Raina.

"I most certainly do." Raina touched Kendall's cheek with her hand. "You're such a sweet girl."

He should have known better than to jump to conclusions about anything, especially when his love life was involved. He shook his head and laughed.

"Something funny?" his mother asked.

"Not a thing," he said wryly. He'd just have

to enjoy Kendall's company before her duties as a parent resumed later on. Duties she'd obviously taken to with more ease than either of them had anticipated.

Though she and Hannah had rough patches, Kendall had an innate understanding of her sister's needs. She had the ability to give the young girl a special life, if only she'd step back, realize and accept it. She'd make a great sister. She'd make an amazing mom. The thought stopped him cold, like a shot upside the head.

He glanced to his side where Kendall and Raina were in deep discussion about video rentals and the possibility of Kendall's borrowing a VCR for the night in order to entertain the girls. From his mother's wide smile, she approved of Kendall, of that Rick was certain. Although he'd never in his life let his mother's input dictate his choice in a date or relationship, it eased his mind knowing that he'd made her happy and hadn't added to her stress or weak heart. In fact, he made her happy. By choosing Kendall.

What unbelievable irony. He'd begun his relationship with Kendall to deter his mother and the women she'd encouraged in order to marry him off and get herself grandchildren. And he'd ended up wanting those very things for himself with the woman who he'd used to foil his mother's plan. Now if only Kendall wanted those same things.

If only.

Kendall parked her car in the spot behind the guest house and walked to the front door. The day had been more fun than she'd had in a while. Successful too, she thought and smiled. As she unzipped her bag, a low whining sound reached her ears. She glanced around, but didn't see anyone or anything. She shrugged and put her briefcase down so she could search her purse for her keys, which she'd stupidly tossed back in her bag so she could get her things out of the car.

The first thing she came up with was the real estate card given to her by Tina Roberts. The young woman had ordered an ID bracelet and then gone on to solicit business, asking Kendall what she planned to do with her aunt's house and without waiting for a reply had offered to come by to give her an estimate should she decide to sell. She'd also boasted her many accomplishments and the reasons why she'd make the perfect listing broker. No hesitancy, no shame. No wonder she'd made Realtor of the Month, Kendall thought wryly.

But she couldn't sell a house for above market value if it wasn't worth the money and the broker's card brought home an important point. Kendall hadn't bothered to do any more work on the house in days. And she hadn't given another thought to putting the place on the market.

The only thing she *had* decided was to put

Pearl and Eldin in the guest house and make their living there rent-free a condition of sale. She didn't know who would accept such terms, but there was no way Kendall would displace the older couple completely. She just hoped they'd be happy in the smaller residence, but with Eldin's bad back, maybe they'd be better off in a one-level place with less maintenance to deal with.

After her incredible day here, Kendall just wasn't ready to deal with selling the house. Not when she'd just begun to let herself think about other possibilities in life besides running. Not when she'd just begun to play *What If* . . .

She had time. Kendall stuck the card back in her bag and continued to poke around until her fingers wrapped around her keys when the pitiful noise sounded again, closer now. Glancing down, she saw a dog. A sandy-colored, shaggy-looking dog staring up at her with deep, soulful eyes.

"Hi there," Kendall said, approaching cautiously.

When the dog's tail began a metronomic wag with no menace in sight, Kendall bent down to pet her. Her coat was matted as if she hadn't been cared for in ages but her demeanor was warm and friendly. She wasn't afraid of Kendall and after a few minutes of head scratching, she rubbed against her legs and next thing Kendall knew she'd rolled onto her back for a belly rub, exposing her private parts for the world to see.

"Well, looks like I was wrong, Mr. Man. You're a boy." Kendall laughed. She felt beneath the matted fur on his neck. "No collar or ID. What am I going to do with you?"

She rose and he followed. She walked back to the front door and he tagged along. Twenty minutes later, after she'd given him a bowl of water, cleaned up the mess he'd made by the door because she hadn't realized the single bark meant he had to do his business, and called Charlotte for the name of the local veterinarian, Kendall and dog were in Dr. Denis Sterling's office.

"I didn't know what to do with him," Kendall explained as the doctor finished up his examination.

"Well, I'm glad you called. I never mind coming in for an abandoned pet."

"I can't tell you how much I appreciate it."

Dr. Sterling gave the dog a friendly pat on the head and Kendall an equally reassuring smile. Everything he did reinforced her initial impression of him as a kind man. He appeared to be in his late fifties, a good-looking man with blond hair, no gray, and a weathered face and gentle disposition.

"I didn't want to page you but Charlotte promised you wouldn't mind."

"And she was right. Charlotte's instincts are good ones." His voice held warmth.

Charlotte had mentioned that the local vet

had a crush on her mother, but Annie Bronson hadn't returned his feelings. Instead she was working on repairing her broken marriage to Charlotte's father. Dr. Sterling seemed no worse for the rejection though.

"Here's what I can figure about your friend here," the doctor said. "He looks like a soft-coated Wheaton terrier. You can tell by the beige- or wheat-colored coat and the terrier face. From his weight, I'd say he's full grown, about two or three years old, tops. And from his exuberance around strangers, I'd say he hasn't been abused."

"Thank God." Kendall released the breath she hadn't been aware of holding.

Dr. Sterling nodded. "The wagging tail's one clue. Wheatons stay puppies forever personality-wise, so this happy-go-lucky disposition won't be disappearing anytime soon." He placed the dog down on the table, forcibly rolling him onto his back. "See how he's letting me pet his stomach and examine him? He isn't afraid of this nondominant position. He's a good, friendly dog. No worries there. You can feel comfortable having him in your home."

"But . . ."

"I don't have any reports of a missing dog and after you called me with a description, I made some inquiries to some friends and shelters in other towns nearby. No luck there either. But they all took the information and said they'd call if they hear anything."

"Dr. Sterling, I'm . . ." *Not a permanent resident*. She paused, the words not coming as easily as they would have a short time ago.

"Yes?"

"I'm not sure I can keep him. What about a shelter?" Even as she asked, the idea didn't sit well. He was too cute and lovable to send away. But what would she do with him when she left? If she left . . .

"A shelter's only an option if you want to risk having him put down. The Harrington Shelter is full to bursting in capacity. They'll take him but the little dogs get taken home first. It's a risk putting him there."

As if he understood, the dog whined and began more furious tail wagging. Begging to be taken home, Kendall thought. With her. After hearing the doctor's description, there was no choice. "Okay, no shelter."

"I could ask around and see who wants a dog, but with you being engaged to Rick and all, I can't see the problem. Rick's a dog lover. When he was a boy, he'd bring home all sorts of strays. Drove his mother crazy."

So Rick was rescuing even back then. "I wonder how many of the animals he saved were females," she asked wryly.

Dr. Sterling laughed. "It takes a strong woman to handle one of those Chandler boys. You and Rick will be just fine."

She realized then she hadn't told Dr. Sterling they weren't engaged nor had she corrected his assumption that she'd be around to handle Rick Chandler. Not because he wouldn't listen like most people in this town but because the thought of taking care of Rick, of being the woman to handle him, held a great deal of appeal. More than she'd admitted to herself until now.

"Of course I'll post some signs in case someone's missing this fellow," Dr. Sterling said, unaware of her inner turmoil. "In the meantime, he'll need a bath and tomorrow when my assistant's in we can update his shots to be safe." Assuming she'd keep him.

And she would, Kendall thought, making a spur-of-the-moment decision. Of course she'd have to make it clear to Hannah that if his owner reclaimed him they'd have no choice but to give him back. But if not, she had herself a dog. A responsibility and a commitment unlike any she'd undertaken before.

She eyed Dr. Sterling warily. "I don't know anything about having a pet. And I don't have dog shampoo or food or . . ."

"Relax. Like infants, dogs don't come with instruction manuals but just like babies, they let you know when they're unhappy. They like to be cleaned, fed, and loved. I'm certain you can handle that. Plus you have me at your disposal. Rick too." He gave her a reassuring smile, not realizing he'd hit at her weakest spot.

How could she trust anyone to be there for her? She'd never trusted anyone, never relied on anyone except herself. Oh, there was Brian, but because he'd needed something in return, she'd been guaranteed his cooperation. As for Rick . . . they'd passed the point of a bargain and Kendall felt as if she were free-falling without a net.

"Now for the specifics," the doctor continued. "Any mild people shampoo will do just fine on him and I have a bag of food for you to get started. Wait here," he said before disappearing out the examining-room door.

"What am I going to do with you?" she murmured to the dog who merely wagged his tail happily. Half an hour ago he was wandering the streets and now he looked at Kendall, trusting her to take care of him. Apparently they were taking that leap of faith together.

His tail swished back and forth. Happy. It seemed to be his permanent disposition. "Okay, Happy. I think you've named yourself." She pet his head again, he licked her free hand and Kendall fell a little bit in love. Another jump into that new train of thought.

"Here's a book. *Seven Days to Successful Dog Training.*" Dr. Sterling walked back into the room, dog food under one arm, book in hand. "I have a feeling you'll be needing it."

She laughed since the first thing she'd told the doctor was about his accident in the entryway. He'd told her to bring in a sample so they could check for disease. She shuddered at the unpleasant memory and had a hunch there'd be more incidents like it before she and Happy were through. "Thanks, Doctor."

"Denis, please. And you're welcome. I'll see you tomorrow. Call at nine to make an appointment. At least your aunt's house has a big yard for him to run in. Rick can play catch with him. Wheatons need daily exercise."

"No apartments?" she asked, thinking of her normal lifestyle when she wasn't in Yorkshire Falls. A lifestyle that was beginning to seem more lonely and confined than she'd ever imagined. Yet how could having a huge stretch of highway and endless possibilities ahead seem lonely? The answer lay in this town, its people, and in her relationship with Rick. Whether she had the ability to trust in it all was something else altogether.

"An apartment is doable just not preferable. I always urge people to ask themselves what's fair to the dog. This guy's thirty-five pounds but he's underweight. He'll gain when you take good care of him and he's an outdoor-type dog. He needs his space."

Just like Kendall did. Or thought she did. Confusion swirled inside her. Her business had taken a huge step forward, her sister had made friends, and she'd inherited a dog.

"Will I see you at the slide show tonight?" Dr. Sterling asked.

"I'll be there."

"Good. Any questions that arise, you can ask me there." He grinned and opened a drawer, pulling out a collar and a leash. "You'll be needing these too. Once you pick up your own things, you can return them. No rush."

Kendall nodded, dazed. In one short day, she'd further cemented herself into the fabric of this small town. She didn't know if she was ready for Yorkshire Falls any more than Yorkshire Falls was ready for her.

Rick picked Kendall up at eight-thirty, knocking on her door as usual. An effusive barking greeted him from the other side of the door. If the sound of a dog wasn't enough of a surprise, seeing Kendall swing the door open, her hand wrapped around the leash of a hairy pooch shocked him even more.

"Come on in before he gets out." The dog shuffled to escape his confinement and Kendall struggled to keep him inside.

Rick slipped in and slammed the door shut behind him. "Where'd he come from?" No sooner had he asked than the four-legged dog leapt up and put both front paws on his chest.

Kendall laughed. "He likes you. Happy down!" She yanked the dog off him.

"Happy?"

"Look at that tail wag. Can you think of a better name for a dog like him?" She shrugged. "I don't know his real name since he wasn't wearing a collar when I found him."

Kendall had taken a stray dog into a home she didn't plan on staying in and she was smiling about it? Rick figured he'd worked one too many long shifts or he was seeing things. "You found him?" he asked, dumbfounded.

"Actually he found me. Outside. Either way, I think he's mine. Dr. Sterling says he'll put out some more feelers but preliminary calls haven't turned up anyone missing a pet." As she spoke, she absently rubbed Happy's neck with her hand. She'd obviously done this before and perfected the motion since she knew just the right spot and the dog nearly rolled over in ecstasy and delight.

Happy absolutely loved Kendall's hands massaging his body. "I know just how you feel, man," Rick muttered.

"What?" she asked.

He shook his head. "He's yours?" he asked instead, repeating her earlier words.

"Yep. Dr. Sterling gave me food and I borrowed a crate from your mom's basement on my way home." She clasped her hands behind her back, seeming pleased with herself.

Happy seemed pleased with her too as he'd settled at her bare feet.

"How'd you know my mom had a crate in the basement?"

"Dr. Sterling said you were a sucker for strays, which I should have known considering you found me."

She grinned and he wanted to kiss that smile on her lips.

"Ready to go to the show?" she asked.

He reached out and placed his hand over her forehead. "You don't feel warm to me."

She crinkled her forehead in confusion. "What's wrong?"

"Kendall, what do you plan on doing with the dog once you leave?" He forced himself to ask the question no matter how much he hated the notion.

Her serious gaze met his. "I'm impulsive but I'm not stupid. I *have* thought this out. A little bit." She bit down on her lower lip.

"And?" he asked, holding his breath.

"I'm not so sure I'm going anywhere after all." She turned away too quickly, not meeting his gaze.

Obviously she wasn't certain of her words but the fact that she'd say them at all gave him a ridiculous shot of hope.

She patted her leg and the dog rose to trail after her as she started for the other room.

"What are you doing?" he asked as she disappeared into the kitchen, leaving him to focus on the denim jeans drawn tight over her behind and the sassy sway to her hips.

"I'm going to lock up Happy so we can get going. And I'm giving myself some space before I hyperventilate," she called over her shoulder.

"Hadn't planned on admitting you might like to settle here, huh?"

"It's happening fast, Rick. Just give me time to think some more."

He nodded. He could do that. After all, with a house, a dog, and a sister to take care of, she wasn't about to perform any of her impulsive disappearing acts anytime soon.

CHAPTER TWELVE

Fresh air, inky night sky, and Rick by her side. In such a perfect atmosphere, Kendall was able to breathe just fine as they approached the football field. For the first time in her life she allowed herself to give in to the idea of belonging somewhere and to someone — and to enjoy it without fear of either being taken away.

She glanced around. As Rick promised, a huge screen covered what had once been the scoreboard and people with blankets had collected on the grass. Holding her hand, he continued past the crowds, not stopping for more than a quick hello.

"Where are we going?" she asked him.

"You'll see." He tugged on her hand and led her toward the bleachers that were also filled with people.

"So far I'm not impressed with the privacy level," she teased.

They rounded the stands, walking behind and then underneath the bleachers where only the echo of footsteps against the metal slats above reminded her they weren't alone. He'd found them a modicum of privacy amid the crowds. "Okay, now I'm impressed."

"Hey, I told you I wanted a secluded place where we could be alone." Warmth resonated in his voice and in the trembling heat of his body as he wrapped his arms around her waist and pulled her close.

The relief of finally being in his arms along with the possibility of being caught making out like two teenagers upped her level of excitement and awareness. Her heart fluttered rapidly in her chest and white-hot darts of fire sizzled in her veins. It was always this way with Rick. Whether she was thinking about him or actually with him, the heat was all-consuming.

"Well, you found the perfect place for us." She nuzzled her nose into the warm spot in his neck, between his shoulder and his ear, eliciting a distinct groan of pleasure in response. "I don't know how we're going to see the slide show and at this moment I don't care. But we're alone like you promised."

"I'll always keep my word, Kendall."

"Then you're going to have to find someplace else to hang out," a familiar male voice called out. "Because we were here first."

"Roman?" Rick asked.

"Who else?"

"Shit," Rick muttered.

Kendall wasn't able to stifle a laugh. "So much for originality."

"Like I said, we were here first."

Rick snorted in disgust. "And you think that gives you squatter's rights?"

"Is this what they call sibling rivalry?" Kendall wouldn't know considering she hadn't grown up with a brother or sister in residence long enough to experience the phenomenon firsthand. But despite the unwanted interruption, she was enjoying the heated yet humorous exchange between the brothers.

"It's what they call males marking their territory," Charlotte explained, laughing along with Kendall. "Besides, neither Roman nor Rick can claim this spot. According to town lore, it was Chase who put the Chandler mark here first."

"Ooh, do tell." Kendall couldn't imagine serious-minded Chase getting into trouble. However, even if Kendall preferred Rick's more outgoing personality, she could see many girls falling for Chase's strong, silent demeanor.

"Well, I heard that back when Chase was in school here, he got caught with a girl beneath the bleachers. They were cutting class and he was suspended," Charlotte said.

Kendall let out a whooping laugh. "You're kidding."

Rick shook his head. "It's the last kidlike story we really know about Chase before he took over as head of the family."

"Before he became the straitlaced, stern-faced brother we know and love," Roman added.

"I wonder what it takes to tame that Chandler man," Charlotte mused.

Roman let out a low growl. "I'm the only Chandler you're going to be taming. Now hit the road, Rick. No offense, Kendall."

"None taken." She laughed. How could she not? She liked how possessive Roman sounded when thinking about Charlotte. And she appreciated that Charlotte had tamed her wanderer, and now trusted him not to betray her as she'd feared her father had done with her mother. All of which made Kendall wonder what it would take for her to make that ultimate leap of faith in any person.

In any man.

In Rick.

She was so close, she knew. Close to believing she too could have the happily ever after and stability that she'd always viewed from the outside looking in.

But lingering questions remained. Like what would she do with that all-encompassing fear of abandonment and betrayal? Where would she put the memories of being left and how could she overcome the years she'd spent teaching herself that being alone and moving from place to place was safer for her heart?

"Let's go," Rick muttered, breaking into her thoughts. He grabbed her hand and started for the field. "You owe me big time, little brother." He was clearly not happy with being displaced by Roman.

Ten minutes later, they'd retrieved a blanket from the car and had joined the masses on the field. Despite the fact that they were surrounded by people, Kendall cuddled on a blanket with Rick. Music played from speakers around them and she couldn't be more content. The show finally started with slides of Yorkshire Falls dating back to its founding.

Rick had been right. Though many of the pictures and some of the narrative were interesting, it made for more intimate moments under the stars than a movie that held anyone's interest. Still, Kendall could see why it had become a town tradition and she was glad to know she'd been a part of it.

Rick pulled her closer, his arms wrapped around her waist and his face buried in her hair. "Did you mean what you said earlier?" he asked.

She could pretend to not know what he meant but that wouldn't be fair, not now that she knew his past and understood his latent fears. Turning so she could see his face, she met his serious gaze. "You mean about staying here?"

He nodded, saying nothing. But the way he looked at her — so full of longing and desire — sent shivers running through her. He waited for her to respond, like Rick, so full of patience and understanding.

And while he waited, his strong hands moved upward, brushing through her hair, tugging at her scalp, and creating both an erotic sensation and a sense of bonding and trust that slashed through her fears and reservations.

That made her want to trust for the first time. "Rick, I . . ."

He placed a finger over her lips. "Before you answer, there's something I want you to know."

He didn't need to say anything. Everything she needed to see and hear was written on his expressive face. But he obviously needed to talk. "What is it?"

He cupped his palms against her cheeks. "I love you, Kendall."

Her heart nearly stopped beating. Just as she'd reached a tentative agreement within herself, he offered her the ultimate, permanent expression of faith and commitment. One she wasn't sure she knew how to return considering she'd never been shown how.

But she wanted to. He was a special man who deserved so much from life and he'd been denied it all for too long. He loved her. "Rick, I . . ."

Loud gasps all around cut off anything she'd been about to say. Kendall turned to see what the cause of the commotion could possibly be and jerked around toward the large screen that seconds earlier had held black and white, then sepia-toned pictures of the town. But instead of muted, boring photos, there was a huge, blown-up photograph Kendall recognized well.

She should considering she'd posed for it. Back when she'd needed money to get her aunt into the optimal nursing home and before Brian had come up with classier shoots, Kendall had posed for a lingerie catalogue in a variety of outfits. Some had included leather. In this one she held fur-lined handcuffs and a silk scarf. And though she'd never choose to wear or use the products she'd modeled, at the time, none of the photos had embarrassed or shamed her. Until now.

Because back then she'd been viewing the pictures in a sales catalogue, not in what was meant to be a display of town pride. The thought brought her back to her surroundings and she realized she was practically naked on screen, on display for the entire town to see. In front of all the people who respected Officer Rick Chandler and the rest of his family. It wasn't just her reputation at stake, it was theirs too.

"Oh, my God. I have to get out of here." She jumped out of Rick's arms and stood, but as all eyes turned her way, she realized her mistake immediately.

Whoever had been focused on the photograph now turned their attention on the subject herself. Pointing, whispering, laughing. Kendall had become the immediate object of ridicule. Her face heated and flamed and waves of nausea washed over her. How had this happened?

Rick wrapped an arm around her waist and tried to nudge her forward. "Kendall, let's go."

But his voice barely penetrated the fog suddenly surrounding her. Glancing back, she saw the photograph had been replaced by a more recent one of First Street. The evidence was gone but the damage had been done, Kendall was forced to acknowledge. "I thought . . ."

"You can tell me whatever you thought later. Let me get you home first."

She felt him push at her again, to get her to move but she remained rooted in place. "I thought I could finally belong."

But obviously *belonging* wasn't a word she'd ever have the right to use. The laughter, shocked gasps, and muted whispers of people she'd come to know and care about still rang in her ears, reminding her of her first day in the beauty salon, when folks had made it clear she was an outsider.

She always would be.

"You *do* belong," Rick told her, hoping his words would penetrate. She belonged here in this town and to him.

Rick knew the people in Yorkshire Falls well and for the most part they were a warm, welcoming, forgiving lot. Minus a select few. Their reaction to the photograph had been borne of shock but no one would penalize Kendall for her choice in modeling jobs, of that he was certain.

However that didn't take into account the photo's immediate impact. The picture had been taken for the purpose of enticing buyers — men and women whose tastes ran for the extremely hot and sexy, and to the more eclectic games in the bedroom. And it had done its job well. When Rick closed his eyes, he saw

Kendall in a leather bustier, her plump cleavage enticing him, her flat stomach calling to him. And though no one in town would hold a benign photograph or job against her, they wouldn't quickly forget what they'd seen either.

Hell, he wouldn't forget the sight of her in all that leather. Leather. He flashed back to the last time he'd seen a leather getup — on Lisa Burton. *Come let me show you my props,* she'd said and dangled a pair of fur-lined handcuffs at him. Son of a bitch, Rick thought.

"I belong?" Kendall asked on a high-pitched laugh. "Ask these people if I'm one of them." She shook her head and he realized her entire body was trembling.

He wrapped his arm around her shoulders. "We're going home." Much as he wanted to settle things with Lisa once and for all, he needed to take care of Kendall first. "I don't know for a fact who did this," he told her. "But I have a hunch. You need to realize it feels bad now, but it doesn't mean a damn thing."

She jerked out of his grasp, staring at him with a wide, incredulous gaze. "Are you serious? It means *everything.*"

His stomach churned at the force of her words. Obviously she believed this had changed things for her. For them.

She'd not only withdrawn but he could see her flight mechanism kicking in, something ingrained in her from her past. When things got tough, her relatives shuffled her from one house to another. When her life as an adult got shaky, she got into her car and ran. With this photograph, Kendall was facing her biggest challenge — would she gather her inner courage, stay and fight?

Or would she continue to withdraw from him until she felt justified in leaving?

"I'm not going to argue with you now." He tugged on her hand and forcibly pulled her away from the staring eyes and the not-so-hushed whispers, and led her toward the car.

He couldn't force her not to run again. He just had to remind her of how he felt before that damning blown-up photograph. He loved her and he'd damn well tell her again, when she was ready to listen. Right now, the shock and pain were still acute. After she'd had time to absorb and deal with this embarrassment, he'd divulge his feelings once more.

If she left after that, at least he could tell himself he'd given her everything he had to offer. Just as he'd done once before with Jillian.

And so much more was at stake now.

They pulled up to her house and Rick started to get out of the car.

Kendall turned toward him, her eyes vague and blank. "You don't need to walk me inside. Besides, I need some time alone."

His stomach plummeted at her plainly spoken words. "To pull further away?"

"You should really check on Raina," she said

325

instead of answering him. "The shock of seeing that picture couldn't be good for her heart."

"The only thing that will happen to my mother's heart as a result of tonight is that it'll hurt for you. I'm sure she can handle this." He clenched his fists at his sides.

"You should still check on her."

He couldn't argue that point any more than he'd be able to get through to Kendall tonight. Her walls were miles high and excluded him. "You'll call if you need me?" he asked.

She nodded. But as she got out without a word, slamming the car door behind her, he knew he wouldn't be the one hearing from her tonight or any other night soon.

Raina paced the floor of her kitchen. Her unwilling co-conspirators in her health scheme surrounded her. Eric sat beside her at the white Formica table while Roman and Charlotte stood by the cabinets across the room. They'd met up here after tonight's fiasco and though no one had seen or heard from Rick since Kendall's picture had been plastered across the screen for the entire town to see, all were concerned.

The only person missing was Chase. Since he'd had an employee covering the slide show for the paper, he'd missed the action and wasn't here now. Thank goodness since Raina wasn't ready to deal with her oldest son and her own lies tonight. Tonight she wanted to help the child who needed her most.

"Tonight was a disgrace," Raina said. "A complete and utter disgrace. I can't believe anyone would do such a thing." She frowned at the memory of what she had seen flashed upon the screen.

"I hardly think posing for a lingerie catalogue constitutes a disgrace," Charlotte defended Kendall. "Isn't that true, Roman?"

He cleared his throat. "I agree. Even if the . . . uh . . . props were somewhat kinky, I think Kendall looked hot." Charlotte jammed her husband in the ribs with her elbow.

"Great. I mean Kendall looked great," Roman corrected on a forced groan. Then he reached out and pulled his disgruntled wife into a hug. "You know what I meant. I adore you but a guy would have to be dead not to look."

Raina rolled her eyes.

"You should have quit while you were ahead, son," Eric said, chiming in at last.

"She wasn't a disgrace," Roman said.

"I agree." Eric propped an elbow on the table.

Raina smiled. She'd knowingly taken the temperature of the room and it had registered high on Kendall's side. "Okay, now that we're all on the same wavelength, what are we going to do to help Kendall out? Lord knows the poor woman must be mortified."

"The most we can do is cut off any gossip we

might hear and support her. Beyond that I'm sure she'd like the whole thing dropped," Charlotte said.

"Dropped?" Raina said, outraged on Kendall's behalf. "First of all, someone set the poor girl up."

"And it's up to her to figure out who did it," Roman said in a stern voice meant to warn Raina to mind her own business.

She ought to know considering she'd been on the receiving end of his outburst before. But she'd given birth to him and that gave her some seniority and the right to continue her thoughts. "Second of all she's like family and I'm sure Rick would appreciate it if . . ."

"We all minded our own business," Eric finished for her.

Raina scowled his way. Considering they'd grown close over the last few months, he understood her burning desire for grandchildren and happy marriages for her sons. Neither of those things would happen if Kendall got spooked and tried to run off now.

"I agree, Raina. As much as you love Rick and Kendall, you can't make decisions for them and you can't change what fate has in store." Charlotte spoke softly but in a pleading voice.

"I beg to differ. If you'll recall, a little thing like a fake heart condition got my sons to participate in that ridiculous coin toss and put Roman on a wife hunt. Glitches aside, you two are extremely happy. I'd call that altering fate."

And though she still felt awful about lying, the cause and the end result had been positive, thank God. Given the opportunity to do it all over again, she'd take a different course of action. However, she couldn't deny it had worked.

"You will mind your own business, Mom." Roman's deep blue eyes, so much like his father's, bore into hers.

She exhaled hard. "What's so wrong with giving support to people you love?"

Charlotte crossed the room and placed a hand on Raina's arm. "Listen. I've spoken with Kendall and from what I can figure Rick had his hands full with keeping her in town, and that was before someone put her on display for everyone to see. He's going to need your support but not your meddling. You're going to have to trust me on this one."

"I wish someone would trust me," Rick said.

Raina gasped and everyone turned at the unexpected sound of Rick's voice.

"I'm not sure whether to be more insulted that you're all here discussing *my* life or that you've been keeping secrets." He stepped into the kitchen, arms folded across his chest and a scowl on his face.

Raina hadn't heard him enter the house and from the shocked expressions around her, neither had anyone else. He leaned against the door frame, looking exhausted and distraught. Defeat wasn't in a Chandler's vocabulary, but it was obvious that whatever had happened between him and Kendall hadn't gone well.

And judging by his obvious displeasure now, things here wouldn't go much better. "How long have you been standing there?" Raina asked. But the sinking feeling in the pit of her stomach had already provided the answer.

"Oh I arrived somewhere around the time you mentioned your fake heart condition." His jaw clenched in unmistakable anger while his eyes flashed with betrayal and hurt.

"Rick . . ."

"Not now, okay? I've been through enough tonight. I don't need to deal with this too. I'm glad you're healthy. Thrilled in fact." Shaking his head in disbelief, he turned to leave.

"Rick." Roman stepped toward his brother.

Rick didn't glance back. "Unless you're going to tell me you had no idea she was faking, we have nothing to discuss either."

"Charlotte, I'm taking my brother out for a drink. Eric will make sure you get home okay." Roman glanced at the other man who nodded in silent assent.

"I'd rather drink alone," Rick muttered.

"Don't worry about me. You two need to talk." Charlotte's blue eyes flashed with compassion and concern for her still-new family. "Rick, you know we love you."

"You all have a funny way of showing it."

"You're right. And there's no excuse but . . ."

Raina's voice trailed off.

"I'll handle it, Mom. Just relax and get some sleep, okay?" Roman laid a hand on her shoulder. She appreciated his concern.

Though he'd never condoned her charade, he wasn't turning on her now and she appreciated the loyalty. She loved her sons, too much if causing them pain was the end result of her good intentions.

"Where's Kendall?" Charlotte asked the unspoken question Raina was certain lay on everyone's mind.

"Home. Probably packing," Rick muttered.

Raina winced. "If it would help I could take a ride over and talk to her." Even as she offered, even as Roman gestured for her to zip her mouth shut, she knew what her son's answer would be.

"Don't you think you've done enough?" Rick asked.

His disappointment shot straight through to her heart, the organ she'd used to manipulate him. Poetic justice, Raina realized, the thought bringing no consolation and an extreme amount of pain.

Rick was suffering too, from a combination of Kendall's withdrawal and Raina's revelation. Her own predicament and feelings now paled in comparison to the agony her middle son must be feeling.

Whether or not Rick forgave her, Raina needed to help him and Kendall find their way back to each other. Unfortunately she had no idea where to begin.

Somehow Kendall survived the night with two teenagers, a new dog, and her own heartache. The girls helped give Happy a bath and the activity helped keep Kendall's mind busy and off the humiliation she'd suffered — at whose hands, she wondered, for the millionth time.

Though Rick insinuated he had a hunch regarding the culprit, Kendall had no idea who hated her enough to post her nearly naked picture on a billboard-sized screen. The only person who overtly disliked Kendall was Lisa Burton and Kendall couldn't see the schoolteacher risking her job or her own reputation to pull such a juvenile stunt.

By the time the girls' giggling subsided and they'd fallen asleep, oblivious to what had happened at the slide show, Kendall came to the conclusion it didn't matter who'd set her up. The fact was, the person had done her a favor. They'd shown her proof of why daydreams could never be reality and why Kendall Sutton didn't belong living in a small town with a good, decent man like Rick Chandler.

By the time daylight streamed through her still-open shades, the slide show and the photograph had replayed itself over and over in Kendall's mind. She wasn't ashamed of her past career or even the particular picture displayed. No matter how badly she needed the money, Kendall would never have agreed to an assignment she felt would devalue her own self worth or that of her family. But the fact remained that she'd been plastered half naked for the town to see, for people who'd been good to her to be affected.

And the Chandlers deserved better. From Charlotte who ran her own business, to Raina who had class and morals and a heart condition that couldn't handle stress, to Rick, whose reputation as a good cop was unsurpassed and untarnished. Until he'd hooked up with Kendall.

She shook her head and walked to the windowsill, looking out at the dew-soaked grass. For the first time in her adult life she'd let herself believe in possibilities. She'd wondered if she should stay, if she could become a part of Rick's town, Rick's family. Rick's life. Last night she'd been given her answer. Shown it in living color and those possibilities had been taken away from her. Just as she'd been taught as a child, she'd learned again last night, family and stability existed for other people, not her.

Thank God Hannah had missed the display. Kendall would have to break the news to her before Hannah heard it from someone else. Nothing would be more embarrassing to a teenager and Kendall wished she could spare her sister completely, but she couldn't. The most she could do now was soften the blow when Kendall explained that she had been a poster girl at the town's historical display.

Then she and Hannah would move west, away from this town before either one of them got any more attached — or suffered any more disappointment.

"Morning, Kendall." The young girls bounced into the kitchen with all the exuberance of teenagers facing a new day.

Kendall wanted only to crawl back into bed, but she forced a smile. "Good morning, girls. Can I get you something to eat?"

"Nah. We can make cereal," Hannah said.

"How was the slide show? We were so busy with Happy last night I forgot to ask." Jeannie patted the dog's head. "My mom usually goes but she's so sick of the same old building pictures year after year that she said she'd take us to the movies instead."

Kendall had no intention of filling Hannah in while her friend looked on. "It was . . . interesting. So what's on today's agenda?"

Kendall's cell phone rang and prevented the girls from answering. "I gave the number to my friends so I've got it," Hannah said as she dove for the phone on the counter. "Hello?"

Kendall waited, hoping Rick wouldn't decide to call her first thing this morning.

"Who's this?"

"Who is this please?" Kendall mouthed, then stifled a groan. Hannah would learn manners or Kendall would die trying, she thought wryly.

"No. No. No! This house is not for sale and it's not going to be for sale. No you can't speak to the lady of the house because *I'm* going to speak to her myself." Hannah clicked off the cell phone and turned to glare at Kendall. "How could you?"

Oh, she didn't need this now. "I didn't list the house, Hannah."

"Not yet. I heard that Tina Roberts lady on the phone. You're gonna list and sell. And then what? I go to another boarding school? How could you?" she wailed again, sniffed, and brushed her hand beneath her now smudged eyes.

Kendall's heart clenched with her sister's pain. She knew all too well what it was like to feel abandoned and unwanted and those were emotions that Kendall was determined to protect Hannah from ever experiencing again.

Jeannie looked from Kendall to Hannah, absorbed by the family argument. Nothing Kendall could do about it. She certainly couldn't hold her sister off until they were alone this time.

Stepping forward, Kendall put her hand firmly on her sister's arm. "I'm not sending you to boarding school."

"You're not?" Hannah glanced up at her, wide-eyed and hopeful.

Kendall shook her head. "Definitely not." There wasn't much Kendall was certain of in this life, but after a few weeks with her sister, she couldn't, wouldn't send her away again. "I'm going to contact Mom and Dad about becoming your legal guardian so I can look after you and make the right decisions on your behalf."

"I knew it," Hannah squealed in delight.

Then she threw her arms around Kendall's neck and held on tight, her arms feeling so good against Kendall's skin.

"I knew you wouldn't send me away," Hannah said in her ear.

How quickly a teenager changed her mind. A woman's prerogative, certainly, but more a teenager's whim. Hannah stepped back, looking at Kendall with all the love and warmth she had in her heart. A lump rose to Kendall's throat, that feeling of being needed threatening to choke her. She didn't want to get into a bawling fest with her sister nor did she want to let the fear of somehow losing Hannah consume her. As blood relatives and as the older sibling, Kendall had more control of the situation.

It wasn't like Rick or Yorkshire Falls, both places she'd be putting *her* faith in. This time it was Hannah who was putting her faith in Kendall and she was determined not to let her down. "I'm not sending you anywhere, Hannah. I'm keeping you with me wherever I go. We're a team, you and I." She shot her sister a smile, glad they had each other at least.

"What do you mean, wherever you go?"

Hannah pushed back, crossing her arms over her chest. "I thought we'd stay here. I've made friends. I like it here. *You* like it here and Rick loves you."

I love you, Kendall. He'd said as much last night and then that damn picture had flashed across the screen. And she'd been so wrapped up in her shock and misery, in her determination to believe she didn't belong, she hadn't given his words another thought. He loved her but how he felt after the repercussions of that photo hit was anyone's guess.

She turned to her sister who stared at her, betrayal replacing the love and gratitude in her flashing green eyes. "What makes you think Rick loves me?" After all, Hannah hadn't been with them last night.

"It's obvious to anyone who looks at him. Just as it's obvious to me you don't care about anyone but yourself." She stomped toward Jeannie who still stood staring, openmouthed. "Let's go."

"Where?" Jeannie asked.

"To town. To your house. I don't care as long as I get out of here," Hannah said.

Kendall sighed. "Hannah, don't. We aren't finished."

"Oh, yes we are. I'd rather be in boarding school than live with you. At least there people don't pretend to care when they really don't. I'm outta here." And as if to prove her point, Hannah grabbed Jeannie's hand and pulled her out of the kitchen. Seconds later the front door slammed behind her.

The sound coincided with the churning in Kendall's stomach as her sister stormed out of her life.

CHAPTER THIRTEEN

Rick's mouth tasted like cotton, his head pounded hard, and he still felt a hell of a lot better than he had watching Kendall withdraw from him last night.

"Rise and shine." Charlotte's too-cheery voice carried to him from across the house.

After getting him drunk and not making him talk, Roman had brought him back to his town house to sleep it off. Rick was still pissed at his brother, but as drinking buddies went, Roman had done his duty.

"Get up, sleepyhead." Charlotte walked into the room and opened the shutters on the family-room windows.

The sunlight hit his eyes first and Rick groaned aloud. "Aww, God, Charlotte, have a heart." He rolled over and covered his head with his hands.

She walked up beside him. From his prone, facedown position, all he saw were her bare toes. Unfortunately she sounded like she'd strapped tin cans to the soles of her feet.

"I have a heart. Look what I brought you." Leaning down, she put a glass on the table in front of him.

"What's that?" He squinted at the dark liquid through slitted eyes.

"Something edible. I was going to make you my father's old remedy which included raw egg and milk."

His stomach rolled but he managed not to gag.

"But I took pity on you and brought you flat Coke instead. I also brought you aspirin." She held out her hand palm up to reveal two tablets that he gratefully grabbed. "Hey, did you drink the water I gave you last night?" she asked.

"I don't remember." Pushing himself off the couch, he somehow managed to rise despite his reverberating head. He swallowed the pills first and the Coke second, filling his empty, growling stomach.

Then forcing himself to focus, he met her amused gaze. She was a glowing vision for any man first thing in the morning. Add to that, she'd given him a hangover remedy without making him scavenge and fend for himself. He couldn't appreciate any woman more.

Unless she was Kendall, but that was a problem for when he'd recovered a little more. "Did I ever tell you my brother's a damn lucky man?"

"Tell me yourself and quit ogling." Roman walked into the room without regard to tiptoeing or to Rick's obvious hangover.

"Who says I can see well enough to ogle? Everything's a blur," Rick muttered.

"Which means you're seeing two of her. Lucky you." Roman's voice took on a distinctly amused tone. Coming up beside Charlotte, he put a hand around her waist and squeezed her close against his side.

"Don't laugh at me after all you've done." As Rick spoke, he recalled the punch in the gut feeling when he'd heard his mother admit to faking her heart condition. He remembered the relief mixed with betrayal, the urge to hug her and throttle her at the same time, and the unbelievable sense of disbelief that his brother would go along with his mother's scheme. "How the hell could you let me think Mom was sick?"

Roman pulled up a chair while Charlotte settled on the arm cushion beside him. "We owe you an explanation," Roman said, then paused as if gathering his thoughts.

Rick waited. The desire to tap his foot in annoyance was strong but he figured his pounding head deserved some preferential treatment.

"This is complicated." Roman shook his head in obvious exasperation. "At first I didn't tell you because we were in Europe on our honeymoon." He reached out for Charlotte's hand and she placed her palm in his.

Rick had all but given up the dream of having that camaraderie, that sense of oneness with anyone, especially Kendall. So seeing his brother and his wife together now was bittersweet. Rick massaged his aching temples. "You could have called," he said in an attempt to focus on his family problems and not his even more messed-up love life. He'd have many empty days and nights ahead to figure out where he'd gone wrong there.

"I could have. Hell, I probably should have. In Charlotte's defense, she begged me to call and tell you."

"So why didn't you?"

"No excuse that'll stand up in court," Roman said wryly. "I was wrapped up in being happy. And I figured a few more weeks of keeping quiet wouldn't hurt anyone. Hell, I even deluded myself into thinking maybe Mom would succeed and hook you up with someone as great as Charlotte. That you'd be as happy as I ended up being. Despite Mom's meddling."

Rick raised his eyebrows, ignoring the pain ripping through his skull. "You should be shot."

Roman shrugged. "You're probably right."

"What happened after you got back to the States? What stopped you from spilling Mom's secret then?"

Roman winced, then with a groan, leaned back in his seat but still held on to Charlotte's hand. He probably needed her support since he was damn wrong and cornered. How he'd justify his actions, Rick hadn't a clue.

"Well, you have to remember we were away for a good month," Roman continued. "I didn't want to give her much leeway but Charlotte and I were busy setting up the apartment in

D.C. I was getting used to the new job. And you have to admit, at first you seemed fairly amused by her attempt to find the right woman for you." He shrugged. "So I let things go. For longer than I should have."

"Damn right." Rick tipped his head to one side, a mistake he regretted immediately when the brass band began playing again. "*Then* what stopped you from coming clean?"

"You and I both know part of Mom's reason for playing this charade was because she wanted us happily settled, but she also wanted —"

"Grandchildren," Rick said, stating the obvious. After all, Raina had drilled the idea into their heads for ages now.

"Right. And I didn't think after faking her illness that she deserved to have her heart's desire — grandchildren — come so easily. I wanted her to sweat a little. If I told her Charlotte was pregnant, I figured she'd . . ."

"Back off of myself and Chase?" Rick asked. "That would be the obvious assumption, right? So why not tell her she got what she wanted, that Charlotte was pregnant? Then blow the whistle on her scheme and give Chase and me some peace?"

"Because Raina isn't most mothers and you can't make obvious assumptions when dealing with her. I happen to know for a fact that she wants us *all* settled and happy. Not just one of us. If she knew Charlotte was pregnant, she'd just be more certain she knew what was best for us all and go after you and Chase even harder."

Recalling Lisa's dominatrix outfit, inspired by his mother's words of encouragement no doubt, Rick shook his head hard. He saw stars. Damn, he had to stop doing that. "I'm not sure Mom could have gone any harder," he muttered. "And if you'd been living here, you'd know that."

Roman's gaze darted away from Rick's. "Well, I didn't know how bad it had gotten. So I told Mom that Charlotte and I wanted time alone together before we started working on a family. So I wanted to make her sweat a little."

If Rick's head was spinning before this explanation, things were even worse now. But one thing finally jumped out in his mind. Charlotte was pregnant with the first Chandler grandchild. Pride and pleasure for his baby brother suffused him along with a fair amount of envy he figured was normal and he refused to analyze. Instead he glanced at his sister-in-law. Other than the beautiful glow in her cheeks, he never would have known. He started to rise, to wrap her in a huge hug and congratulate her but his head refused to cooperate.

She came to his side and placed a stern hand on his shoulder, chuckling as she said, "Congratulate me later. Get better first." Then she settled in beside him. "Rick, there was more to our silence than just making your mother pay for manipulating us. I know we should have told you. But once we got home, I realized that

344

my mother's mental health was still shaky. Her depression . . ." She shook her head. "The medication wasn't working yet. And I wanted to wait a few months to reveal the pregnancy. Until she could appreciate the news. So then *I* asked Roman to wait before telling anyone about Raina's health. Or my pregnancy."

Rick turned to this woman who'd made his brother's life complete. She stared at him with wide green eyes, apology and regret etching her features. How could he remain angry at her? He exhaled a groan and put a comforting hand on Charlotte's shoulder. "I don't blame you."

She shot him a grateful smile. "We were still wrong."

Roman nodded in agreement. "And by the time we were ready to tell you everything, you'd met Kendall. There was no way in hell I was going to tell you that Mom had been faking her heart condition."

"Why the hell not?"

Roman rolled his eyes as if the reason were obvious. As if anything about this situation could be obvious, Rick thought with no small amount of frustration.

"I couldn't tell you once you met Kendall because she was the first woman you'd trusted since Jillian. The first one who really interested you. You seemed to have a shot at what we have." Roman gestured back and forth between himself and Charlotte. "And I wasn't going to be the one to give you an easy excuse to claim distrust in women and back off from Kendall. Not when it was so obvious you were already head over heels. So when Mom wanted to tell you the truth, I put a stop to it."

Rick shook his head in disbelief. "Mom wanted to come clean?"

Roman raised his hands in the air. "What can I say? She's had it with pretending to be sick because it's putting a crimp in her social life. So I told her to keep her mouth shut. I figured making her keep up the charade of being sick was damn good punishment for meddling in our lives."

Rick pinched the bridge of his nose. Thank God the aspirin had begun to kick in and the pounding had lessened enough for him to relax and think more clearly. "I don't believe this. You played psychologist and matchmaker." He wanted to throttle Roman.

But as brothers, they'd always understood one another and thinking about the whole messed-up situation, Rick supposed his younger sibling's reasoning made sense. In an ass-backward sort of way. "You do realize this makes you no better than our mother?"

Roman actually flushed red. "Hindsight is twenty-twenty," he muttered.

Charlotte sighed, placing a hand on Rick's shoulder. "So here we are."

Rick groaned. "Yeah. Here we are. Did you know you two could give a sober man a headache?"

346

Roman laughed and though Rick glared, he joined his brother. Putting all the pieces and reasoning together, he couldn't hold Roman responsible for a situation Raina had created and one he'd believed he had no choice but to perpetuate. After all, Chandler brothers stuck together when they could. Nothing would change that — except a woman. In Roman's case that was Charlotte and knowing what Rick would do for Kendall, he wasn't about to pass judgment on his younger sibling.

"I take it the family feud is over?" Charlotte asked, staring at Rick until he was forced to meet her bright-eyed gaze.

"I'll think about it." Let Roman wallow a little while longer, Rick thought. For as long as his hangover lasted seemed a fair exchange to Rick considering his head still hurt like a son of a bitch. "Scratch that. No thinking today."

Roman laughed, obviously reading Rick and knowing things between the brothers were fine once more. "I need to do some errands in town before Charlotte and I head back to D.C. tomorrow. Finish your soda, take your aspirin, and I'll drop you off at home."

Rick picked up the glass and polished off the entire drink in almost one gulp, aspirin along with it. "That's better." He stepped toward the front door when realization bypassed the mugginess in his brain. "We need to tell Chase about Mom."

Together Roman and Charlotte winced. Rick

understood. When his oldest brother discovered the extent of their mother's games, things wouldn't be pretty. He wasn't thrilled himself, but exhaustion, body aches, and other hangover-related ailments prevented him from focusing too much on Raina's antics. Besides, if he was capable of concerning himself with anything at this particular moment, it would be Kendall.

Twenty minutes later, feeling just as crappy as when he awoke, Rick climbed out of Roman's car and headed around the side of the building to his apartment.

To his surprise, when he arrived he had a visitor waiting. Hannah sat, head bent, her hair hanging over her face. He paused on the step below her. "What's wrong?" he asked, concerned that she'd show up out of the blue and wait for him to come home.

She raised a tear-stained face to his, pain etched in her expression. "Kendall's going to sell the house and leave town." Her voice cracked on the last word.

Rick hadn't realized he was still holding out any real hope for a future with Kendall until he heard the finality in Hannah's tone. And though the heartache was great, her words weren't a surprise. Instead of shock, he felt let down instead. Disappointed in Kendall and her decision not to stay and fight her demons, not to fight for them.

Rick had spent last night drowning his emotions and this morning learning about his family situation. He hadn't dealt with anything yet, but it could wait. Right now Hannah needed him more. He knelt beside the young girl, wishing he could offer comfort when he knew there was none to be had.

Not for Hannah and not for him. After wrapping an arm around her, he pulled her close. "Your sister loves you, you know."

"Yeah right." She snorted in his ear and ended with a sniffle.

Despite his disappointment in Kendall, Rick knew it was in Hannah's best interest that he put a positive spin on a hopeless situation. Normally Rick didn't give up without a fight but Kendall had left him with no alternative. He'd done his best to show her the life they could have together. She was the one walking away. And though he thought he'd been preparing for this moment since Kendall's arrival, the burning in his gut told him he was wrong.

Regardless of how she felt about him, Rick was certain Kendall did adore her sister. But before he could begin to make Hannah see the truth, he needed to know what Kendall planned. "Well, where did your sister say *you'd* be going when she takes off?" His stomach churned as he used words that put an end to their time in Yorkshire Falls.

Hannah sighed. "Kendall said she'd take me with her but I don't want to go anywhere." Her voice trailed off in a long sigh.

Clearly she wanted more than Kendall was willing to give. Join the club, Rick thought silently. But knowing Kendall was doing right by Hannah filled Rick with relief and eased the vise gripping his heart. If Kendall was giving up her solitary roaming, then she'd begun to face her fear of commitment and stability. She was fighting harder than he'd given her credit for, but he didn't delude himself into thinking she'd take that next step and do right by herself. At least she'd opened her heart and her life to her sister at the moment the young girl needed her most. That counted for a lot in Rick's book.

He glanced at Hannah out of the corner of his eye. "You know your sister's way of thinking. She doesn't know anything other than a transient kind of life. For her even to take you with her is a huge leap. You need to go. To bond with her. Get to understand her."

He drew a deep breath, forcing himself to make a bleak situation look great to a teenager. "Besides, I hear Arizona has amazing weather, no humidity, and you'll be able to learn horseback riding," he said, figuring Kendall planned to head west as she'd told him a while back. He put his hand beneath her chin. "Look at me."

She glanced up but instead of excitement he saw desperation in her young eyes. "You have to try and stop her," she said, pleading with no shame.

He'd grown to love Hannah like he loved his

own family and he'd do anything for this kid. Anything he could, Rick amended. Unfortunately that excluded what she wanted from him most of all. "I can't."

She blinked and turned away, that mutinous, stubborn tilt to her chin returning. "Because you don't care if we stay or go either." Her stubborn bravado faltered when her voice caught on her words.

"Untrue and you know it." He still held her tight, no matter that she tried to pull away and put distance between them. She obviously wanted to blame him, force him to share the brunt of her anger.

"Then why won't you help me get Kendall to stay?"

Because Rick refused to shoulder the burden for Kendall's impulsive actions. She obviously wasn't facing her feelings and Rick wouldn't be the one to make her life any easier. She didn't deserve it. If her pint-sized, hellion sister wanted to torture her a little, maybe she'd be forced to take a good look at her decisions and their consequences.

"Because Kendall's a grown woman," he explained, gentle in tone but firm in his intention. "She knows her own mind. I can't make your sister do something she doesn't want to do, Hannah."

"Yeah, yeah. Thanks for nothing." She jerked out of his grasp and rose to her feet.

Rick followed, standing on the step above

hers. "Promise me something?"

"Maybe."

He loved this kid despite her wise-guy mouth. He shook his head and stifled a laugh. "Just think about what I said and give your sister a chance. She loves you."

"Says you." She turned and started to bound down the stairs.

"Hannah, wait."

The young girl pivoted back to face him. "Yeah?"

"I just want to know where you're going." He couldn't help looking out for her.

"To Norman's for a soda. Jeannie's there and since I don't know when Kendall will decide to take off, I want to hang out with her as much as I can."

Rick nodded. He'd felt the same about Kendall. "Need money?"

Hannah shook her head. "I earned some yesterday. But thanks anyway."

His cell phone rang, disturbing their exchange. "Hang on a sec." He unclipped the phone from his belt and answered on the second ring. "Chandler."

"Hi, Rick." There was no mistaking the soft voice on the other end.

"Kendall." His heart picked up rhythm, kicking into high gear, and his mind began a steady whirl of questions. Had she changed her mind? Decided to stay? Did she need a friendly ear?

Did she need him?

All of those things, he hoped. "What's up?" he asked her.

"Have you seen Hannah?"

His personal hopes plummeted and common sense took over. This was Kendall and she didn't want to stay in town or with him. She never had. To her credit, she'd been honest about her intentions from the first. If he had anyone to blame for falling into a deluded trap, it was himself.

After all, he'd done it once before, with Jillian. "Your sister's here." He covered the receiver and gestured for Hannah to come closer. "In case she wants to talk to you," he whispered.

"I have nothing to say to her," Hannah said, her lips set in what he figured was a permanent pout.

"I heard that," Kendall said, obvious disappointment and hurt in her voice.

And it was the hurt that got to him. Considering the woman was breaking his heart, he shouldn't care. But he did. Too much.

"Can you get her to meet me at Norman's?" Kendall asked, keeping things between herself and Rick strictly business. As if they'd never made love, as if he'd never declared his.

He swallowed hard. "Sure thing."

"Thanks. I'll see you both in a few minutes." She hung up, dismissing him as if he meant nothing to her.

Get used to it, buddy. Rick turned to Hannah. "We need to meet your sister at Norman's."

She folded her arms across her chest. "I'm not hungry."

He rolled his eyes. "Then don't eat. Besides, you were going there anyway. I'm sure Kendall just wants to talk, so for your own sake, try meeting her halfway." He braced his hands on her shoulders and looked her in the eye. "I know it isn't easy and I know you're not happy. But this is your life and only you can make it better."

"Geez you are so full of it."

He cocked an eyebrow, knowing he could only allow her big mouth to go so far. "Excuse me?"

"So full of wisdom, Officer Chandler."

She grinned and in her beautiful smile he caught a glimpse of her sister. Hannah would be a knockout one day soon. She was well on her way. He only hoped she had more confidence in the world around her than Kendall did.

"Full of wisdom." He shook his head and despite the screwed-up mess of his life, Rick laughed. "I see. In that case, you're pretty full of it yourself. Now give me a minute to change and I'll meet you downstairs."

Hannah gave him a smart salute, turned around, and headed down the stairs. Rick would do the same. He'd meet up with Hannah at Norman's, meet up with Kendall, pretend he was fine with her choices, then get the hell out.

He'd already scrapped his prior plan. No way would he tell Kendall he loved her one more time. He'd told her once. He'd shown her in many ways. Why set himself up to be trampled on again?

He might love Kendall but it was time he cared for himself more. Time to start rebuilding the walls around *his* heart.

If not for her sister, Kendall wouldn't have willingly walked into Norman's the day after her slide show unveiling. She wouldn't have willingly called Rick. But she'd known better than to search Hannah out in person or ask her to come home until they'd talked. Hannah was hurt and angry.

The last time she'd acted on those emotions she'd taken Kendall's car. This time around Kendall hoped to circumvent a major catastrophe. And she hoped to avoid a huge scene by meeting her sister in a public place.

By the time Kendall had parked and walked inside, Hannah and Rick had already taken a table in the back. Drawing a deep breath, Kendall held her head high as she passed the tables of people, heard the whispers again, and noticed the pointing. She wasn't imagining being the center of attention, she knew, but she didn't have time to worry about it now.

Whereas her sister wouldn't meet her gaze, Rick did. Those gorgeous eyes stared into hers.

From a quick glance, he looked as if he hadn't slept well. Razor stubble covered his face and dark circles swept beneath his eyes. He looked as awful as she felt and she hated being the cause.

"Hi." She forced a smile.

He didn't return the gesture. "Hi, yourself."

Kendall didn't know what to say to him and apparently the feeling was mutual because silence descended, making her stomach cramp and her nerve endings tingle. Without warning, Hannah rose from her seat, pushing her chair back with a screech, making a huge amount of noise, and breaking the charged, silent connection between Kendall and Rick.

Without a word, Hannah started to walk away from the table.

"Where are you going?" Kendall asked.

"Bathroom. You two make me gag." Then she glanced at Rick. And winked.

Kendall sighed. The little traitor was leaving on purpose, to give Kendall and Rick time alone. Before she could stop her, Hannah stalked toward the back hall.

"I didn't put her up to that." Rick leaned back in his seat.

"I didn't think you had." Since Kendall knew she'd shut him out of her life last night, he wouldn't orchestrate time alone with her now.

Rick's eyes had twinkled with laughter at her sister's antics but when he focused on Kendall, his expression turned blank. He'd drawn a shutter over his emotions and closed her out. Though she deserved the reciprocal wall he'd erected, she hated the strain between them, hated more that she'd forced him to put distance between them. She simply didn't know how to handle things now.

He stretched an arm over the back of his seat in a casual, masculine gesture that flexed the muscles in his forearms and pulled his T-shirt tight across his broad chest. "Hannah tells me you're selling the house and leaving town." His voice held not a hint of emotion or caring.

After the intimacy they'd shared, a virtual stranger sat across from her. She hated that too and a huge lump formed in her throat and remained. *This is what you wanted, Kendall,* she reminded herself. *No ties, no strings, no attachments. Just the freedom to pack up and move at will. No one close enough to leave you behind or push you away.* No one who held the power to hurt her at all.

Exactly the life she'd always chosen and the one she'd opted for again since last night. But if she'd gone back to a lifestyle she preferred, then why did she feel so god-awful now? Kendall had a hunch and the answer scared her so much that she refused to deal with the strangling emotions hovering just out of reach.

Focus on the mundane, she told herself. "I haven't listed it yet but Tina Roberts called and she thinks she can get a nice amount of money for the house and property. Less because of the stipulation I insisted on but a good enough amount for Hannah and me to start over. Somewhere." Her own thoughts and words threatened to choke her and she had to forcibly swallow over the lump in her throat before continuing. "Arizona's probably where we'll head next."

He nodded and clenched his jaw tight, obviously unwilling to give her the satisfaction of letting her see an emotional reaction to her words. "What stipulation?" he asked instead.

"Pearl and Eldin get to move to the guest house and live there rent-free. As long as they maintain the place, I'm hoping someone will agree. I can't displace them." She couldn't imagine the elderly couple who lived in sin residing anywhere but Aunt Crystal's house.

"Did you tell them yet?"

She shook her head. Another thing she couldn't bring herself to face. But no matter her own feelings, she owed Rick an explanation for her sudden remote behavior. He'd been so good to her and her sister, and he'd suffered much in the past. She didn't want him to think he'd done anything or was the cause of her inability to stay around. "Rick, listen. I just want you to know —"

"Don't." His eyes flashed angry sparks, hurt and betrayal evident in his stare and his taut expression. "Don't apologize or tell me how much you care."

"Even if I do?" She rubbed her hands against her jeans.

He shrugged. "What good does it do me? Or you for that matter? Besides, you told me up front you wouldn't stay. I just thought this town and its people would grow on you. That I would grow on you."

She blinked back tears. "You did."

His stern expression didn't falter. "So what? Your words don't change a damn thing. You're unable to commit, unwilling to face your fears." Without warning he rose from his seat, towering over her, a giant in both stature and strength of emotion. "And you know what?"

"What?" she whispered.

"I'm disappointed in you."

The dim light in his eyes backed up his harsh words and she flinched. Kendall had expected many emotions from Rick, anger being the primary one. She hadn't anticipated his intense disappointment nor could she believe how small and defeated she felt, having let him down.

Every experience she'd had since coming to this small town had been foreign and new. Frightening for someone who'd never known stability or family. How dare Rick condemn her for it? "Well, I'm so sorry I'm a disappointment, Officer Chandler. But like you said, it's not like I wasn't up front with you from day one."

"And you backed up your words with actions. Congratulations." He clapped his hands in a slow round of applause. "You came here running from a situation in New York, and you'll leave here the same way. Running from me." His palm came to rest on the tabletop as he leaned in closer. "But remember something, Kendall. You can't run from yourself or your own feelings. Someday they're bound to catch up with you. Excuse me if I don't wait around for that time to come."

He straightened his shoulders and met her gaze with a lingering look. "Sorry to sound like a cliché but we could have had it all." He shook his head, turned, and walked away.

Not once during his exit from the restaurant did he look back. But his words remained long after he was gone, reverberating inside her head until it pounded.

"Oh, God." She lay her forehead against her hands.

"You blew it, didn't you?" Hannah's verbal condemnation came on the heels of Rick's abrupt departure.

Kendall lifted her bleary gaze and glanced around before dealing with her sister. Every surrounding table was filled with eavesdroppers eager to catch the gist of Kendall's next confrontation. Heck, she wondered if they weren't taking notes.

Since this day just seemed to get better and better, she might as well face Hannah now, she thought, meeting her sister's expectant gaze.

"Well? Did you blow it with Rick or not?"

"I suppose it depends on your definition of blowing it."

Hannah had obviously reapplied shocking pink lipstick while in the ladies' room and her full, colored lips turned downward in a frown. "I left you alone with him. All you had to do was say you'd stay. Say you loved him. Say anything but you didn't, did you? And now he's gone," she said, her voice rising along with her hysteria.

"Hannah, please." Kendall clenched her fists and fought down the rising tide of embarrassment. Kendall had come to care what these good people thought. "Can you lower your voice?"

"Why?" Hannah practically shouted. "Everyone's already watching you. Which reminds me. I heard someone in the bathroom say something about you and that picture last night. What picture?" She barely paused for breath. "What'd I miss? And how bad did you screw things up with Rick?"

Kendall groaned and rested her head in her hands, massaging her aching temples. She was dizzy and nausea rose quickly.

"Kendall?" Hannah asked, more quietly this time.

"Hmm?" She barely raised her gaze as she answered. Her head hurt, she was emotionally spent yet Hannah had an agenda that wouldn't be deterred.

"Did I mention I stuffed Norman's toilet and it's overflowing?"

"Oh, God." That got Kendall's adrenaline flowing again and she jumped up and flagged Izzy down.

"Just a second," the older woman called.

"But . . ." Kendall tried to catch her but Izzy disappeared into the kitchen before returning with food on her tray and heading in the opposite direction.

"It wasn't my fault. I mean it was an accident, I swear," Hannah continued at full speed.

"An accident? This from the girl who stuffed the toilet in the teachers' lounge at Vermont Acres?"

Her sister had the good grace to blush before going on with her rambling explanation. "The garbage was full and the paper towels from washing my hands kept falling onto the floor." She gestured wildly with her hands. "And I wouldn't normally care, ya know? But you're always saying to be polite and clean up after myself, so I tried to flush them down the toilet instead. See? An accident." She shrugged too innocently in Kendall's opinion.

"Isabelle!" Norman's voice bellowed from the back hall. "Damn toilet's overflowing," the owner of the restaurant yelled in an extremely pissed-off tone.

Kendall lowered herself back into her seat. She tried unsuccessfully to blink back tears and when that didn't work, she lay her head back in her hands so she could alternately cry and laugh hysterically.

Her life had become a complete and utter mess. And based on Hannah's acting out, her inquisitive questions, and push for Kendall's reconciliation with Rick, things weren't about to get easier anytime soon.

CHAPTER FOURTEEN

Kendall dragged herself home after the episode at Norman's. She'd let Hannah leave with Jeannie and her parents while Kendall had stayed until the plumber arrived and she'd been successful on insisting he send her the bill. She walked up the front stoop, pausing when the obvious aroma of chocolate assaulted her senses, giving her a needed boost of energy.

She knelt down in front of the foil-covered plate on the stoop and lifted the white note taped to the top, reading aloud. "Kendall Dear. Your favorite comfort food at a time you need comfort badly. It's the least family can do. Ignore the gossips and they get bored quickly. Hugs and kisses, Pearl and Eldin."

It's the least family can do. "Family."

The word seemed to come up again and again, mocking her. Until her move here, Kendall had considered herself more a loner than someone with connections, especially family connections. She had kept everyone on the periphery of her life, even Hannah. And they'd both paid for that lapse, Kendall thought sadly.

Yet here were Pearl and Eldin, whom she'd just met, worried about her feelings and taking her into their life because they cared. Just like

Raina Chandler, like Charlotte and Roman, Beth . . . the list of people who cared for Kendall seemed to go on and on. Yet wasn't she equally concerned about them?

She wiped a tear from her cheek, one she hadn't realized she'd shed. And what about Pearl and Eldin, she thought, taking in the brownies. How could she tell them they needed to move out of the large house into the smaller one just so she could sell the home out from under them?

The same way she'd told her sister she was taking her away from Yorkshire Falls, that's how. And the same way she'd ignored Rick's words. *I love you,* he'd said. And she'd walked away anyway. She shivered despite the heat, realizing she still stood on the porch.

With a sigh, she picked up the plate of brownies and let herself inside. Happy made a beeline across the house to greet her at the front door. Tail wagging, he jumped on her, his front paws nearly hitting her plate.

"Happy, down."

Her stern voice worked. The dog settled at her feet in a sitting position, but his tail still wagged with glee. "At least someone's happy to see me today." After putting her things down in the kitchen, she gave the dog the attention he craved, and he reciprocated, the laps of his tongue and his furry acceptance almost more than she could handle.

He loved her unconditionally and all he

asked in return was that she love him back. Despite the fact that she'd been a perfect stranger until last night, he trusted her to provide him with that safe haven and love he sought.

And she would. So why couldn't she trust the same way? When had her life become so complicated, Kendall wondered. She walked to the window, Happy at her side, and looked out at the backyard, at the stretch of green grass and trees she remembered from childhood. The sight brought her back to the tea parties with Aunt Crystal where the stuffed animals were the guests. Kendall realized now that her aunt had used the animals as weights to prevent the towel they sat on from blowing away in the wind. But she didn't care. The animals had consumed her tea and they hadn't answered back or interrupted her stories.

Neither, she remembered, had Aunt Crystal. A smile tipped her lips at the wonderful memory. One that didn't bring her pain, only comfort, and she hugged the dog close. With the memory came the answer to her earlier question. Kendall couldn't give blind trust the way Happy did because she was human. She had memories, both good and bad, which shaped the person she'd become. An empty, distrustful person, she thought sadly.

Even Rick, who'd been burned badly once before, had opened his heart. And she'd destroyed any love and respect he'd once had.

You're unable to commit, unwilling to face your

fears, he'd said. *And I'm disappointed in you.*

His words had been like a punch in the stomach, then and now. They'd had the same emotional impact Aunt Crystal's words had when she'd told Kendall she couldn't stay in Yorkshire Falls. The same impact her parents' second departure had had, the day they'd packed Hannah off for boarding school and left again for parts unknown. Kendall wrapped her arms around her waist, trying to get past the remembered pain.

Rick was right. She couldn't trust because she hadn't faced her fears. She hadn't dealt with her past, but she was dealing now. Because she'd already lost Rick, was on the verge of losing Hannah, and she realized, probably too late, that she no longer wanted to be alone.

The irony was clear. *The very life she'd always run from was the life she'd secretly craved.* The startling thought ricocheted through her brain. The little girl who'd loved tea parties had subconsciously dreamed of having a family of her own. People who loved her. People she trusted to be there in good times and bad.

But since her parents hadn't been those people in her formative years and Aunt Crystal couldn't be, Kendall had closed herself off to any more hurt, disappointment, or pain. Her first step had been to convince herself that by the time she was eighteen and her parents left again, she was already so estranged that she didn't care where they went or what they did.

But she'd lied to herself, she realized now.

Losing parents in any way, at any age, hurt badly. She'd lost hers twice, both times because they'd rather travel than be with her, and the effect on her psyche had been devastating. She'd withdrawn so far from her emotions it was amazing Rick had been able to break through at all.

But he had. And she loved him too. She swallowed hard, the pain in her chest and the knot in her throat hard to bear. She loved him yet she'd pushed him away. In falling back on old habits and patterns, she'd hurt a man who'd taken the greatest risk of all and reached out to her despite his past hurt.

There was no possible way Rick could ever forgive her nor could he begin to understand what drove her need to remain in a self-contained cocoon of safety. Unfortunately she no longer felt as safe or protected as she once had. Instead she felt ripped raw, exposed, and she hurt badly. But if she hurt, she was feeling. For the first time.

Which meant just maybe she had a future.

Raina sat in the living room of Eric's house while he made himself busy doing heaven knew what. She didn't mind, rather she enjoyed the solitary time she spent in his home. It had been too long since she'd enjoyed the sounds of a man puttering around her and she savored the feeling. Soon she'd have even more family around her when Eric's daughters and their children arrived.

Raina couldn't wait to spend the time with them and her heart swelled at being included and accepted. Eric planned a quiet afternoon at home and dinner at Norman's in deference to her charade. He didn't approve of her faking a heart condition but he accepted, his only stipulation that if ever directly questioned by Raina's sons, he refused to lie.

Which was why his associate, Dr. Leslie Gaines, was now her doctor of record. Personal and professional lives should be kept separate anyway though at this point, it didn't much matter. Roman knew, Rick had just found out, and no doubt they'd fill Chase in next.

"I'm sorry to have kept you waiting," Eric said as he joined her in the living room and sat by her side on the white sofa.

In his striped polo shirt and khaki pants, he looked handsome. Her heart fluttered each time he walked into a room, a sensation she still hadn't gotten used to after being a widow for twenty years, but a feeling she definitely enjoyed. Eric's attention made her feel years younger and she thanked God every day for a second chance at happiness — the same happiness she wanted for all three of her sons.

"I had some paperwork I had to finish up. But now I'm yours for the day," he said, a pleased smile on his face.

"That's wonderful."

"Then why do you sound so miserable?" He turned toward her, taking her hand in his.

She shook her head. "Not miserable. Just a bit worried about Rick and Kendall."

He let out a sigh. "I understand. That display the other night was completely inappropriate. Is Rick any closer to finding out who switched pictures?"

Out of respect for her middle son and his hurt over her actions, Raina had tried hard not to meddle more or ask him too many questions. But this one she did know the answer to. "He has a hunch it was Lisa Burton but he can't prove anything."

"Lisa?" Eric's eyes opened wide. "Now that's a shock. I'll assume jealousy was the motive but I can't believe she'd go to such extremes to find information on Kendall's past. She had to have dug deep or how else would she have found something to embarrass poor Kendall with?"

"Well, she may not have had to dig too deeply. Apparently Lisa's got a kinky fetish not many people know about."

"Then how do you know?" Eric asked.

Raina chuckled. "I overhear things. Rick's not the only one drawing the same conclusion about Lisa. It seems Mildred in the post office got tipped off immediately since she's been putting those *smutty* lingerie catalogues in Lisa's mail for years. Those are Mildred's words, you understand."

"I certainly do. You're searching for information to redeem yourself with Rick." He shook his head, clucking his tongue at the same time. "Raina, Raina. When are you going to take my advice and get more involved in your own life than in your sons'?"

She sighed. "Not this again. You know good and well I read to kids at the hospital children's ward once a week, I exercise when I'm not in fear of being caught, and I see you whenever you aren't working. My life's very full and rewarding." Very rewarding indeed, she thought, staring into his dark eyes.

"Is it now? Then how about making it even richer?" He reached over to the lamp table beside the sofa and picked up a small box she hadn't noticed earlier.

Coming up on sixty in a few years, she'd been around and Raina had a hunch she knew exactly what kind of jewelry sat in that box. As her pulse rate tripled, she thanked God she didn't really have a heart condition or she'd find herself prostrate on the floor right now. As he held out the box, she accepted it with shaking hands.

"It's different when the surprise is on you, isn't it?" he murmured.

She met his amused gaze. "I'm not sure what to say."

"That's a first," he said wryly. "Then don't speak. Just open it."

The smooth material glided against her skin as she lifted the box top and revealed a round sapphire blue ring that sparkled in a traditional platinum-looking setting. "It's . . . it's spectacular." She blinked back tears, knowing she didn't deserve anything so beautiful or precious.

"I thought since this is the second time for us both we could dispense with the expected and go with the more personal touch. The sapphire reminds me of your blue eyes," he said, his voice suddenly gruff and husky. Unexpectedly he dropped to his knees. "Would you do me the honor of becoming my wife?"

The beauty of both the ring and the gesture took her off guard and emotion swelled inside her chest making it difficult to breathe or talk.

"You're silent." Eric waited a beat, then took her hand, anxiety obvious in his eyes. "Can I take that as a stunned yes?"

Somehow, she managed a shaky nod. "Yes. Yes." Before she could act on her feelings and throw her arms around him in a hug, the doorbell rang, interrupting the moment.

He sat back on his heels. "Timing," he muttered. "That must be my kids."

"We can't tell them just yet." She held the box reverently in her hands, staring at the ring that represented the start of a whole new life. A happy life as a couple, the wife of a man she loved.

"Not until we tell our children together. We could plan a dinner, perhaps."

Warmth suffused her at the notion. "Oh, a

family dinner. I could cook and have everyone over . . ." After Chase found out about her perfect health. "But I need some time. Until Rick and Chase get themselves settled first. Please, Eric. I need my boys happy before I can completely be the same."

The doorbell rang once more.

"Hang on," Eric called. "We'll be right there."

He glanced at her and narrowed his gaze. "I'll tell you what? I'll wait until Rick and Kendall have gotten themselves settled one way or another. Good or bad. And then, regardless, we're announcing this."

She'd known she'd have to bargain him down and was grateful he understood her need to wait at all. But he also understood the compulsion to assure herself her boys weren't depriving themselves of the best things in life.

Grandchildren, she assumed, would come soon after. She hoped. She treated him to a beaming smile. "I love you for accepting me."

He brushed a soft, endearing kiss over her lips and her stomach fluttered with a combination of newness and familiarity at the same time, then sat back and smiled. "Accepting is the least I can do since you'll become familiar with my faults in good time." He laughed, his smile wide and pleased. "Besides, I do love you, Raina."

She sighed, her heart full with more happiness than any one person had a right to in this lifetime. And she'd found it twice. "I love you too. Now let your daughter and her family off the front porch."

He rose from his knees, grimacing.

"Don't worry, darling. I'll keep you young."

He chuckled, then snatched the velvet box out of her hands. "And I'll keep this until you're ready to divulge our little secret." He slipped it into his pocket. "Added incentive for you to up the time frame." He winked and strode for the door.

"I don't even know if it fits," she thought aloud and allowed herself a moment to pout. But she knew she'd given him no choice. Having seen the ring and the love in Eric's eyes, she wanted so badly to wear it and let the world know she was fortunate enough to have this man love her.

A tremor of awareness rippled through her along with an idea. He wanted her to up the time frame and she would. By pushing Rick and Kendall in the right direction.

Kendall ripped the real estate broker's card in shreds and let the tiny pieces cascade into the trash. She wasn't moving, wasn't leaving Yorkshire Falls, wasn't going to run. Arizona would just be running away and her future was here. For the first time in her life she was facing her fears and reaching for her unspoken dreams. And though the idea scared her to death, she'd never been more sure of any decision.

Her cell phone rang, interrupting her thoughts. First thing to cement her status as a resident, she'd get herself a permanent phone line and a real telephone, she decided as she flipped open her tiny cell phone. "Hello?"

"Hi, Kendall. It's Raina. I don't have long to talk, so just listen."

Kendall chuckled. She loved Rick's mother and her unobtrusive way of handling things. "Is everything okay?" Kendall asked.

"It's not like me to meddle," Raina said, then quickly retracted. "Okay, it is like me to meddle, so forgive me for doing it again. Even if you're leaving town, I have some information I think you'll want to hear."

Kendall drew a deep breath. "Raina, I'm not selling Aunt Crystal's house."

Only Rick didn't know that yet and neither did her sister. She hadn't seen Hannah, who'd opted to sleep at Jeannie's instead of being in Kendall's company. And she hadn't yet faced Rick. She had no way of knowing how badly she'd hurt him. She'd taken a man who'd been betrayed, one who'd reached out to her anyway, and trampled on his heart.

Kendall shook her head. She didn't deserve his forgiveness or his love, though she desired both. But even if Rick rejected her, Yorkshire Falls was her home and had been since Aunt Crystal had taken her in. Too bad she'd taken so long to acknowledge the truth. She might have saved everyone a lot of grief.

"Kendall, did you hear me? I said it's wonderful news that you aren't selling! Your aunt would be so pleased," Raina said, her exuberance and honest emotion traveling through the phone lines.

"Thank you." Kendall exhaled, grateful for the older woman's warmth and compassion. "But can you please let me be the one to tell Rick?"

"Of course. And now that I know, my information seems more important than ever."

Raina's words piqued Kendall's interest, as the older woman no doubt intended. "What do you know, Raina?"

"I know who switched the photos at the slide show the other night. Who set you up. Hang on. I'm in the hallway at Norman's and I don't want anyone to overhear."

As Raina paused, Kendall's anticipation grew. Now that she planned to build a life for herself, beginning with the decision to remain here, she had decisions to make about how to move forward. Confronting the person who so obviously wanted to run her out of town would be a tremendous start. Then she'd face Rick.

"It was Lisa," Raina whispered.

Kendall shook her head. Rick had hinted at the same thing but Kendall still had a hard time imagining a schoolteacher resorting to such extremes over any man. Then again, it would make more sense and give Kendall more comfort if it was Lisa, someone who didn't hide her contempt, than someone in the shadows with no reason to hate her. Lisa's jealousy had been apparent from the start.

"That seems absurd though," Kendall said, voicing her uncertainty to Raina. "I'm not doubting you mean well, but I can't confront someone without proof."

"Well, how's this for evidence? Mildred down at the post office has been putting — how can I say it delicately? She's been putting eclectic lingerie catalogues in Lisa's box for years."

Kendall inhaled deeply. "Did Mildred mention any one in particular?"

Raina laughed. "I knew you'd ask me that, so of course I questioned Mildred further. It seems Lisa gets everything from *Victoria's Secret* to *Feminine and Flirty* to *Risqué Business*. Any of those ring a bell?"

"Yes." The photo at the show had come straight from *Risqué Business*. Kendall cleared her throat, acceptance settling in. At least the enemy had a face and a reason. "Thanks, Raina. You're so sweet to tell me about this."

The other woman sighed. "Well, I wasn't sure whether you'd be better off not knowing but when I walked into Norman's and saw Lisa acting all haughty, like she was so perfect . . . well, I decided she didn't deserve to get away with it. And I'm embarrassed that I encouraged her to go after my son at all. I needed to make amends. Now I have to go join Eric's family."

"Thanks again, Raina."

"You're welcome, Kendall. You know your aunt was like family to me. So are you. Bye, bye."

Seconds later the connection severed, Kendall lowered the phone from her ear. She glanced down and realized she was shaking, not in fear but in anger. Anger at herself and at Lisa.

Kendall had caused the rift with Rick on her own. She couldn't blame anyone else. Lisa Burton couldn't have come between them if Kendall hadn't been running scared and she had a hunch that if Lisa hadn't plastered Kendall's half-naked body on a screen for the town to see, Kendall would have found another excuse to run. That had been her M.O., after all. But no more, Kendall thought, proud of herself at last.

Still, Lisa ought to be held responsible for her actions and she'd had no right to sabotage the town's annual slide show any more than she had the right to publicly humiliate or harass Kendall in the name of jealousy. Kendall might not have current rights over Rick Chandler's body but he'd made himself clear to Lisa. She had none either. And she never would.

If Kendall was going to stay in town, it was time she asserted herself as a person with rights, feelings, and personal goals — one of which included Rick Chandler.

Which meant she had to tell Lisa Burton to back off.

Rick walked into Norman's. When his mother called him at the station a few minutes ago and asked him to come and join her and Eric's family after work, he couldn't refuse despite the fact that he was still damned angry she'd faked a heart condition.

But knowing she had his best interest at heart, no matter her warped way of showing it, he wasn't about to turn around and hurt her in return. She was his mother and he loved her.

No sooner had he stepped inside the restaurant and met up with his mother than she grabbed him in a huge hug, her gratitude and relief evident. "I'm so glad you came. Thank you."

He hugged her back, silently thanking God her body was healthy even if he wished her mind wasn't quite so conniving. Then he stepped back. "So where's Chase?" Rick assumed Raina had also invited him to dinner with Eric's family. Roman's turn would probably come next time he and Charlotte returned from D.C.

"Your brother will be here," she said without meeting Rick's gaze.

Rick hadn't yet told Chase about Raina's charade. Amazing since he'd chastised Roman for holding out on him, but Chase had been busy on deadline and in meetings and there'd been no time for Rick to break the news. Now he had his mother to deal with again and she was back to exhibiting signs of mischief.

This dinner suddenly reeked of a setup. "So where's Eric's family?" Rick asked, wondering if they were even here.

"They're sitting at the round table right there." She gestured over her shoulder to the large group of people in the corner. "But I think you should know that when Kendall walked in —"

Rick groaned. His mother had just confirmed his hunch. She'd conned him into coming to Norman's. Oh, she wanted him to have dinner with Eric's family, all right, but the idea probably hadn't come up until she'd walked in and seen Kendall. At heart, his mother was a matchmaker extraordinaire.

Kendall. His stomach had plummeted at the mention of her name, a feeling he knew he'd have to deal with for a few more weeks. Or at least until she packed up and left town. He placed a firm hand on his mother's shoulder, wanting her to back off. He'd given up on Kendall meeting him halfway or any way for that matter. He needed to move on with his life without his mother trying to interfere.

He squeezed her shoulder lightly, wanting to make sure he had her attention. "Where Kendall goes and what she does is her own business. We're through, she's leaving town and she doesn't want me butting into her life. Let's leave things at that."

Raina frowned. "Okay, but if you don't want

to make sure Kendall's confrontation with Lisa doesn't turn into a catfight in Norman's back hall, that's your business." And with that declaration, she turned and started for the round table where Eric's family sat.

Rick exhaled a groan. Would he ever not fall into his mother's trap? She'd baited him and he knew it. But she had a point. If Kendall was in the back hall with Lisa, someone needed to referee. And that someone had better be him.

As he turned the corner in the back, Kendall's voice traveled loud and clear. "If you ever harass me again, I'll sue you."

"For what?" Lisa asked, sounding bored.

"Oh, I'll start with something simple like intentional infliction of emotional distress and then I'll move on to filing charges with the police. Harassment would be a nice start. I'm not sure it really matters since Yorkshire Falls is such a small town and the people have long memories."

Rick didn't want to risk stepping into plain sight by taking a peek, but he heard the joy in Kendall's voice as she laid down the law with Lisa, who merely let out a long-suffering sigh.

"I've lived here longer, have a sterling reputation, and besides you can't prove I did anything," Lisa said in reply.

"Are you so sure? I have a friend at the post office."

Rick narrowed his gaze.

"And you know how the magazine companies

put the name and an address label on the front cover? Anyway, this friend wouldn't mind ripping off the front cover of your next monthly delivery of *Risqué Business*. You know, the cover that proves you get a subscription to the same magazine I modeled for?" The glee in Kendall's voice was clear. "I'm not a lawyer but that should be enough to prove opportunity. Everyone in town knows you have a thing for Rick, so motive's no problem. Trust me, Lisa. You do not want to mess with me on this. Back off." She said the last, her voice deepening.

Rick blinked in shock. He'd never heard Kendall take such a strict, don't-screw-with-me tone, not even with her sister. Pride welled in his chest along with the acknowledgment that something inside Kendall had changed. She'd obviously faced some of the demons instilled since childhood and come out stronger for the experience.

He wished he could draw hope from the thought but Kendall had wanderlust in her veins. Even if fear motivated her running and some of that fear seemed to be gone, he'd been burned too many times to let himself believe she might change her mind and stay. With him.

But he took pleasure in knowing that when she left town, it would be with her head held high. "That's my girl," he said under his breath, then realized that she was no such thing, and never would be.

"Once you're gone you do realize that Rick will forget all about you," Lisa said, as her parting shot.

Rick took a step forward, instinct compelling him to correct Lisa and protect Kendall. But Kendall replied first, proving she didn't need him to look out for her. She'd always gotten along fine on her own.

"Let's get a couple of things straight," Kendall said. "One, I'm unforgettable, two, I'm not going anywhere, and three, keep your hands off Rick. He's mine."

Rick chuckled at the same time Kendall's words registered, and that elusive ray of hope found its way inside him after all. Kendall's use of words like *not going anywhere* and *he's mine* provided a jumpstart to his adrenaline and his doubts. Not that he'd take those words of hers at face value.

Turning, he walked into the hall so he could confront Kendall himself. Lisa stormed past him and he let her go. Kendall had said everything that needed to be said — and more. But the question remained, would she say it again, this time to his face, or would she turn and run?

He glanced over. She'd leaned against the back wall and shut her eyes. Rick knew confrontation wasn't her favorite form of recreation but she'd done well. He was proud of her. He didn't know if Lisa had pulled her last prank, but at least Kendall had put the other woman on notice. There would be consequences next time.

Kendall breathed deeply, then exhaled. Her breasts rose and fell beneath the lemon-colored tank top she wore. One delicate strap dipped off her shoulder, revealing her smooth skin, and the urge to kiss every inch of her exposed flesh grew strong inside him.

"Easy," Rick said under his breath. They had a long way to go before he'd indulge in kissing of any kind with this woman who held his heart in her hands. He'd do best starting with the basics. "Congratulations."

Her eyelids flew open wide. "Rick." She blinked, obviously startled but not unhappy to see him if the hesitant smile on her face was any indication. "Congratulations about what?"

"You tamed the witch," he said, speaking of Lisa. A smile tugged at his mouth. "That deserves a round of applause." He clapped to prove his point as well as to break the tension between them.

"I don't know if I tamed her." Kendall laughed, her eyes sparkling. It had only been a few days but God he missed the light in her eyes and her easy laughter. "But I did set her straight."

He nodded. "So I heard."

"You were eavesdropping?" she asked, obviously surprised.

"Listening in a public place."

She rolled her eyes. "Same difference. So . . .

how much did you hear?" she asked as she bit down on her glossed lips.

He wanted to take a nibble too. "How much do you want me to know?" he asked instead.

She sighed, shifting from foot to foot, her discomfort obvious. "Rick, I don't want to get into a game of twenty questions."

"Neither do I." He also didn't want to stand here pining for a woman who'd just reject him again. "So how about you just answer my question. Tell me whatever it is you want me to know." He stepped closer, taking the biggest risk of his life. But if he'd heard her correctly, she'd finally taken a risk too. If not, this was Rick Chandler's last stand. "Talk to me."

Kendall stared at Rick, taking in his beloved face, serious expression, and gorgeous mouth. Now that he stood before her, she didn't know what to say so she opted for the truth. "I'm scared," she admitted.

He reached out a hand and stroked her cheek. His roughened skin sent awareness shimmering throughout her body, reminding her not just of their physical connection but the emotional one as well. Obviously their bond remained despite her attempts to shut him out and the relief sweeping through her veins eased her mind a little bit. This was Rick and she could tell him anything.

As she looked into his eyes, she realized how much hinged on her reply. Though she feared he'd reject her, ironically she also feared he'd accept her. The life she'd always wanted and feared at the same time hung just within reach and she wouldn't be human if she didn't admit to being petrified.

Drawing a deep breath, she took a huge leap of faith, hoping Rick would be there to catch her. "I'm not leaving Yorkshire Falls after all."

"Really." He raised an eyebrow. "Do tell."

An adorable smile tipped the corner of his mouth and Kendall knew he'd heard her entire conversation with Lisa. But he still deserved to be told firsthand and in a much different tone and manner than she'd taken with the witch, as Rick had aptly called Lisa.

"I . . ." Kendall paused and cleared her throat, nerves nearly paralyzing her. What if he turned away? What if he didn't?

As if sensing her distress, he reached forward and clasped her hand in his, squeezing tight. For courage. For comfort. "Go on."

She forced a smile that became easier and more real as she spoke. "I decided to stop running."

"Because?"

He squeezed her hand harder and she appreciated his show of support, gaining hope. "I don't know why. One minute I was looking at that blown-up photo and convinced myself the time had come to leave. That you and your family deserved better."

"Did any of us tell you we wanted better?" He growled and a fierce scowl replaced his smile. Clearly he wasn't pleased.

"Well no." No one had planted the idea in her mind.

"But you figured you'd make the decision for us. Thank you very much." He shook his head.

"It was an excuse for me to run."

"It was an excuse for you to run," he said at the same time.

She laughed, the lump in her throat disappearing. "You know me so well."

"That's what I've been trying to tell you all along." His voice grew somber, serious, and even more sexy if such a thing was possible.

"I wish I could promise you this would be easy." She gestured back and forth between them. "That I'd have no trouble adjusting."

"If I wanted easy I'd be with Lisa." He grinned, slapping his thigh and laughing hard at his own joke.

"Very funny."

"I thought so," he said, then shrugged. "Seriously, sweetheart, all I want is you, in one place. With me. The rest will come naturally, I promise. A few bumps in the road maybe, but every married couple deals with those sooner or later."

"Married?" She stepped back in surprise and hit the wall behind her.

He followed, leaving no room for retreat. "We can do this one of two ways. Slow and easy or fast and hard." He braced one hand on the wall over her shoulder. "I don't want to push you into more than you're ready for but I do have to lay my cards and intentions on the table so there's no mistake."

She nodded. She wanted that too. Honesty, up front, no mistakes, no surprises. No retreat.

"I want to marry you." He stroked her cheek with his other hand. "I want to spend the rest of my natural life with you. I want to help you raise your hellion sister along with a couple of kids of our own. And I want to do it here, in Yorkshire Falls." He tipped his head close, his forehead touching hers, his breath warm against her cheek.

She inhaled deeply and felt as if she'd come home. "I want those things too." Her voice cracked and a tear dripped down her cheek. "But what if I panic? I've never lived in one place for very long, never looked to the future. The first sign of a problem and my instinct is to run — to reject a person or a place before they can reject me. I realize that now. What if —"

"Shh." He placed a finger over her lips. "There are no what ifs. Not now that you understand why you've been running. If that panic comes over you, I'll know it. Or you will and you'll come to me because that's what people who love each other do. And I'll talk you through it," he said, then sealed his mouth over hers, promise and love evident in the broad sweep of his tongue and the possessive way he took command of her senses.

He knew her, he understood her, and he accepted her in spite of it all. She brought her hands upward, cradling his face between her palms, giving herself better, deeper access to the moist warmth of his mouth before finally pulling back. "I never thought I'd find home," she whispered.

"It's right here, sweetheart." His lips hovered over hers. "With me."

"Mmm." Despite the lingering fear she knew she'd spend more time coming to terms with, Kendall felt safe, loved, and wanted for the first time in her life. A feeling she'd pass on to her sister and to kids of her own. Warmth filled her chest and expanded inside her.

"Cool beans!" Hannah's yell echoed in the hallway. "Jeannie, get in here and see this! And bring Mrs. Chandler. I mean Raina. Bring Raina. Woo hoo!"

Kendall felt herself blush, the heat rising fast and furious to her cheeks while Rick merely straightened to an upright position and laughed. "Guess I'd better get used to this kind of an interruption, huh?"

"Maybe she'll learn to knock?" Kendall asked hopefully.

"We're staying? Are we staying?" Hannah asked, her eyes huge and hopeful.

Kendall grinned. "We're staying."

"Where are we gonna live? Can we move to the main house? Pearl said Eldin's back would do so much better in the guest house but she didn't want to tell you that with the scandal on your mind," Hannah rambled on.

Kendall glanced up at Rick, her head spinning.

"We haven't gotten that far, squirt," he told Hannah.

"Okay well fine. We can talk about it later. I want my room to be purple. Can you paint whatever room I get purple, Rick?"

Kendall stared in shock at her suddenly exuberant sister. "We'll discuss the purple room another time. How did you get in here anyway? Didn't Norman say he didn't want to see your face around here until next century?"

"Yeah but I charmed him," Hannah said with a huge amount of sass.

Rick turned toward her sister. "And how'd you do that?"

"I helped him wash a few dishes this morning and he was putty in my hands. Does this mean I can call you Dad? Or Uncle Rick? Or how about Hey Copper?" Hannah giggled, happier than Kendall had seen her. Ever.

"I don't know what you should call him, but you'd better call me Grandma," Raina said, coming up behind Hannah. She met Rick's gaze. "You see? I told you I had grandchildren in my future." She wrapped her arms around the young girl, squeezed her tight, and kept squeezing.

"I can't breathe," Hannah squeaked.

"And she can't talk either. Keep hugging her, Mom." Rick chuckled while Hannah shot him an annoyed scowl that quickly turned back to a big smile once Raina released her.

"Does this mean you'll lay off Chase?" Rick asked. "You've got Roman and me settled. I think we should go on over to *The Gazette* and tell him the truth together."

"What truth?" Kendall asked, lost and curious.

"I'll tell you later," Rick whispered in her ear. "When we're naked and alone," he said in an ever softer voice. He nuzzled her cheek as he spoke.

"Eew," Hannah said, watching them. But the grin didn't leave her face.

And as Kendall met Rick's heated gaze, she knew exactly how her sister felt. Giddiness, happiness, disbelief, and a tremendous amount of love settled inside her when she thought about her future. All possible because she'd faced her past.

Kendall had come to town running and ended up finding the life of her dreams and the home and family she'd never had. She'd tamed both her personal demons and the town's playboy. Not bad, if she did say so herself.

About the Author

Award-winning, best-selling author Carly Phillips is an attorney who has tossed away legal briefs in favor of writing hot, sizzling romances for Harlequin and Warner Books. Since her first sale in 1998, Carly has sold a total of eighteen books. She lives with her husband, two young daughters, and frisky Wheaton terrier who thinks he's child number three. When not spending time with her family, Carly is busy writing, promoting, and playing on-line! She loves to hear from her readers and you can write her at P.O. Box 483, Purchase, NY 10577 or E-mail her at carly@carlyphillips.com.

JUN 0 4 2003 DATE DUE		
SEP 0 2 2003		
OCT 1 4 2003		
MAR 0 2 2004		
JUN 2 2 2005		
OCT 20		
SC AUG 2006		
AUG 0 8 2007		
MAR 1 2 2009		
DATE DUE		
SJ OCT 2009		
SF MAR 2010		
WC JAN 2012		